ANGEL CITY BEAT

ANGEL CITY BEAT

EDITED BY
BARB GOFFMAN

Contents

Introduction

By Naomi Hirahara

More than nine million people like me call Los Angeles County home. While some outsiders love to hate us, no one can argue that our region is the cauldron of reinvention. We are known for being the original center of Hollywood television and film. Southern California also boasts a gorgeous coastline—perhaps not as jaw-dropping as Monterey's or the Mendocino coast in the north, but much more accessible and, as a result, more crowded and embraced by the masses.

This curated collection, edited by the queen of the short story, Barb Goffman, whose observant and discerning editorial eye has improved some of my own short fiction, is focused on "beats." In its solicitation for anthology submissions, the Sisters in Crime Los Angeles (SinC LA) chapter suggested that writers explore cops on their beats, reporters on their beats, screenwriters' beats, beats of LA's music scenes. "If it's an LA mystery and it's got a beat, write to it."

The fifteen selected short stories in *Angel City Beat* have certainly answered SinC LA's call. There are protagonists with a law-enforcement background, but not your typical men and women in blue. Norman Klein's police detective in "Crime Doesn't Play" is from out of town, but is called to aid the Beverly Hills Police Department in an investigation of stolen artifacts because of his bookish sensibilities. In Sybil Johnson's "Fatal Return," a volunteer must rely on her former experience as a police detective in solving a crime in a library. Amy Kluck, in "The Missing Mariachi," explores Boyle Heights and beyond in the case of the kidnapping of a female trumpet player.

The beats of music are also covered in Anne-Marie Campbell's "Settling the Score," in which the competition to determine the next director of the Los Angeles Philharmonic becomes deadly.

Hollywood is well represented in "Underbelly," Jacquie Wilver's tale of warring screenwriters, as well as in Daryl Wood Gerber's writers'-room mystery "Murder Unjustified," which also happens to be the name of the television show the characters are working on.

While print journalism has had its challenges in the twenty-first century, a reporter for the *Los Angeles Times* is featured in both Nancy Cole Silverman's 1998-set "Byline for Murder" and Kate Mooney's "Getting Warmer." Each protagonist has a slightly different newspaper beat, yet for both, the full truth doesn't make it to their respective investigative stories.

More unusual beats are covered in some of the stories. Ken Funsten, CFA's "A Dead Line" follows a high school student's summer gig cold-calling retirees about senior-living packages. Funsten, CFA, also has a second story in the anthology, "What's Really Unforgettable," which features a Connecticut-based fund manager who returns to LA to identify a potential client who has been hospitalized. And in Meredith Taylor's "Death Beat," observations of a hospice nurse reveal unexpected events in some patients' final days.

In many of the stories, Southern California's academic institutions, most notably USC and UCLA, but also Caltech, are mentioned. Academia is the star in Paula Bernstein's "A Thesis on Murder," which uses Santa Monica Beach and Westwood as settings.

Los Angeles's reputation as a culinary mecca is not forgotten in Gail Alexander's celebration of Italian cuisine in "The Feast of the Seven Fishes." The region's constant thirst for water has spurred Jenny Carless to create a dystopian world in "Everything's Relative," where people literally fight for this vital rationed resource. And finally, Melinda Loomis's "Unbeatable" perhaps nails the most LA character of all—a pet psychic who is hired to communicate with a racehorse at the Santa Anita racetrack.

The stories in *Angel City Beat* are entertaining and imaginative. Their unique sleuths and situations even have potential for becoming the solid foundation for a novel-length work. Sisters in Crime Los Angeles has again fulfilled its mission to encourage members to further develop the craft of writing mysteries. My hope is that publication in this anthology will encourage writers to reach their creative goals and continue to set stories in our wild and wonderful world of greater Los Angeles.

THE MISSING MARIACHI

By Aimee Kluck

The call came in at 8:05 p.m. as I was heading home to my empty house from the Hollenbeck Police Station after a dull day of sifting through missing-persons reports. My mind ached for some action, either a riveting police detail or an all-night party. Neither of which I was getting much of lately.

"Isabella, we got an abduction in the parking lot behind Casa Valdez. Adult woman. Blues are on the scene interviewing the witnesses. How fast can you get there?"

I had told my partner, Manny, not to call me that name. I go by Izzy. He did it to tease me. As if I looked anything like an Isabella, with my short-cropped hair, muscular pecs and arms, Dockers pants, and steel-toed work boots. Occasionally sporting a plaid, button-down flannel shirt when I could get away with it. A detective-worthy navy blazer and a starched white blouse when I couldn't.

"Ten minutes. On my way."

"I'm across town. I'll get there as fast as I can." With traffic, that could be an hour.

Usually, when an adult woman is kidnapped, it's by someone she knows, to terrorize, intimidate, or subjugate her. Everything I fought against. At least we had witnesses.

I hightailed it to Boyle Heights, my hardscrabble Latino beat and homey

1

community. In the parking lot outside the banquet hall, I pulled up beside the cruiser with flashing lights. Got out and approached two officers standing under the streetlights, trying in vain to get clear statements from a gaggle of teen girls outfitted in frilly party dresses.

The girls squealed simultaneously and babbled over the officers. "Oh my God, he kidnapped her."

"She was screaming her head off."

"You have to save her."

I nodded to the harried officer, then addressed the girls. "One at a time, please. You." I pointed to the teen in the red dress, who seemed calmest. "Do you know who the woman is?"

"She's the trumpet lady in the mariachi band at the quinceañera we're attending." Red Dress pointed toward the building adorned with colorful murals depicting Mexican artists and heroes. "We came out for some fresh air while she was loading her gear. Then, from literally out of nowhere, this guy ran up and forced her in the trunk of her own car, jumped in the driver's seat, and sped away."

"What did he look like?"

The girls glanced at each other and shrugged. Red Dress spoke. "Chubby guy, wearing a hoodie and dark clothes. I didn't see his face, but I think he's White."

That description fit a thousand men in Los Angeles.

"Honestly, I was so shocked, it took me a while to get my camera ready, but I did take this photo." She showed me a picture of a blue Honda Civic driving away. When I enlarged the license plate, the numbers blurred.

I texted the pictures to my cell phone and handed hers back. "Do not post that on social media. We don't want the kidnapper knowing we're on to him. And thank you."

I motioned to the officers. "Let's find out who's our missing person and get a BOLO out for her car. I'm going inside to talk with band members and party organizers. Can you give me a hand?"

One officer stayed behind, securing the crime scene, and the other followed me. We strategized how we would conduct our investigation while minimizing disruption of the event, a major highlight in any Latina's young life.

With the help of the party organizer, we located the celebrating girl's parents and the band leader. The officer took the parents aside. I guided a tall middle-aged woman dressed in a *traje de charro*—tight-fitting pants, ruffled shirt, and a jacket with heavy embroidery—to the lobby, where we could speak without the deafening noise of reggaeton from the dance floor. Another woman, wider but clad in the same black-and-silver mariachi outfit, followed us.

"I'm Izzy Zavala, detective in the Major Crimes Unit, LAPD. By the way, I saw your group, La Rosas, in the parade this year. Totally refreshing: an all-female mariachi band."

Time was of the essence, but I figured I might get more cooperation if I took a few seconds to pay her a compliment. She smiled. Yep, all artists like recognition and praise.

I explained what happened to their trumpet player in the parking lot. "Who is she?"

"Ay, *Dios mío*." The tall woman made the sign of the cross and fanned herself. "Sonia Sanchez. A lovely girl, a good person."

"You have any idea who would kidnap her?"

The wide mariachi member pushed forward. "It's that *pendejo bruto* she goes around with."

"Details, please."

"Sonia does not pick acceptable men. The latest, Hector Hernandez, hit her. Busted her lip, right where she must press to blow her horn." She grimaced in disgust. "He's the type of thug to pull a stunt like this. He's got a record. I told her to leave him."

"Know where I can find him?"

"At the gates of hell." She snarled. The tall woman clutched my arm. "There was a man, a *fluencia*, at the event, hanging around Sonia. Dark hair greased back like a gangster, dressed in a suit too big. Shady, like he had bad intentions. He gave me the creeps. I was about to call security to have him removed, but he disappeared. Ay, I should have. Maybe I could have stopped this terrible thing." She fanned herself.

"Don't blame yourself. Either of you know who he is?" They shook their heads.

Two leads, Hector and the stalker.

The tall woman gave me Sonia's address. I called Manny and heard the Lakers game on the radio in the background. I gave him the details I knew so far.

"I'm on my way to the kidnapped woman's home. Can you track down Hernandez?"

He yelped. "LeBron scored another three-pointer. Okay, Izzy, I'm on it."

Driving down Indiana Avenue, the main drag struggling with gentrification, where mom-and-pop *tiendas* mixed alongside trendy cafés, jealously rose up in me as I observed the Saturday night revelers. I tried to remember the last time I ventured out to carouse and enjoy life. Not since Elena left me. Nights off these days, I stayed home, licking my wounds and wondering if I could possibly win her love back. If I could be less stubborn and more fun. I almost ran a red light thinking about it.

On Houston Street, I parked in front of a low stucco house lit by the porch light and walked the path among the aloe bushes and orange trees. I knocked on a green door, and a young woman holding a sleepy toddler on her hip answered.

I flashed my badge and introduced myself. "Are you related to Sonia Sanchez?"

"I'm her sister, Ines. Is Sonia okay?" She looked puzzled, with a frown line forming between her deep-brown eyes.

"May I come in?" Police were not generally welcome in this neighborhood, often the bearer of bad news or about to cause a major disruption in people's lives. But maybe my Latina credentials gave me a little more credibility with this family.

Ines opened the door and called for her mother. Inside, the house smelled of homemade cooking—stewed meats and spicy beans. Tamales and enchiladas. Churros on rainy days. My stomach moaned. Those scents reminded me of my mother's kitchen, a place I hadn't visited in a while, ever

4

since she disowned me for bringing Elena home for Easter dinner. In my mother's eyes, a good Catholic girl like me should not love a woman.

A sad cumbia song filled the air. The memory of my father teaching me to dance before I attended my first school event flashed. I hadn't thought of my parents in a while and found myself feeling sentimental.

A stout woman in a flowery housedress and apron emerged from a back room. We sat in the living room, a cozy confluence of overstuffed furniture, paintings of saints hanging on walls, and colorful drapes. I cleared my throat, readying myself to deliver the startling news. "Senoras Sanchez, it appears your daughter and sister, Sonia, has been abducted this evening after her performance." I explained what we knew so far en Español, my first language.

The mother sat wringing her hands like an old dishcloth, perspiration dotting her furrowed forehead, lips trembling. Ines interrupted me repeatedly asking questions, her voice rising in pitch and shrillness each time.

I asked about Sonia's relationship with Hector, of which they knew little. Maybe Sonia knew better than to bring her not-so-desirable friend home. I trusted Manny would locate the lowlife's address and beeline it to his house.

"Do you have a picture of Sonia?" The mother, sadness spread across her wrinkled face, waddled to the bookcase, took a photo from a frame, and handed it to me. "Have you had anyone in the house recently that you don't know well, repairmen maybe? Or have you seen any strangers watching the house?"

They said no.

"Any other friends I should speak to? Has Sonia had disputes with anyone?"

"Sonia doesn't socialize much. Our father is sick. She helps my mother." Ines laid the child down on the couch between them and patted her back. "Sonia's been having trouble at work. She told me there's something wrong with the production line, but no one's listening to her. She's afraid she'll get fired if she blows the whistle. They've threatened her."

"Threatened her how?"

"She didn't say exactly, but she has a bruise on her mouth. She said it's a cold sore, but it looks like a cut."

Two versions of the injury: the man she went with or someone at work. I jotted down the information about Sonia's workplace, Gibeon, a manufacturer of airplane parts located in El Segundo, and her role in the Quality Assurance section.

Ines frowned. "Her boss is Bill Colton, but he won't help you. He's the one she complains about."

Sounded to me like a suspect I needed to check out. What was going down at work? Sexual harassment? Physical or psychological abuse?

I thanked them for the information and explained a team would be setting up a phone trap in case the abductor contacted them. I left the worried women with a heavy heart, knowing how tense the next hours would be while they processed this disturbing news and telegraphed messages to extended family and close community asking for help in finding Sonia. Latinx families united in a time of crisis.

Back in the car, I called HQ to arrange the trap and get demographic info on Colton.

"Lives in Culver City." Dispatch recited his address and phone number. "No priors."

I called Manny. "Making any progress?"

"Found Hernandez's place, but no one's there. I put in for a warrant. So far, nothing on his car or Sonia's. I'm canvassing the neighborhood to see if I can spot him, and I sent some undercovers to search the bars." As usual, during a pursuit, Manny spoke in an excitable, high-speed cadence. I prided myself on keeping an even keel.

"Although, if he's with our victim, they may be hidden away." Sonia could disappear anywhere within the five hundred square miles of this city.

"Maybe they headed out of town."

"I think the suspect might want to ditch Sonia's car. Must know we'll be looking for it. Get in touch with Highway Patrol. Have them check the freeways. Keep going. We need to find Hernandez. He's our main suspect."

I called the officer in charge of interviewing the quinceañera guests. "Any luck identifying the stalker?"

"Evidently a party crasher. Security reported they've seen him before.

They tossed him out two months ago. Checked his ID at the time and recorded his name in their report."

"Go by and pick him up. Bring him in for questioning. I'll meet you there." After I paid a visit to the boss. I tried calling Colton's cell phone, but it went straight to voicemail.

One thing about working in LA, you better like driving. Colton lived nearly fifteen miles west. I traveled down I-10, past the Convention Center beaming like a tin can in the sky, and wove through the mess of the 110 interchange, where cars darted across four lanes to make their exit. I tuned the radio to the channel playing corridos, those romantic ballads Elena and I used to dance to in the kitchen on Friday nights. A pang of longing for my best friend and lover gripped my heart. I brushed it away.

A half hour later, I pulled in front of a WW II bungalow with a rickety picket fence, in the shadow of the old MGM water tower. The curtains were closed, but I could see the blue tint of the television peeking through. I knocked. After a few minutes, I knocked again. The porch light blinked on, and the door cracked open.

"Whatcha want?" A woman in yoga pants and an oversized sweatshirt, her hair in a high ponytail and holding a cigarette, peeked from behind the opening allowed by the chain guard.

I badged her and asked to speak with Bill Colton.

"He's not here. He's never here." Saturday night, out on the town. She started to push the door shut. I slid my foot forward and forced it open, as far as the chain would allow.

"Where can I find him?"

"How would I know? I'm just his wife. Ya think he tells me anything?" She took a drag on her cigarette. "Probably taking one of his little chickadees back to his pitiful office. Like I don't realize what he's doing behind my back. The perv." She puffed out smoke rings. "I oughta divorce the louse."

Chickadees? His office? Sonia's busted lip? While wifey rattled on, the hairs on my neck rose. I learned long ago not to ignore those sensations. Nothing concrete, just a notion that something was amiss.

"Do you have a recent photo of him?"

"Why?"

"To identify him."

"If he's in trouble, he better not come crying to me. Wait here." She closed the door, and after a few minutes, she returned and presented a photo of an overweight guy on a boat with a large fish in hand. "We all done?"

I handed her my card. "I need to talk to him immediately. Can you contact him?"

"Not likely, but I'll try."

"Thank you."

She shut the door. Not sure she'd get my message to him, so I tried his cell phone again to no avail.

The interviewing officer called back while I was heading east again. Our stalker was in custody, and he was falling apart. I drove like wildfire, changing the car radio to a station playing huapangos. The foot-stomping, fast-beating rhythm compelled me to rush.

At HQ, I stomped into the interrogation room and slammed a folder on the table. Took a seat across from trembling Ivan Ochoa. Even in this rancid room, the stench of his fear and BO toppled my senses.

"What were you doing at the quinceañera party this evening? You weren't an invited guest."

He eyed me momentarily, then lowered his gaze. "I like to go out. It's near my house."

"Why were you bothering the trumpeter?"

He shook violently. "I didn't. I was digging the way she played." His eyes wide and wild.

"Did you kidnap her?" I got the feeling Ivan would have trouble catching a fly.

"No way." He tugged at his greasy hair, hard as if he'd pull it out.

"Where did you go after the party?"

"Home to get online to game with my friends."

The young officer who had joined me in the interview leaned over and whispered. "I can check his time online. Another thing, Ivan never had a driver's license. Claims he doesn't know how to drive."

Figures. "Do it. If his alibi checks out, let him go. In the meantime, get him a cup of tea or something to chill him." I lowered my voice. "He looks like he's about to implode. Don't leave him alone. Who knows what he'll do."

I hustled back to my desk, stretched my arms, and wiggled my stiff back to the annoying pop song that had been stuck on an endless loop in my head since this morning. One suspect down, two MIA. And poor Sonia out there in trouble. I couldn't rest. I called Manny.

"So where would you hide her? Close by the party venue? Or as far away as possible?"

"Good question. I'm sticking close, driving from Casa Valdez to Hernandez's hole, which is about a mile away, and back again. I'll stay out all night till I find the shithead." Manny loved working the night. Loaded up on endless thermoses of coffee, refilled with the worst burnt crap and scads of sugar from places like 7-Eleven and all-night diners. Me, I preferred going home, relaxing. Except these days, living alone again was not relaxing. I ended up watching a lot of bad TV.

"Meet me in the banquet hall parking lot." Better than sitting still, with those minutes ticking away. On the way, hoping to settle my growing anxiety, I listened to those melancholy songs on the oldies station—the music the cholos blasted from the ginormous speakers in their lowriders. It was just after one in the morning. Almost five hours since Sonia had been taken. Everybody knew the longer the person stayed missing, the bigger the chance she wouldn't be found alive. Time was not on my side.

In the lot of Casa Valdez, where Sonia's car had been parked, Manny paced the cordoned-off area, examining the ground. His shaved head gleamed under the streetlight.

"Detective Rodriguez, find anything useful?"

"Not a trace."

I faced the street. "The witnesses said the car took off toward the west. Freeway's about a ten-minute drive if traffic's not heavy. He could have gone in any friggin' direction from there." Searching for a single car in Los Angeles was like looking for a particular star in the sky.

"If the car is on the road, we'll find it. Everybody's out looking."

"And if it's stashed away in some garage or some empty warehouse, we'll... wait a minute." The idea light flashed in my brain. "Warehouse. Gibeon, where Sonia works, is a manufacturing firm. They got warehouses."

"What are you saying?"

"I spoke with Sonia's boss's wife. She put this bug in my mind. Her creepy husband takes his 'chickadees' back to his office for you-know-what. Maybe he took Sonia there. The guy is overweight, which matches the description from the witnesses. And Sonia's sister said she's been having trouble with her boss."

"*Hijo de puta.*"

I nodded at the apt description of Colton. "He might not be our guy, but I'm going to call in for a warrant."

Manny's phone rang. "Rodriguez." His eyes lit up. "You got Hernandez?" I swear he started panting. "You at his house? Look for the girl. Tear apart the whole damn place. We're on our way."

We jumped in his car and took off. He screeched through the streets, running his siren and lights. At the house, Manny jogged ahead while I locked the car and prayed a silent wish Sonia was unharmed.

Inside, an officer reported our missing victim was not on the premises. Hernandez, with beady, bloodshot eyes and rumpled hair, sat on the couch in a ransacked room that had clearly been worked over by my colleagues, his hands cuffed behind him, an officer lurking above him.

"Where's Sonia?" Manny yelled at our suspect, inches from his face. I wouldn't stop him yet. Sometimes the bad cop, good cop worked. Not usually on sleazebags, though.

"I wasn't with her tonight."

"Where were you?" Manny looked like a pit bull ready to bite.

"With someone else. I can't say."

"Then you got no alibi. I'm taking you in." Manny grabbed Hernandez's sweatshirt and tugged him to his feet.

"Okay, I was with a chick. Stephanie Wright. But she's married. Her old man don't know."

"He's going to know now. Where does she live?"

Hernandez revealed his "chick's" address and phone number. We sent him to lockup on suspicion of abduction till we could verify his alibi.

Before we drove to the adulteress's home, I had to deal with my niggling notion that Sonia could be hidden in a warehouse.

"Let's head out to Gibeon. Check it out."

While I called the overnight judge to lay out our evidence and get the search warrant approved, Manny took the 10 until we switched to the 110, then the 105. Traffic flowed like a stream of red-lit insects, marching along on route to their destination. Even at this late hour, going on three a.m., the LA freeways hummed with ceaseless activity. He drove with his left arm slung out the window, his right hand tapping to the beat of the salsa music playing alongside the scratchy buzz of dispatch. With my window open, a cool night breeze drifted in, caressing my face. We didn't speak. We didn't have to; we'd been partners long enough that we honored each other's silence.

We were stopped at the gate to Gibeon by the guard and showed our IDs.

"Hey, Scowcroft, how's retirement treating you?" Manny spoke in a friendly voice.

"Bored as a tossed peanut shell. Picking up a few hours here and there just to get out of the house."

"Listen, we're looking for Bill Colton. Wife says he's working late. You seen him tonight?"

The guard shook his head. "Can't say I have. But I just started my shift."

"We got a verbal from Judge Littleton. Where might we find Mr. Colton?"

He pointed to the yard. "Second building to the right."

Manny thanked the man and drove through the gate,

Slow as a rush-hour traffic jam, we cased the warehouses. Motion lights flicked on, revealing metal buildings with loading docks and a few roll-up garage doors. We parked and walked the perimeter. From under one door, a crack of light seeped out. I drew my service weapon as Manny crept forward and placed his hands under the door, moving it slightly. He motioned to me, and I positioned myself, poised to cover him and storm inside.

He raised the door in one fell swoop. I barged forward. "Police. Stay where you are and raise your hands."

Nothing moved. Manny swung his flashlight across the warehouse space until it landed on a blue Honda Civic. The trunk door was flung open.

"Plates match. It's Sonia's car."

We spread out and worked our way to the back of the cavernous space filled with Bobcats and other moving machinery and floor-to-ceiling shelves laden with airplane parts. Along the back wall, a row of closed doors led to more rooms.

Manny opened each one and flashed his beam inside the darkened spaces while I held my gun ready. On the fourth try, we found a room filled with crates and pallets, lit by the full moon streaming in through overhead skylights.

Up against the back wall, a woman dressed in a mariachi outfit sat tied to a chair, duct tape over her mouth, her dark hair hanging loose, blood smeared on her forehead, her eyes tight with fear. I recognized Sonia from the picture her sister had given me.

I swept the room for the kidnapper, but found no one. Manny covered me while I slipped toward the woman and gently removed the duct tape, whispering, "It's okay. We're police."

Sonia coughed and choked. "My boss, he's here."

I cut through the ropes with the switchblade I kept hidden in my boot. When the ropes loosened, the exhausted woman fell into my arms. Manny placed his jacket over her shoulders and, to my surprise, produced a water bottle. I held it while Sonia sipped.

Manny tried to call headquarters for backup, but he had no reception inside the warehouse. "I'm going to step out."

Moments after he left, a gunshot rang loud in the echoey space and buzzed past my ear. I dove to the ground, keeping hold of my flashlight while shoving Sonia behind me. She landed with a thump and an "oomph." I aimed my pistol in the direction of the noise.

"Colton. Drop your weapon. You're surrounded. Give up."

Something stirred behind rows of boxes. I swung my flashlight toward the movement. Sweat dripped down my neck. My heart thrashed in my chest. But my grip on the gun held steady.

"It's over. Come out with your hands up. Don't make this hard." I motioned to Sonia to crawl toward the wall, into the shadows. She lay frozen and immobile.

"Go." I jostled her and imitated a combat crawl, wincing at her head wound, which had started bleeding again. She scrunched her belly forward, and I followed in a crouched position, moving backward. Kept my gaze focused on the crates. Where the hell was Manny? Didn't he hear the ruckus?

Another bullet zipped by us, close enough to elicit a scream from Sonia but not within striking distance. She lay in the dark, her breathing fast and erratic, her eyes distant. Undoubtedly in shock.

Grunting, Sonia pushed herself up on her elbow and yelled, "Mr. Colton, please, stop."

He appeared at the edge of the pallets, his pistol pointed at us, his expression maniacally exuberant. He fired in our direction.

Crouched low, I aimed at his thigh and shot. Didn't aim for his heart as I normally would under threat of life because I didn't want him dead. I wanted him to account for his misdeeds. His leg buckled, and he fell.

Manny rushed in.

"Colton's hit. Let's get Sonia out of here."

He grabbed her legs, and I lifted her under her arms. Staying within the shadows, we stumbled outside. From a distance, the roar of police sirens approached.

* * *

The EMTs tended to Sonia, but before they took her away, she spoke to us in a weak voice.

"There's a problem with the parts we've been sending out to factories. They're faulty. They didn't pass inspection, but Colton pushed them through anyway. Had to meet the production contracts." She grimaced. "I reported him to the feds. This must have been his retaliation."

"He wanted to silence you." Had Colton intended to keep Sonia tied up long enough to convince her to retract her statement and cooperate like a good girl? Or had he planned on torturing her and then eliminating her? I trembled at the thought.

Sonia thanked us and asked that I tell her family what happened and direct them to the hospital.

The EMTs took Colton, too, his leg a bloody mess. Would be a while before he walked straight again. I didn't regret shooting him. I had a duty to protect my charge, his victim, Sonia.

Manny invited me for a celebratory drink at a cop bar he knew opened early, but I declined. I was tired, and I needed some alone time to think.

To reflect on Sonia's family and fellow musicians, who banded together to care for each other. To wonder about couples who stayed with each other for the wrong reasons. To consider how alone I felt in the world.

Maybe I didn't have to go solo; I could choose another way.

Maybe I'd call my mother tomorrow. Maybe I'd stop by and see Elena.

Five o'clock, heading home along the freeway. The traffic had waned, and only the latest night owls and early-morning Sunday workers drove steadily along, lost in the world within their cars. I turned to the Cool Latin Jazz station and grooved to the soothing sounds of the band Maqueque while I cruised along. The sweet, jazzy tempo lulled me to a place of comfort, calmed me down after the excitement of the evening.

I opened my window and breathed in the hot, concrete, throbbing scent of the city.

Hell, I rescued a woman tonight. That ain't nothing.

MURDER UNJUSTIFIED

By Daryl Wood Gerber

"**S**uzy's dead?" Tears welled in my eyes. My throat constricted. My best friend was dead? How was that possible? After leaving work early to celebrate surviving the first day in our latest writers' room, Suzy and I went to dinner at Musso & Frank's. When I'd hugged her goodbye a little over four hours ago, she was fine. Sure, she was upset with me for giving her unsolicited advice, but she was healthy. "How, Max? Heart failure?"

"Murdered," he said. "The police just left here. They're coming to you next, Angelica."

* * *

Earlier in the day

"Angelica!" Richard Dickson, Jr., producer of *Murder Unjustified* and a sixty-year-old clotheshorse—today's getup included a pin-striped linen shirt, Italian silk trousers, and chunky O-ring gold necklace—marched into my office. "Assemble the team."

Richard was an egomaniac who thought he could write better than anyone. Honestly, he couldn't tell a beat in a script from a hole in his you-know-where. His father could, but Junior couldn't. Richard had a bad rep. He would throw things at directors who ran over budget, actors who messed up lines, and cameramen who were slow. Yet the network loved him because

Richard's last show, thanks to his late father's involvement, was a ratings bonanza. But that didn't make his staff love him, and Richard no doubt knew it.

"Got a problem with that?" he asked.

"Nope," I said.

"Do you, Suzy-Q?" Richard asked.

Suzy was reading *The Hollywood Reporter* on the couch. "No, sir," she said solicitously. She'd locked horns with men scummier than Richard.

"Now," Richard demanded and exited.

Death doesn't become anyone. Especially me. So why had I said yes to being the showrunner for *Murder Unjustified*? The director was hot for me because of the way my last show, *Band of Thieves*, had flipped the genre on its head. With more money thrown at me than I'd seen in my career, I folded. My occasional boyfriend, Jared, had been against it, but he didn't get a vote.

Once we were assembled, Richard said to my writers seated around the table, "Story beats. Who can tell me what those are?"

The eye-rolls were hysterical. We all knew what story beats were.

Suzy, who was so pretty she should've been an actress, raised her hand. I was happy she hadn't gone into the glam side of the biz. I'd met her ten years ago in a screenwriting class and knew immediately she was going to be the Cagney to my Lacey. We riffed off each other without even trying.

"Yes?" Richard said.

"A story beat is a shift in the narrative."

"Good girl."

I almost vomited at his misogynistic reply.

"Anyone else?"

Griffin, one of the best writers in Hollywood and the gentlest lover I'd ever encountered—years ago, after my foray with a chef and way before I met Jared—raised his hand. "They can even be shifts in narrative tone."

"Good, good."

I glowered at Richard. Why was he torturing us by treating us like noobs?

Max, a former *CSI* writer who got booted off that show but was beholden to me because I'd discovered he could write grisly scenarios blindfolded,

16

said, "Story beats can be emotional turns, incidents, or events."

"Textbook screenwriting answer, kiss ass," I whispered.

He kicked me under the table.

Richard eyed me. "Honey, care to contribute?"

Honey? I clenched my fists. "Nope. They nailed it."

"I believe they missed one. The primary definition."

"There's a primary definition?" I winked. "Who knew?"

He put both hands on the boardroom-style desk and glared at me. "Story beats are small moments that move the story forward."

"Well, yeah. Not to be confused with script beats."

Max tattooed the table. "Ba-dum-dum."

"Don't give me lip, Angelica," Richard hissed. "I never wanted you on this project."

"And yet, Dick—" I shot to my feet. "May I call you Dick? Your father's name was Dick, wasn't it? Which makes you—" I stopped short of uttering the term *little Dick*. I was clever. Not suicidal. "Look, Dick…Richard…I'm being paid the big bucks to lead the team, which means the network wants me."

With everyone's eyes on me, Richard couldn't see Max mouth, "So why don't you make like a drum and beat it?"

Then Suzy whispered behind her hand, just loud enough for me to hear, "Don't you mean whip it like a drum?"

I bit back a laugh and continued. "Leave it to me, Richard. We will put together fantastic stories for you to deliver to the network, beats included. Cool?"

It took Richard nearly thirty seconds—I counted, *one potato, two potato*—before he said, "Make the magic happen, people."

* * *

"Why are the police coming to question me?" I said into the phone, still stunned by Max's news. Suzy was dead.

"Because Suzy was sleeping with Jared."

17

How could the police know about Suzy and Jared? I'd only learned that at dinner.

* * *

Inside fifteen minutes of when we were seated at the restaurant, Suzy downed two daiquiris—for liquid courage, I'd realized, once she'd started spilling her guts.

"When did you two hook up?" I asked her.

"Seven months and three days ago." She signaled the waiter for another drink.

Jared and I weren't exclusive. Our open relationship was my doing. A year ago, when he asked me to marry him, I said no because my parents had had a crappy marriage, and his parents' marriage hadn't been any better. A couple months later when he asked again, I turned him down flat.

"You like sex with multiple partners," I stated.

"I used to."

"Are you ready to settle down with one guy? With Jared?"

"I think so."

"Forgive me for giving you advice, but I don't think it's a good idea."

She pouted. Then glowered. Then apologized through crocodile tears, saying she truly hadn't seen herself ever falling in love until it happened.

* * *

"That's all the cop would tell me," Max said, bringing me back to the present. His voice sounded thick, like his tongue was too big and he was tired. "If it's not true, they shouldn't suspect you."

"Why'd they question you first?" I asked.

Max waited a beat. I could picture him pressing his thin lips together, his go-to move whenever he tried to keep quiet.

"Max?" I coaxed. He was a great writer, but he was lousy at keeping secrets.

"I loved her and sent her tons of text messages telling her so."

Whoa! He was better at keeping secrets than I thought. "Did you make a pass and she turned you down? Is that why the police suspect you?"

"They don't anymore. I have an alibi. I was here. At my place."

"That's not an alibi."

"With Jared. Doing gummies and binging *Star Trek*."

Jared did love *Star Trek*. He knew the lines from every episode. He was an actor. A good one. Ryan Gosling good. He didn't work enough and tended bar to make ends meet, because he refused to do commercials or be an extra, saying that'd be demeaning to a classically trained actor like himself.

"He knew you and Suzy were going out to dinner tonight and called me up," Max added.

I'd sent Jared a text to tell him about the dinner. He'd replied: *Cool.*

Suzy. What was I going to do without her? Even putting aside that she wouldn't be in my life anymore—I couldn't contemplate that right now—she would be a huge loss at work. She was the most creative writer on the staff. She understood story and character development. Heck, she understood why audiences were obsessed with murder mysteries. Without her input, *Murder Unjustified* would suffer.

"How did she die?" I asked.

"The killer bashed her in the head."

"With what?"

"Police didn't say."

There was a loud knock on my door.

"Who is it?" I yelled.

"Police."

"Call Griffin. Fill him in," I said to Max, and pressed End. The whole team should be told what happened. Of course, that included Richard, but I would take care of that call myself. Eventually. I checked myself in the mirror on the wall. I didn't look like a murderer. I didn't have blood anywhere on my person, and I was still in the clothes I'd worn to work. I opened the door.

The guy who introduced himself as Detective Hart could've been right out of central casting. Dark hair, bedroom eyes. I pegged him for a daily sit-ups and push-ups guy who did at least two or three long-distance runs a week. No partner, I noted. He was riding solo.

I said, "Max Duff called. He told me about Suzy—"

"Where were you tonight?"

"Come in."

He followed me into the foyer. I told him, beat by beat, about my day. Work; then Musso's from five-thirty to seven thirty; then home. No stops along the way. No grocery store. No gas station. If only I'd Ubered like Suzy had, I'd have a witness to my whereabouts immediately after leaving dinner and to the fact that I'd come home instead of going to Suzy's.

"Max said Suzy died from blunt force trauma. What was the weapon?"

"An Emmy for Outstanding Drama Series. You've won three, right?"

Instinctively, I glanced over my shoulder at where I displayed my awards. I'd earned a trio for *Band of Thieves*, and my name was engraved on each one. When I saw only two, my knees buckled. "I didn't kill her. She was my best friend. Someone must have swiped it."

Hart asked if I'd had a break-in. I hadn't, not to my knowledge anyway. But the statue had been there this morning. I'd dusted it. Then he asked who had keys to my place. Jared had one, I told him, but I couldn't see him killing Suzy. Besides, he'd been with Max. Griffin also had one. Hart took Griffin's details. "Were there prints on the Emmy?"

"Wiped clean."

Hart checked the locks on the front door and sliding doors leading to the terrace, which provided a view of Universal City Plaza. From that vantage point, he surveyed the rest of my townhouse. "You and Ms. Sanders ate at Musso & Frank's. A witness overheard you two arguing."

Suzy and I hadn't argued. Okay, I might have raised my voice.

* * *

"The Tiffany heart bracelet you're wearing," I'd said to Suzy as she started her first drink. "That's new. When did you get it?"

She covered it with one hand, and somehow, I knew.

"Jared gave it to you?" My voice sounded a little screechy.

She reached for my hand, remorse etched in her gaze. "Oh, Angelica, I've been wanting to tell you for ages." Tears bloomed in her eyes. Real tears.

* * *

"We didn't argue, per se," I said to Hart. Before finding my path as a writer, I'd spent a year in law school, dead set on defending people's rights; hence, the legalese coming out of my mouth. "Hold on. Was the witness Richard Dickson?" Good old Dick had been sitting at a table three down from ours. His back was to us, but I could envision him weaving a tale that would put me in hot water.

"Dickson?"

"Our producer."

Hart didn't confirm or deny. "The witness heard you and Ms. Sanders discussing the fact she was seeing your boyfriend."

"Jared and I have an open relationship." Yes, I might have called Suzy a lousy friend for hooking up with him—after all, she could have any guy in town—but I hadn't meant it.

What had this supposed witness heard? That I was ticked off Jared couldn't date someone other than my best friend? Someone less smart? Someone less pretty? On the other hand, once I'd calmed down and listened, the way Suzy told it, they were perfect together. He respected her. He didn't maul her like…

I jolted. Suzy hadn't finished the sentence. She'd downed her daiquiri, ordered the third, and gone silent.

Without enough evidence to arrest me, Hart gave me his card, warned me not to leave town, and left. And I collapsed on the couch.

Mauled you like who, Suzy?

* * *

My mind was moving like at warp speed. Hart must have suspected *I was set up since only an idiot would leave a murder weapon with their name on it*

21

at the crime scene. Besides, he went to see Max first, so Max must have been deemed a more likely suspect. Max said he sent tons of text messages to Suzy proclaiming his love. Did she rebuff him, which angered him? Would Jared corroborate Max's alibi?

Who else could have done it? Griffin? He'd set his sights on becoming the showrunner on *Murder Unjustified* and had been bummed when he found out I'd gotten the green light. Did he kill Suzy so he could pin the crime on me?

That's a stretch, Angelica.

What about Richard Dickson? He'd needled Suzy at every turn, calling her ridiculous nicknames and saying things like, "Pretty girls should be seen and not heard."

Suzy's and my friendship had to be the connection, right? Why else would someone kill her and frame me? I ran through a list of people we both knew but couldn't come up with anyone else who might have had a viable reason.

Curiosity taking hold, I went to Suzy's to view the crime scene. I was surprised to find no police presence at her bachelor-style house. It dawned on me that I hadn't asked *where* she was murdered. In an alley? A parking lot? At the gym? She'd been obsessed with her weight.

Even though I knew how guilty I'd look if I stole inside and the authorities found me, I had to risk it. I needed to see if Suzy left a clue as to who killed her.

I slipped on the latex gloves I'd thought to bring along, retrieved the key Suzy hid in the planter by the front door, and entered. Using my cell phone flashlight, I toured the house. I peeked in the kitchen cupboards. Rummaged through the medicine cabinet. One container of birth control pills, two left. The good news? She probably hadn't been pregnant with Jared's child.

I checked the dresser drawers in the bedroom. In the bottom one, I found a jewelry box filled with chokers. Suzy had invested in expensive ones. Silver, gold, black velvet studded with diamonds. Once, when I'd asked about her obsession, she'd said she liked kinky sex. I'd laughed and said, "Yeah, right."

I eyed her bed. Neatly made. Pillow fluffed.

I opened the drawer of the side table and discovered an empty box of condoms…and a diary. Suzy had kept diaries every year of her life, starting at the age of ten. Claiming they were precious gems and that she planned to write a memoir one day, at the end of each year, she secured them in a safety deposit box at the bank. This had to be the current one.

"What do you write about?" I'd teased once. "Being a TV writer in Hollywood? Big yawn."

"My secrets."

What kind of secrets did you harbor, Suzy?

Drawing in a deep breath, I opened to the first page, dated January first of this year.

An hour later, I was sitting on the floor crying. I knew Suzy's secret. She'd been in a relationship with someone who hurt her. Who? Not Jared. There were glowing pages of their budding relationship.

I flipped to the middle and reread a passage.

Cloaked in the irony of seduction, he wooed me. It was a complex experience. He did everything he could to make me desire and then detest him. It was like walking a tightrope between attraction and detachment. Did he want me? Would the beatings continue?

Anger gnawed at me. Had this creep killed her? I pressed the book to my chest and vowed I would find out who killed Suzy and murder the SOB.

With diary in hand, I slogged to my car. Yes, I knew I was stealing possible evidence, but since the murder didn't happen in her house, I felt I was justified.

I called Jared, even though it was one in the morning. He answered right away. He'd heard the news. I cut to the chase. "Were you with Max tonight?"

"Yes. I split right before the police questioned him. He called me when they left. He says you're the main suspect. The murder weapon was your Emmy."

So Max had known but hadn't told me. Interesting. "Are you high?"

"Not anymore."

"Did Max ever leave you alone?" Max could've borrowed Jared's key to my place and stolen the award. He knew where I lived. I'd invited him and the entire gang over two weeks ago for taco night.

"No. The guy is as much of a *Star Trek* nerd as I am. We were glued to the TV. Except when he passed out for a few minutes." Jared chuckled. "Too many gummies."

"Did you lend the key to my place to anyone?"

"Why would I…" He grew quiet.

"Who?"

"Suzy borrowed it once. She needed an ingredient for a recipe. She never gave it back. Maybe she took your Emmy, and the killer found it at her place, and—"

A sob escaped Jared's lips, and my heart melted. "Did you love her?"

"Yes. I know it hurts you to hear that."

"It doesn't, but Jared, we're through."

* * *

Fifteen minutes later, I pounded on the door of the third-best writer on my team. "Open up, Griffin!"

He did, wearing only pajama bottoms. I'd forgotten how massive his chest was. I averted my eyes. "We need to talk."

"Hello to you, too. I was sound asleep."

Can a murderer sleep soundly?

I pushed past him. "Where were you tonight?"

"Here."

"Alone?"

"I'm always alone since you—"

"No. Don't go there. I'm not the reason you don't date."

He shrugged.

"Do you still have a key to my apartment? The one you wouldn't give back when I…"

When I broke up with him, it wasn't pretty. He'd called me names like *hack* and *grind*. He was angry because I'd gotten the gig on *Band of Thieves*. It took us a month to make amends so we could work together without rancor. How ticked off was he that I got hired to run *Murder Unjustified*? Did he kill my best friend to not only frame me but to break my heart?

No, no, no! He wasn't petty.

"Sorry. I lost my key ring two weeks ago. Right after you and I had lunch at the studio cafeteria. One second I had them. The next, *poof.*" He flicked his fingers. "Lots of people were there shooting the Coliseum scene for the remake of *Gladiator.* Anybody could have picked them up."

Jared had gone on an audition for a small role in that movie. He hadn't gotten it, though they'd said he could be an extra. He had passed.

"I always carry a spare condo key in my wallet," Griffin went on, "and I keep a duplicate car key under the tire well of my Mustang, so I thought *big deal.* If anybody found them, they wouldn't know they were mine. The key fob was a Dodgers helmet. Lots of people have those. What's the big deal about your key?"

"Suzy's dead."

"I heard. Max called."

"Whoever killed her didn't break into my house to steal my Emmy. They must have had a copy of *my key.*"

"Your Emmy? I'm not following."

I stared at him. He hadn't asked how I was doing or said he was sorry about Suzy. Nothing. Who does that?

He moved past me into the living room. Everything was white. The furniture. The walls. It wasn't an artistic choice. It was because of me. When he asked me to move in with him, I cut the cord, and he became a blank.

"Did you ever make a pass at Suzy?" I asked.

"Are you kidding? I knew how close you were. I'm not a heel."

Unlike Jared, I mused. "You didn't try to seduce her?"

"Babe, I'm rough edges. There's nothing smooth about me."

* * *

I couldn't eat. Couldn't sleep. I sat on the couch and reread Suzy's diary, front to back, but I couldn't find a clue to the identity of her seducer. Was he someone in the industry or a nobody?

25

At six a.m., my cell phone rumbled. Richard was calling. I answered.

"Gelly, is it true?" he rasped. "Suzy's dead?"

Gelly? He was giving *me* a nickname now? I preferred *honey.* "Yes."

"I heard the police have questioned all you writers."

You writers? Alarm bells went off in my brain. Was he trying to distance himself from us riffraff, as if he barely knew Suzy, so Hart wouldn't consider him a suspect? Was it possible he was the guy who'd seduced Suzy? Had he lured her to his place, saying he wanted to talk about the script? To promise her a higher position? To maul her?

"Listen," Richard went on, "why don't you come over? I'll make coffee. You can cry on my shoulder, and then we'll talk about who you'll hire to replace her."

Wow. His rush to fill the position was downright cold.

"Why don't we meet at the office?" I suggested.

"I'm not going in today."

As rash as it might be to go to his lair, I needed answers. "Sure. I could use a good cry."

* * *

To be cautious, I left a message for Hart before heading over, asking again if he'd questioned Richard. He hadn't answered when I'd asked the first time. I added that Richard wanted me to find a replacement for Suzy ASAP, which I found disturbing, so I was going to his house to discuss the matter. I signed off, saying if Hart had questions he wanted me to ask Richard, I'd be happy to help out.

Thankfully, I had GPS. The Hollywood Hills were hard to navigate without it. Richard lived in a Spanish Colonial revival. I'd visited once before, when he threw a party to welcome the cast and crew of *Murder Unjustified.* Champagne flowed. Fresh hors d'oeuvres appeared with regularity. All the guests gushed over his exquisite taste, with the exception of me and Suzy because, as I'd confided to my pal, every detail, down to the beautiful rotunda and cascading staircase, had been designed by his father.

26

Richard opened the door seconds after I rang the doorbell. He was dressed in tan slacks, ecru shirt opened two buttons to reveal his gold chain, and loafers. No socks. "How are you holding up?" He threw an arm around me, the first physical contact we'd ever had. He was bonier than he appeared.

I shimmied out of his grasp. "I can't believe Suzy has been murdered."

"Tragic." He shook his head. "Coffee's brewing." He started toward the kitchen.

I peeked in the dining room as we passed. The view was incredible. A canyon separated him from his closest neighbors.

"What do you take in your coffee?" he asked nonchalantly, as if we weren't meeting to discuss Suzy's murder.

"Black." I didn't intend to drink any of it. My stomach was rancid.

I'd spent most of my time in Richard's kitchen during the party. Expansive blond wood island. An eight-burner Wolf stove. A gleaming set of Wüsthof knives. A container filled with spatulas, mallets, and spoons.

I glanced past Richard at the laundry room, which lay just beyond the kitchen. My gaze landed on the cuff of a pin-striped shirt poking from the laundry basket. The same shirt he'd worn to work yesterday. It had a pink stain on it.

Richard, who was pouring coffee into two mugs, followed my gaze. "What a klutz. I spilled a raspberry daiquiri down my shirt last night. That'll teach me to give the maid the night off."

"You were drinking daiquiris? Alone?"

"I had company."

"Who? The woman you had dinner with at Musso's?"

"A gentleman never tells." He handed me the mug. No comment on how I'd known he was there. So he had seen me and Suzy.

How could I ask him the question burning in my brain. *Did you dump your date, invite Suzy over, and kill her?* But that couldn't have happened here, or there would be police crime-scene tape.

I ambled around the room, checking out the subzero refrigerator. The glass-paneled cupboards. I paused by the built-in desk, shocked to see a picture of Suzy and Richard by the pool. She was perched on his knee, dressed in a skimpy bikini.

Nauseated, I set my mug on the counter. "Bathroom?"

"First door on the right."

I hurried to it. I wasn't going to vomit, but I needed something to calm my insides. I opened the medicine cabinet. No heartburn remedies. I spun around and tugged on the knob to the storage closet. It wouldn't budge. Was it locked because Richard was afraid guests would steal rolls of TP? I looked around for a key, saw one resting on top of the door frame, stood on tiptoe to retrieve it, and unlocked the door.

What I saw inside made me gasp. It wasn't a storage closet. Well, not for household items. Bondage equipment hung on hooks. Cuffs. Harness. Mouth gags. Chokers. Ropes. Whips. I knew what the items were because an actor in *Band of Thieves* had overshared photos of his obsession.

I recalled yesterday's staff meeting, when Max whispered to me, "Make like a drum and beat it," and Suzy had joked back, "Don't you mean whip it like a drum?"

Had she been trying to clue me in that Richard was the man referred to in her diary, a way to share her secret without really sharing it? Had he promised her the position of showrunner if she let him dominate her? Had she played along to get the dirt on him so she could expose him? Or had she enjoyed it? When she'd told me she liked kinky sex, I hadn't taken her seriously. Should I have?

I pictured the shirt in the laundry basket. What if Richard hadn't spilled a drink? What if the stain was Suzy's blood that he'd tried to wash out?

Boner move, Richard. You should've thrown your precious shirt away.

I sent a quick text to Hart, then studied myself in the mirror. "You can do this." My hands were trembling. "You made a promise to Suzy."

When I returned to the kitchen, Richard was standing beside the desk, staring wistfully at the picture of Suzy and him.

"You and she had sex," I said.

He jolted as if I'd wakened him from a trance.

"You beat her."

"No."

28

"Is that your fetish? Making younger women submit to your whims?"

"You've got your facts wrong. It's me." His voice cracked. "I'm the one who submits."

I eyed his gold necklace and recalled the actor in *Band of Thieves* saying O-ring collars were worn by submissives to indicate they were in a steady relationship. Had Suzy loathed herself for dominating him and detested Richard for consenting? Was that why she'd written that the relationship was complex?

"Where'd you and Suzy have sex last night?"

"We didn't."

"No final fling before you killed her?"

His mouth dropped open. "I didn't—"

"Liar!"

"I thought you killed her. When the police called to tell me she was dead, I told them about your argument."

"Why call you? I was her direct supervisor."

"I was her producer, and she was killed—"

I lunged at him. Hooked my finger into the O-ring. Tugged. Hard.

He gagged and dropped to his knees. "Do it, Gelly, baby," he rasped. "Do it!"

Oh, I was going to do it all right. I had to avenge Suzy. I twisted until I was cutting off his air supply.

At the same time the pervert offered an air-starved death grin, I heard a door squeak. Soft footfalls in the hall. Had the maid come? I released Richard. He collapsed on the floor, coughing.

Jared appeared, a pocket pistol in the palm of his hand. His face was contorted with anger.

I gasped. "What are you—"

I stopped. In his other hand was a key ring. With a Dodger fob. In an instant, everything came into focus. Jared, so tired of bartending, must have taken a job as an extra on *Gladiator*, after all, and saw Griffin and me having lunch. In all the time we'd been together, I'd only seen Jared act jealous twice. Both times were in regard to my past with Griffin. To punish me for my latest offense, he must have swiped Griffin's keys, sneaked into my place, and stolen the Emmy.

But why would he murder Suzy? He'd loved her.

On the other hand, he had a history of mistrusting women. His mother had cheated on his father.

"Jared, did you know Suzy was doing the nasty with Richard?"

A growl escaped his lips, meaning, yes, he'd found out. It must be why he'd killed her. Why he was here. He thought we both needed to die.

"You went to Max's to establish an alibi. Then you roofied him." In retrospect, Max's voice had been slurry. "After which, you lay in wait outside the restaurant. When Suzy appeared, you told her to forget the Uber. You'd drive her home. But you took her...I don't know where. And you killed her."

"Quiet!" Jared wagged the gun.

"That's a tiny pistol. About the same size as your—"

"Shut up!"

I spotted Richard's set of knives and container of kitchen tools. When I'd dated the chef, he'd cooked for me, and I'd assisted. I was pretty good at slicing and dicing, but tenderizing meat was my specialty. I dashed to the counter and grabbed the heavy aluminum mallet.

Jared fired. The bullet went wide.

"Suzy loved you," I said. "She wrote about you in her diary. She wanted to marry you."

"You're lying."

I ran at him and whipped the gun with the mallet. The gun crashed to the floor. I pounded Jared's arm. Struck his shoulder.

Richard, still on the floor, sideswiped Jared with one leg.

Jared plummeted.

"Why did you frame me?" I screamed, but I knew the answer. Because I'd introduced Suzy to Richard. He blamed me. I raised the mallet again.

"Stop, Angelica!" Jared drew into a protective ball.

I had to finish this. I'd made a promise. But I couldn't. In a rage, I walloped the floor beside his head.

"Police!" Detective Hart yelled as he and a female officer raced in.

"Everyone, hands up."

I tossed the mallet aside and obeyed.

Richard tried, but the move pitched him forward.

Jared remained tucked.

"Jared killed Suzy!" I cried.

"We know," Hart said. "We've got proof. Turns out there were hidden cameras in the writers' room."

Richard mumbled, "I told them."

I said, "Jared, why did you take her there?"

"I wanted her to show me where the magic happened."

Poor Suzy. Did he land the killing blow when her back was turned?

Jared let rip with a guttural howl. Grabbed his gun. Aimed it at me.

Hart fired his weapon. The bullet pierced Jared's chest, right where I imagine his heart would've been, if he had one.

"Are you okay?" the detective asked me.

"I am now."

And suddenly, I knew what our next story for *Murder Unjustified* would be.

GETTING WARMER

By Kate Mooney

As Charlie Walter walked toward the yellow tape blowing in the breeze along the Whoops Trailhead, she tried to ignore the sinking feeling inside her stomach. Even though it was after nine a.m., the sun was still tucked behind a hazy layer of Los Angeles fog. Besides the detective and two patrolmen guarding the yellow tape, the trail's dirt path was empty.

Charlie held a cup of coffee in each hand. When she approached the detective, marveling at how he was now wearing his thin layer of hair in a semicircle around his head, she handed one to him.

"Charlie Walter," Detective Galuppo said as he accepted her offering. "Now, how did I know you'd be the first reporter on the scene?"

Charlie shrugged. "Because I'm always the first reporter on the scene?"

"Bingo," he said as he took a sip of his coffee.

"So, what do you got?" she asked.

"Off the record?"

"Of course."

Galuppo walked toward a thicket of trees at the edge of the perimeter. Charlie followed. Once they were out of earshot of the patrolmen, Galuppo said, "A hiker took his dog off trail. The dog was sniffing around, starting digging, and found what looks like a finger bone."

"ID?"

Galuppo sipped his coffee again before he responded. "Eh, nothing official."

Charlie had been bringing coffee to Galuppo's crime scenes for over five years now, and thanks to all those overpriced lattes, Charlie knew when Galuppo was holding something back.

"Come on, you must have a hunch."

Galuppo looked behind him to make sure that the other two patrolmen hadn't wandered over."Between you and me? It could be that Jason Rundell guy. You remember he went missing from USC about ten or so years ago?"

"Yeah, I remember. He was last seen at an off-campus party right before graduation. What makes you think it's him?"

"I caught that case all those years ago and never had so much as a lead. It was like that guy disappeared out of thin air. Anyway, I always kept my nose to ground and told my guys if they ever came across anyone with a Marymount High School graduation ring on to call me. Jason's parents told me he never took it off."

"Let me guess, this guy was found with his high school ring?"

"Yep. We dug up a lot more bones. Just gotta wait for the official ID from the ME. We'll know soon if it's him."

"Right. Well, you'll let me know when you hear?"

"We'll see."

"There's a donut in it for you if you do."

"Thanks for the coffee, Ms. Walter." Galuppo held up his cup and nodded.

"Anytime, Detective Galuppo."

Charlie turned away from the detective and walked back to her car. With each step, she felt like the dirt might swallow her whole.

* * *

Once she was inside her car, Charlie googled Jason Rundell's name. The most recent article was a piece about how his family was holding a memorial on the ten-year anniversary of his disappearance. Charlie swallowed hard before scrolling further back in time. She went article by article, plucking out names of Jason's former friends, a soccer teammate, and even a professor who had provided quotes that relayed their shock and sadness over the young man's disappearance. Once she had a handful of names, she went over to Facebook and typed them in one by one. Jason's old roommate was a surf instructor over in Santa Monica, and the former soccer teammate was an accountant at Skrine, White & Adams.

It never ceased to amaze Charlie how easy it was for her to find out people's information online. With just a couple of clicks, she was able to find addresses and employers of people who were likely unaware of how exposed they were to the outside world.

Charlie reached into the center console to grab a bottle of Tums. She popped two in her mouth and sat back in her seat as the chalky tablets worked their magic on her acid reflux. Then, she plugged in the address of Skrine, White & Adams into her phone, took a deep breath, and put the car in drive, leaving the crime scene behind her.

Forty minutes later, Charlie found herself sitting on a stiff leather couch, waiting for Peter Bryant to come out of a meeting. A large piece of expensive-looking art hung behind the desk of the secretary who guarded the glass doors that presumably led to the rest of the firm.

"He'll be out in just a moment," the secretary said to Charlie for the third time.

"No problem. I'll wait," Charlie said as she relaxed further into the couch, hoping to indicate that she had no intention of leaving.

She checked her phone. By the time she'd left the crime scene and arrived at Peter's office, the news of Jason's body being found along Whoops Trailhead had broke. Charlie rolled her eyes as she thought about Galuppo, too giddy over the prospect of finally closing a cold case to keep his mouth shut. It didn't matter, though, because Charlie was already one step ahead of everyone who was trying to chase down this story.

Just then, a man in a navy suit with slicked-back black hair appeared behind the glass door and swung it open.

"I'm sorry to keep you waiting, Ms...."

"Walter," Charlie said as she stood. "Charlotte Walter."

Peter Bryant held out his hand. His skin was tan, like he had just been on vacation.

"How can I help you, Ms. Walter? I hear you're a reporter with the *Times*?" Peter said.

"That's right. I was wondering if there's somewhere we could talk?"

"Of course, of course. My apologies. Please, let's go into my office." Peter held out his arm, signaling for Charlie to walk through the glass doors. Once she was on the other side, she followed him into one of the dozen offices that lined the narrow hallway.

"Now," Peter said as he sat down in his large leather chair behind his oak desk. "Is this about the merger rumors? As you may know, I am not at liberty to discuss anything like that."

"Oh no. I'm not here to talk about any sort of merger. Actually, I'm here to ask you about Jason Rundell," Charlie said, dropping his name like a bomb in the middle of Peter's office to see how he would react.

"Oh," Peter said as he shifted in his chair. "That's a name I haven't heard in a while."

"I'm doing a piece on him and his disappearance. Do you mind if I record this?" Charlie asked as she put her phone on the desk.

"No, of course not," Peter said as he shifted in his brown leather seat.

"So, what can you tell me about him?"

Peter rubbed his chin. "Well, we were teammates on the intramural soccer team. That much you must know?" Charlie nodded. "And, we were friendly."

"Just friendly?" Charlie asked.

"No, what I mean to say is we were friends." Peter tapped his fingers on the top of his desk.

"What can you tell me about Jason's personality? What was he like?"

Peter's eyes grazed the ceiling. "Jason was a great guy. He liked soccer, he liked going out—he was the life of every party. When he disappeared, we were devastated. He had the whole world ahead of him."

"What about girlfriends?"

"Yeah, he had girlfriends. Or girls he hung out with. I don't know.... This was all so long ago."

"Were you with him the night he disappeared?"

Charlie watched as Peter's eyes landed back on hers. For a moment, she wasn't sure if he was going to answer her, but then he slowly nodded his head. "Yeah. Yeah, I was with him that night."

"What can you tell me about it?" Charlie knew she was making Peter uncomfortable, but she didn't care. She needed to know what he knew.

"We went to a house party off campus. I can't remember whose house it was, but I'm sure I told the detectives at the time." Charlie nodded. Silence spread between them, but she wouldn't be the one to talk first. "And we were just drinking and having fun."

"Who else was with Jason that night?"

Peter rubbed his face like this conversation was giving him a headache, and Charlie knew she was minutes away from him asking her to leave.

"There were some other soccer guys there, I remember. I'm sure they all gave statements after Jason disappeared."

"Anyone else?"

"Jason was with a girl, I think."

"Do you remember her name?"

"Name?" Peter laughed. "No, I don't remember her name. I never got her name. I'd be surprised if Jason even knew it. He met her at the party, I think."

"Could you describe her?"

"Listen, Ms. Walter, like I said, this was over a decade ago. I don't remember. Now, I've taken valuable time out of my day to tell you what I know, but that's that. I'm sorry, but there's not much more I can do for you." Peter rested his folded hands on top of his desk, letting her know this meeting was over.

"I understand," Charlie said as she stood. "Thank you for your time."

"Of course," Peter said as he stood to walk her out.

"I'll show myself out, thanks."

Once Charlie was in the elevator, she checked her phone. She had two missed calls. The numbers weren't saved in her phone, but she knew exactly who was trying to get in touch with her.

* * *

"That guy was a total prick," Scott Nelson said as he walked around the counter of Scott's Surf Shop carrying a surfboard above his shaggy blond hair.

Charlie ducked as he walked by and followed him to the other side of the store, where he put the surfboard down next to others that were leaning along the wall.

"He and I were roommates at the Sigma Chi house for a year, and it was the worst year of my life."

"Why's that?" Charlie asked.

"Because the rules didn't apply to him. He did what he wanted, when he wanted."

"Can you be a little more specific?"

Scott put his hands in his pockets and sighed. "For starters, he never cleaned up after himself, ever. He'd play loud music, even if I was asleep. And he loved playing pranks on people."

Charlie noticed a thin layer of perspiration forming at the top of Scott's forehead, and she wondered why the thought of an old messy roommate would make him sweat.

"Did he ever play a prank on you?" Charlie asked.

Scott laughed. "I was his main target. He'd steal my clothes and hide them all over the house, so I'd have to go on a freaking scavenger hunt to find them. That was mild compared to some of the other stuff, though. He'd put dog shit in my pillow case, spit in my food if I turned away from my plate, and then there was the whole thing with Lydia." Scott walked back toward the counter of the surf shop.

"Lydia?" Charlie asked as she followed behind him.

"Lydia Jacobs. She was a girl in my English Lit class," Scott said. Charlie thought she saw his jaw clench. "Jason found out I had a crush on her, and he started flirting with her. Next thing I know, he's waking me up in the middle of the night telling me to get lost because he brought a girl home. I bet you can guess who it was."

Charlie winced.

"Yep." Scott took a deep breath. "After that, I dropped out of the fraternity and moved to an apartment off campus."

"When was this?"

"Spring of my sophomore year."

"Did you see Jason after that?"

Scott shook his head. "He disappeared a month later."

* * *

Charlie leaned against the hood of her car while she looked up Lydia Jacobs from her phone. There were thirty-eight Lydia Jacobses on Facebook, five in the Los Angeles area, and one who had listed USC as their alma mater. Charlie took a chance and entered in an address she'd found on a sketchy-looking site that came up after she googled "Lydia Jacobs Los Angeles address."

It took her almost an hour to get to Silver Lake. Once she arrived, she drove through quaint suburban streets before she pulled up to a ranch house with a small front porch.

Charlie knocked on the door. There was a swing hanging from the ceiling of the porch on her right and a pair of rocking chairs to her left.

"Hello," a woman with blond hair cut to her chin said as she answered the door.

"Lydia Jacobs?"

"Yes." Lydia cocked her head.

"I'm Charlie Walter. I'm a reporter at the *Times*. I was wondering if I could talk to you about Jason Rundell?"

Unlike Peter and Scott, Lydia didn't look surprised when Charlie said Jason's name. In fact, Lydia looked relieved.

"Is this about what I saw in the news this morning?" Lydia asked.

"Yes."

They stood for a moment in silence before Lydia opened the door wider for Charlie to come inside the narrow hallway.

After Lydia offered Charlie some water, they sat down in the living room full of wicker furniture.

"I guess I knew it was only a matter of time before one of you showed up at my door," Lydia said.

"Why's that?" Charlie asked.

"Because of what happened between me and Jason." Lydia's fingers were intertwined on her lap. "Someone was bound to find out eventually."

"Can you tell me about that?"

"You don't know?" Lydia's eyes narrowed.

"I spoke to Scott Nelson. I know you were involved with Jason a month before he disappeared. I know you went home with him one night. And, I know you were at the party the night he disappeared." Charlie studied Lydia as she told two truths and a lie. When Lydia sighed, Charlie knew her assumption was correct. "It's better if you tell me what happened yourself. If you don't, other people will tell your story for you."

Lydia looked around her own home, as if she was searching for a way out of this, but Charlie had done this enough times to know that Lydia was going to talk. She knew the second Lydia opened the door for Charlie to come inside that she wanted to get this off her chest.

"I met Jason a month before he disappeared. He came up to me after my English Lit class and introduced himself. He fed me some line about how he'd noticed me a while ago and was building up the courage to talk to me. I fell for it. We went on a couple of dates, and he was charming and charismatic. I was smitten. Then, one night, we went to a party." Lydia closed her eyes. "We both drank. Then, he invited me back to his place. I said yes. When we got to his fraternity house, he asked me to wait outside while he told his roommate to leave. I'll never forget the look on Jason's face when Scott came out and saw me standing there. It was the scariest smile I've ever seen in my life. It was like he was amused by Scott's pain. Before that, I didn't know Scott liked me, but in that moment, it was obvious. Jason knew and was using it against his own roommate. I should have left right then and there, but I didn't. I went inside." Lydia opened her eyes and looked right at Charlie. "It's one of the biggest regrets of my life."

39

"What happened next?" Charlie asked.

"We were just kissing at first. He wanted to do more, but I said no. He didn't like that." Lydia looked away. "Anyway, I tried to fight back, but I'm sure you've seen pictures of him. He was a big guy. Eventually, my body just gave out, and I figured the best thing to do was to wait until it was over."

Charlie shook her head. "I'm so sorry."

"Yeah, me too. I can't say I'm sorry he's dead," Lydia said as she reached for her glass of water with a trembling hand.

"Do you know what happened the night he disappeared?"

"You were right. I was at the party that night. After what happened in his room, I fell apart. I stopped going to class, couldn't leave my bed, and barely ate. I followed him to the party that night. I wanted to confront him. I watched from the corner as he laughed with his dumb soccer friends, drank beer, and flirted with girls. I wanted to hurt him like he hurt me." There was an edge to her voice now, and Charlie noticed a throbbing blue vein appear in the middle of her forehead. "But I never got the chance. I went to the bathroom, and when I came out, I lost track of him. I looked everywhere, but he was gone. So, I went home. When I woke up the next morning, I heard he was missing."

"Did the police talk to you back then?" Charlie asked.

Lydia shook her head. "I didn't report the rape, so there was nothing connecting me to Jason. That is, until Scott said something to you."

"Right. Can someone verify what time you came home that night?"

"No, my roommate was out when I got home."

Charlie took a deep breath. "I believe you, but I'm not sure the cops will. You have motive and opportunity. If I were you, I'd work on strengthening your alibi."

"What? How do I do that?" Lydia sat back into the couch as if the weight of Charlie's words hit her square in the chest.

"Are you still close to your roommate?"

"Yeah, she's my best friend."

"Ask her again where she was that night. Maybe you remember wrong. Maybe she was home watching TV on the couch when you came home."

Lydia nodded wide-eyed as Charlie got up and started for the door.

"Hey," Lydia yelled after her. "Are you going to write about everything I told you?"

Charlie turned around and saw tears in her eyes.

"No," Charlie said. "This was off the record."

* * *

Charlie checked her phone when she got back inside her car. She had another two missed calls. She took a deep breath as her hands wrung the steering wheel like a wet rag. Before she put the car in gear, she picked up her phone and dialed.

"Hello?" A gruff voice answered.

"Detective Galuppo, this is Charlie Walter."

"Didn't think I'd be hearing from you so soon," Galuppo said. Charlie imagined him leaning back in his desk chair, the springs nearly giving way to his weight. "Solve my case yet?"

"Not yet, but I've got something for you," Charlie said.

"I'm listening."

"I'll need something in return, though."

"That depends on what you tell me."

Charlie expected him to say that, but she had no choice. She had to tell him what she knew in order to find out what he knew. Besides, it had only taken her a day to find Lydia Jacobs. She was good, but so were the cops. They'd find her by the end of the week, if not sooner. "I spoke to one of Jason's old soccer teammates, Peter Bryant. He told me Jason met a girl that night at the party."

"A girl?" Galuppo said. Charlie could hear the shuffling of paperwork on his end. "I don't remember anyone mentioning anything about a girl back then. Did he know her name?"

"No, but maybe this girl knows something about what happened to him that night."

"Hmm," Galuppo said.

41

"Your turn. Who are you talking to on your end?" Charlie asked.

Silence.

"Come on, Galuppo. You know I can help you."

Galuppo sighed. "All right. We've got a list of names we're going through and interviewing, on the assumption that the bones belong to Rundell. The ring had the year of his graduation engraved on it."

"The list is of the same people you interviewed after he disappeared?"

"Plus a couple new ones."

Charlie swallowed hard, but it didn't alleviate the rock-sized lump that had emerged in the middle of her throat.

"A witness we talked to this morning rattled off a handful of names we didn't have back then, so we're looking into them."

"Any chance you can send me that list?" Charlie asked.

"Keep dreaming, Walter."

"Listen, Detective," Charlie said as she dug around the middle console for her bottle of Tums. "It's barely been seven hours since the hiker called nine one one, and already there's been a lot of media coverage on the case. Trust me, you're going to want to control the narrative on this one, and to do that, you need a good reporter on your side." Her hand found the bottle and popped the top open. "Lucky for you, you happen to be on the phone with one right now. So, send me the list of names of people you're interviewing, and I'll make sure the public knows that the LAPD are doing everything in their power to finally close this cold case." She brought the bottle to her lips and let a couple of chalky tablets fall into her mouth.

Galuppo didn't say anything for a moment, and Charlie knew he was trying to think of an excuse to not send her that list.

"All right. Fine," Galuppo said at last. "But we talk to everyone first, okay? If I hear so much as a whisper that you're contacting these people before us, your ass is grass, Walter."

"You got it."

After she hung up, Charlie's phone dinged with an email notification. She opened the list and scanned the page of thirty or so names. Only when she reached the last name on the list did she realize she was holding her breath.

Before she could put her phone down, it started ringing in her hand. It was one of the unsaved numbers that had been calling her all day. Charlie knew it was time to answer.

* * *

It was nearly nine p.m. by the time Charlie pulled up to Barallo's Italian Ristorante. Inside, a young hostess wearing a white collared shirt looked up from her phone when Charlie approached.

"Table for one?" the hostess asked.

"Actually, I'm meeting a couple of friends," Charlie said as she craned her neck. Just then, Charlie saw Stephanie waving her down from the corner booth. Naomi was seated across from her. None of the nearby booths were occupied.

Charlie slid into the booth next to Stephanie.

"Thanks for coming," Charlie said as the two women each gave a solemn nod in return.

It had been eight years since Charlie had seen Stephanie or Naomi. Stephanie's dark hair was still long, falling well past her shoulders, and Naomi's eyes were the same piercing blue she had remembered. Charlie wanted to say something about how the years had been kind to them. She wanted to ask Stephanie about the pictures of her kids she had seen on Instagram and congratulate Naomi on becoming first violin chair in the Los Angeles symphony, but as Charlie looked between the set of anxious eyes staring back at her, she knew they didn't have time for any of that.

"So," Naomi started, her voice trailing off. "They're sure it's him?"

"They're pretty sure," Charlie said. "Once they run their tests, it'll be confirmed. I got a list of names the cops are going to interview—"

"How'd you get that?" Stephanie asked.

"Doesn't matter. But, Naomi, your name's on the list."

"Fuck," Naomi said as she put her forehead on the table.

"I talked to one of Jason's old teammates who said Jason met a girl that night, but he can't remember her name or her face."

"That's good," Stephanie said as she looked between Charlie and Naomi. "That's good, right?"

"For now, it's good," Charlie said to Stephanie before turning back to Naomi. "I don't know who placed you at the party that night, but there's no use denying you were there. If you do, the cops will label you a liar, and you'll lose all your credibility. That means, if Naomi was there that night, then Stephanie and I need to come forward and say we were there too."

"What? Why?" Naomi asked.

"Because you'll need us to confirm that we all left the party together."

"Well," Stephanie said. "Technically, that's true."

"Except it wasn't the three of us," Naomi said. "It was the four of us."

That night, a little more than ten years ago, Charlie, Stephanie, and Naomi had gone to a friend of a friend's house party to celebrate the end of the second semester. Music blared in their ears as they stood together in the living room full of sweaty bodies, jumping along to the beat. Together, the three of them threw their arms in the air as they belted out the lyrics to the songs that would mark their sophomore year.

A guy in a tank top with his fraternity's letters plastered across the front grabbed Naomi's hand and pulled her in to dance. Her eyes went wide with excitement as she looked back at Charlie and Stephanie, who nodded their approval.

A few songs later, while Naomi was still dancing with the frat guy, Charlie tapped Stephanie on the shoulder and pointed toward the stairs. The two of them went up to the bathroom, then stopped in the kitchen to grab a drink.

"Get one for Naomi," Stephanie said, handing Charlie another Solo cup.

By the time they made their way back to the dance floor, Naomi and the frat guy were nowhere to be found.

"Maybe she went to the bathroom?" Stephanie asked.

"We were just there, w. We would have passed her on the stairs," Charlie said as she scanned the room for her friend's blond hair.

"Maybe she went into one of the bedrooms?" Stephanie said.

"Yeah. Let's just go check on her, make sure she's okay."

Stephanie followed Charlie back up the stairs to where the bedrooms were.

"Naomi?" Charlie said as she knocked on one of the wooden bedroom doors. She waited a moment before she turned the handle.

"Hey!" A guy yelled once she opened the door. He was sitting on the edge of the bed with a woman who wasn't Naomi.

"Sorry," Charlie said as she closed the door.

In the next two rooms they checked, all they found were piles of dirty laundry and unmade beds.

"She wouldn't have left, would she?" Stephanie asked.

They took out their phones to see if they had a text from Naomi saying she was going home, but they didn't. Stephanie texted their group chat, asking Naomi where she was. While they waited for her to reply, Charlie suggested they look downstairs again.

It was Stephanie who spotted the back door off the kitchen. The two of them stepped onto the small back porch and breathed in the hot night air. Even from outside, the music was loud, but not loud enough that Charlie couldn't hear the muffled noises coming from the depths of the backyard.

Charlie took the steps two at a time. Stephanie followed. Once they were in the backyard, they heard small cries that could have been mistaken for an injured animal. Then, a man, grunting, his breath fast and gasping. Charlie took out her phone and turned the flashlight on. There, past the garage, away from the crowded party, was Naomi. She was lying on the ground. The right side of her face was smashed in the dirt. Her one visible eye was bulging and desperate as a faceless man loomed over her with one hand around her neck as he pushed himself against her.

Charlie didn't remember seeing the rock or even picking it up. One minute, her hand was empty, and the next, she was wielding the rock above her head before bringing it down on the back of the man's head.

He didn't scream or cry out. He just slumped over and rolled onto the ground. Free from the man's grip, Naomi gasped for air as she stumbled to her feet into Stephanie's arms. Naomi's small body shook as she pulled up her shorts. Red marks appeared around her neck where the man had held her down, choking her nearly to death.

Charlie stared at the unconscious man at her feet. Maybe it was the fact that he was brazen enough to assault her friend right outside a crowded party, maybe it was a gut instinct, but something told Charlie this wasn't the first time he had done something like this. And, in that moment, she knew one thing was certain: if he did it once, he would do it again. That's when she picked up the rock that had since fallen from her fingers. Once again, she held it over her head and brought it down on the man's head. This time, she didn't stop hitting him until Stephanie and Naomi pulled her away from his lifeless body.

* * *

"Anything to drink?" The waiter asked as he looked between Charlie, Stephanie, and Naomi.

"We need a minute, thank you," Stephanie said.

"I should have gone to the police back then," Charlie said after the waiter walked away. Tears gathered in the corners of her eyes as the weight of the past pressed down on her shoulders. "Maybe it's time I finally tell the truth about what I did."

"What *we* did," Stephanie corrected her. "It was my idea to bury him out at Whoops Trail. I'm just as guilty as you are."

"But I was the one who—"

"Who saved me," Naomi said as she reached across the table and put her hand on top of Charlie's. "You're the one who saved me."

The lump inside Charlie's throat grew as she looked between the women she had known since the first day of college. Even though life had carried them in different directions, for better or worse, they were bonded by what happened that night by the garage. Charlie was thankful that even though ten years had passed, their loyalty to each other remained unchanged.

"So," Stephanie said, straightening her back. "We left the party together."

"That's right," Naomi said.

Charlie nodded. "Together."

WHAT'S REALLY UNFORGETTABLE

by Ken Funsten, CFA

I was talking to Clarissa, who was holding the phone up to our baby daughter Cassie's mouth so she could tell me her newest word. Barely two years old—it was 1998—she'd seemed so happy gurgling gobbledygook up to then. (Remember those long strings of sounds you figured meant nothing but later wished you'd recorded?) Only suddenly, our little jewel had taken to enriching our lives by enunciating whole, understandable, and even complex sentences out of nowhere! Sitting at my desk at work, I could picture her toothy grin, looking at the phone for approval after each one of them. I felt like I was in heaven there but wished I was home instead. And that was the very moment when Mimi, our newest assistant at Acorn Financial, the hedge fund manager I ran in Greenwich, Connecticut, rapped her knuckles on my open door.

"Mr. Kieper, sorry to interrupt you, but there's a gentleman on hold, calling from Los Angeles, and he's getting pretty demanding. And one other thing. He says he's the police."

That got my attention. So I bade goodbye to my "girls"—who were curating domestic memories while I paid for them at work—and told Mimi to put this dedicated public servant through to me. The things you'll do when your name's on the door.

The gruff voice introduced himself as Hank Chinaski, a detective from Parker Center, the Los Angeles Police Department's headquarters at the time. At first, he played nice, tossing his thank-yous as wide as confetti at a birthday party, but then he seemed to let go of his manners when I asked him to get to the point. "Time's money," I said. "Why are you calling me, sir?"

"All right," Chinaski grunted. "Just trying to be nice. So when was the last time you were in LA?"

I flashed back to memories of the town I grew up in before moving east with Clarissa and most of our employees to where the "old money" was, and still is, the East Coast, first relocating Acorn Financial to Midtown Manhattan, then to Greenwich, Connecticut.

"Well, last year. Mr. Nate Hensdorff—Acorn's director of trading—and I were on a West Coast marketing trip. And that took us through Southern California and—"

"And you haven't been back since?"

"No, sir." Work was too demanding—and honestly, I was making too much money, though I wouldn't tell Chinaski that—to be able to afford any travel that wasn't business-related. My discipline had been doubly necessary since Clarissa stopped working and Cassie was born. And now, in addition to the baby, we had a new house, the manse in Old Greenwich, where all the other hedge fund chieftains and their families lived. Who said you couldn't keep up with the Joneses? My hard work sowed the fruits of my labor, though too often, I barely saw the harvest myself.

Detective Chinaski interrupted my reverie by taking another tack. "Okay, look, then let's not beat a dead horse around the bush here. So, just hypothetically, you know, assuming you haven't been to LA since last fall like you say, can you tell me why a man without any other identification would have your business card in his pocket?"

"My business card?"

"That's right. We found the victim in an off-site parking structure near LAX. Beat up with nothing on him but your card. That is, if you're the same Quentin Kieper, CFA, president and portfolio manager of Acorn Financial in Greenwich, Connecticut, like it says on the evidence I'm holding in my hand."

I thought about my last contact with somebody from Los Angeles. It would be a helluva coincidence if this unconscious victim was the man who had come to visit us in Greenwich only a few days before.

"So you haven't been able to identify your victim yet? What's he look like? How old is he?"

There was another long silence from Chinaski, almost as if someone had punched the mute button, and then he came back on and said, "Well, he's Asian."

I waited for the follow-up—the further clue that would move things forward. I figured this Jack Benny from Parker Center had perfected Hollywood's suspense beat. Maybe even written a few spec scripts for *Dragnet*. I figured I'd outwait him—then outwit him.

But I blinked.

"Your description fits over half the world's population," I said…before I again pictured the man we'd met with in Acorn's offices: Wyatt Hu, a world-class entrepreneur. Born in China, emigrated with a wife and three kids from Taiwan, landed a little over thirty years ago in a suburb of Los Angeles, he'd built a company that supplied America's new immigrant communities with homes, which they paid him good money for. He'd come to Greenwich late the previous week to see me about Acorn's investment services. The company he'd built, Hu Holdings, was teed up to go public, and he'd read Acorn's performance record was superlative, bar none. Taking his company public via an IPO, or initial public offering, would create the largest liquidity event of his life, so he was interviewing money managers to invest the proceeds he hoped to receive. I told him Acorn wanted to be one of those managers.

Could the man with my business card in his pocket be that same entrepreneur, Wyatt Hu?

I shared my hunch with Chinaski, explaining how I'd had meetings with Hu just a few days earlier, that business cards had been exchanged, and that, yes, Wyatt Hu was ethnically Chinese. I told him liquidity events like Hu Holdings going public meant potential new business for investment managers like Acorn, and so it was not unusual for us and others to be visited by clients and potential clients like Hu. He'd have my business card because I'd given him one. Additionally, he was the only Asian I remembered meeting with in months. Still, I cautioned, my hunch wasn't a guarantee. "Do you have any photos of your victim you could send me?"

My suggestion prompted an immediate email from the LAPD, with a link bringing up photos of a dark face covered with puffy purple blotches—and yet memorable to me as Wyatt Hu.

"Yes, this might be him," I said nonchalantly. "Of course, I can't be sure with your technology's substandard resolution, but it could be. What kind of shape is the man in?"

I was working to hide my growing anxiety. While Detective Chinaski grumbled an answer, I took my then-new Motorola StarTAC clamshell from my briefcase and, hoping I had reception indoors, dialed the private number we had listed for Wyatt Hu on Acorn's "Marketing Hot List." His phone rang twice, then went direct to a recording that stated he was unavailable and voicemail was full. Acorn Financial's newest potential account, a windfall I'd counted on, was now at best a huge "if."

Losing the Hu account would be a material loss. We needed the additional revenue to pay for all my recent expenses—both business and personal. But my feelings of concern weren't totally commercial. I'd found Wyatt Hu genuinely likable. It was frosting on the cake that Hu's liquidity event would add to Acorn's bottom line. At least, that's what I told myself.

Chinaski, now with a name for his vic, told me he'd order up a search for fingerprint records and next of kin. But before he did, he intended to check in with the medical center where Hu had been taken, the regional hospital then known as County USC, housed in those days in the mammoth Depression-era art deco "castle" east of downtown. Chinaski asked if I'd like to remain on the line.

"Sure," I said. And so, in no time, using his gruff authority, the detective had a sympathetic hospital staffer synopsizing the patient's medical file for us: "John Doe" had been brought in after midnight that day, badly beaten and unconscious. He intermittently had regained consciousness. But remained unable to remember who he was or what happened to him before being brought to the hospital. Preliminary diagnosis was a concussion. Secondary diagnosis, traumatic emotional shock. X-rays had been requested. Prognosis was "TBD"—to be determined.

Hearing all this, I knew what I should do. Acorn couldn't give up. And if not me, who? I had to find a way to score the Hu account, but to accomplish that, I undoubtedly had to be in Los Angeles. It was the city I once called home and where I'd begun my lucrative investment management career. Memories flooded back for me: First meeting Clarissa. Then, my initial investing victories. The fast takeoff of our fund. I told Detective Chinaski that I intended to fly out that night so the next morning, I could provide him with an in-person ID of his victim—*if* I recognized him as Wyatt Hu.

Chinaski said it was a free country, so I could do what I liked. But he'd be looking forward to meeting me the next day at the hospital if I could catch a flight.

* * *

Late the next morning, Nate Hensdorff and I found ourselves traveling by taxi from the glitz of the Loews Hotel in Santa Monica, where we'd spent the night, slogging all the way through LA traffic to the grittiness of Boyle Heights, hoping to identity Wyatt Hu and then to somehow bring the amnesiac's big account back within our grasp.

Nate had decided to come with me to LA at the last minute, begrudgingly admitting markets could survive without him for a few days. I'd been happy to have his company. Starting as my mentor, Nate Hensdorff had become my partner when we'd formed Acorn together, after our former boss, Tommy Candiotti, had died a half-dozen years earlier. During the intervening time, I'd watched Nate's hair turn from gray to white, his frame from thin to thinner. I hoped all the financial excitement I'd gotten us into wasn't the cause. But even then, I knew it hadn't made him any younger. I've come to understand since then, we're all clocks winding down in life. And that once we stop ticking, we're only alive in others' memories.

On the plane, Nate and I had reviewed what we both knew, agreeing that the most likely explanation for Hu's mugging—if it was Hu—was a random robbery. However, we also concluded that the second-most likely explanation was someone wanting to halt Hu Holdings's stock offering. Without its founder and chairman present, the company's plans to go public would be a no-go. Investment bankers who were working the deal would pull the plug. And once that happened, there'd be no liquidity event for Wyatt Hu—and no new account for Acorn.

We couldn't stand by and let that happen. It might sound selfish to some, but we had our own business interests to pursue and protect. That's why we'd paid up for same-day seats on the previous night's last flight to LA.

After we'd checked into the Loews, due to the time difference, it had been too late for me to call Clarissa and Cassie. Wanting to be a good husband and a good father, too, I'd promised Clarissa I'd start working toward a positive work-life balance. A family balance. Once I made the promise, however, she warned me not to forget it. And yet, the next morning, after a late breakfast, a lot of coffee, and still no time for a proper phone call, Nate and I were once again totally immersed in our business venture.

In the front lobby of the great stone monument that was County USC, we met Hank Chinaski. I'd been ready for someone as big as the building, but Chinaski still surprised me. Chinaski was large, with a face worse off than Robert De Niro's in *Raging Bull*, as if he'd gotten into a dog fight when younger—and the dog had won. We shook hands, his large and meaty compared to mine. Chinaski grumbled something, then took us up by the elevator to see the victim and document our positive—or negative— identification.

Standing crunched together inside the small white room, I gazed at the heavily bandaged body on the bed. It was obvious he'd taken a beating. "Beatings are our beat," I'd heard one cop say to another in the airport the night before, as if it were a joke. But this was no joke to the man we saw lying motionless. The Wyatt Hu who had visited our offices had been an impatient man, even by trading-room standards. He'd been quick like a crack analyst, but also eager to dissect our marketing presentation titled "Hedge Funds for Positive Performance in Non-Trending Environments."

The Hu we'd met then had been a man fully engaged while the current figure on the bed was barely breathing.

Nevertheless, Nate and I both confirmed for the LAPD that the patient in the bed in front of us indeed appeared to be the man we knew as Wyatt Hu, the wealthy entrepreneur on the verge of taking his private company public. It was just then that a lanky young man in blue scrubs poked his head into the patient's room, nodding at the burly detective and motioning for us to please step outside with him. There, he introduced himself as Dr. Andy Pasqual, a resident neurologist. Chinaski then introduced Nate and me as "colleagues" of the victim, before abruptly asking, "What's the latest, Doc?"

Moving us farther down the corridor, Pasqual began by saying, "The patient—I still think of him as John Doe, but I take it you've confirmed his name is Wyatt Hu?" I nodded, and the doctor continued, "Well, as you can see, he's badly bruised but physically stable. We've found no major internal issues. Still, it's his memory loss that worries me."

"No family's turned up yet?" Chinaski asked.

Pasqual raised his eyebrows at this question. "We were told you found someone, a child? But no, I haven't seen anyone yet."

"When Mr. Hu's been conscious," I broke in, "how is he?"

"That's the thing. He asks for water, asks where he is. Listens. Nods. Seems content, has no sense of panic about him, but doesn't have a clue when we ask him who he is."

"Maybe the sight of us will jog his memory?" Nate suggested.

"I hope seeing you two will do that. I'd like to try it if you'll stick around. It's interesting," Pasqual continued before we could answer him, "the patient is exhibiting what's called repressed-memory defense mechanism. He understands there's been an accident, but he can't recall anything specific about how it occurred. Amnesia like this can be caused by a hard knock on the head, or it can be the result of a painful emotional trauma. Your appearance might help us determine which it is in this patient's case."

Nate and I looked at Chinaski, and he indicated he'd appreciate any help we could give him.

"What if seeing us again doesn't help?" Nate asked.

"Then we'll be in no worse shape than we are now," Pasqual replied. "We're still awaiting our radiologist's conclusion as to a concussion. But if that's out, it increases the possibility that the memory loss is neurological or psychological in nature. All we know now is that he's in good hands and is cooperating in his own recovery. He seems a very nice man, but to every question we ask him about his family, he says he's forgotten."

Pasqual let this bushel of information be digested, then added, "Memory loss, when it occurs, isn't necessarily permanent. Sometimes it restores itself, and all that's needed is time with no other intervention. But sometimes, memories stay lost—forever unremembered."

Back down the hall, I saw a nurse poke her head out the doorway of Hu's room. She called out, "Dr. Pasqual, your patient's awake now."

"Well? Let's see if we can get some fresh answers."

We re-entered and found Wyatt Hu sitting up in bed. Upon seeing us, neither recognition nor fear lay in his eyes. In fact, his puffy face evinced only a sense of dopey curiosity, appearing more like a baby in front of a TV than a risk-adverse victim of a recent mugging.

"Have you got something for me?" Hu asked, grinning at us as we drew closer.

"Mr. Hu, do you remember Nate Hensdorff?" I motioned in back of me to the lean trader. "Or me, Quentin Kieper?"

The patient looked back and forth from me to Nate. "Should I?"

"Just a few days ago, you visited our offices in Connecticut," Nate tried.

"Ring any bells?" Chinaski asked.

Hu considered all of us for a long moment. "No, no bells. I...I don't remember you," he confessed, gazing at each of us with what seemed real sorrow.

"It's all right," the nurse interceded, giving Pasqual a wink. "You will after a while. Just keep trying, okay? Keep resting." She turned back to the doctor. "I've been told his son's coming to visit tonight."

"Then we don't want to overtire him before that," Dr. Pasqual said. "First visits from family after an accident like this can often be traumatic."

* * *

Less than five minutes later, Nate and I were walking toward the elevators after leaving Detective Chinaski with Dr. Pasqual when we heard a woman's voice in front of us. "No, don't leave. Even if he doesn't know you, it's important for him. Wait!"

Down the hall, we saw a middle-aged Asian man with a nurse. She reached out to him. He swatted at her, knocking her down. Then he took off, disappearing through a door to the building's stairwell.

Nate and I rushed to help the unfortunate woman. "Are you okay? What was that all about?" Nate asked.

"He said he wanted to see the patient in bed twelve and wanted to be alone with him, even if he was unconscious. To say goodbye. But when I told him the patient was now conscious and talking with you, he just took off."

"Did he give you his name?"

"He said his name was Hubert Hu."

* * *

I figured that a family member bolting when he finds an older relation conscious instead of comatose is not indicating relief, but guilt. That was conclusion number one. Secondly, I figured if we could catch him, maybe he'd shed some light on what had really happened to Wyatt Hu.

I looked at Nate. He could read me like a bar chart. "Let's go," I urged my partner. "Maybe we can catch up with him."

But rushing down the stairwell and into the lobby, at first sight, there was no sign of the man. Then we saw him. He had the same strong gaze as Wyatt Hu but a weaker chin.

"Mr. Hu?" I called, and he stopped, turning to look at us, then scowled.

"Leave me alone. I'm in mourning for my father."

"But he's not dead. Your father's not dead. We spoke to him."

"With the injuries he's got, he may be tomorrow. Anyway, I've got to go now. I've got a company to run."

"But if you know he's alive, why the hell don't you go up and see him?" Nate said, staring. "Your dad might have things he needs to tell you, things to do. Maybe some good advice, too."

"It's my business, not yours." Hubert Hu stared daggers back at Nate, then turned from us, pushing through the heavy glass-and-metal lobby doors. We watched as he walked down the steep steps to the street, before giving a man waiting by the curb a handful of bills. Then he took off in the red Jaguar the man had been guarding.

"What was that all about?" I asked Nate.

"I don't know. But I bet we can find out."

So, with his usual charm, Nate succeeded in borrowing a computer with internet access from a young nurse. She even let us sit down to work at her station. There, Nate was able to pull up the preliminary regulatory filings for the Hu Holdings IPO—though no finalized financial audit yet. This was information we hadn't yet considered in our dealings with Hu personally. There, we saw Hubert Hu was listed as the company's chief financial officer, with a total pre-tax salary and bonus of over a half a million a year, which was still quite a nice income in those days.

"He's married with two kids, both in private schools," Nate said after pulling up an *LA Times* article using the Yahoo! search engine. "He lives in Holmby Hills. A ritzy neighborhood, right? He gives a ton of money to his alma mater, USC. His wife, Marji, does volunteer work. There are even some photos of Hubert with his red Jag, as well as some of him with his family on vacation in Maui last Christmas."

"That indicates a lot of spending, even on his salary. How's he afford all that? The interest alone on what's probably a huge mortgage would take a big bite out of his after-tax paycheck every month." I spoke from experience.

"Way big. Total expenses might even exceed Daddy's generosity," commented my friend, the old trader. "But whereas his father's a shrewd businessman, that toolbox hasn't necessarily traveled with the genes."

"You thinking what I'm thinking? Was the elder Hu in any of those Maui photos?"

"Not a one."

"It could be he doesn't like Hawaii," I suggested.

"Or it could be someone else doesn't like going on vacation while Daddy watches him spend all that money."

* * *

For the rest of that day, progress remained slow. Hu's daughters—Hubert's sisters—were located. They'd been visiting family in Asia but were returning now to attend to their father's needs. Hu's daughter-in-law said she hadn't seen her husband for three or four days. No one at Hu Holdings returned the hospital's calls, but Nate and I figured Hubert had told them not to. We tried to sell Chinaski on our suspicions about the victim's son, but he wasn't entirely buying it. Nevertheless, Xerox copies of Hubert's photo had been circulated to the staff, so the son would immediately be identified if he did return. The older Hu was quickly regaining strength, but the amnesia remained. Nate and I couldn't afford to be away from Acorn's offices much longer and needed to find some way to bring Hu's memory back quick, because for both Hu and us, memory was now money.

So I decided to concentrate on the patient, not the crime and left Nate standing guard outside Wyatt Hu's room. What could I do to increase our chances of bringing in the money? Was there something I'd forgotten?

I decided to spend the afternoon at USC's Doheny Library, researching articles on amnesia, repressed memory, and PTSD, which at the time was often still referred to as simply "trauma syndrome." My largest problem was not knowing what had caused Hu to forget. Like everyone else, I was in the dark there. Then, I read a couple of articles in succession that gave me an idea.

Rushing out of the library, I flagged a taxi just off campus to take me back to the medical center, where I shared with Nate my idea to re-stage Hu's mugging. According to articles I'd read that afternoon, reliving an emotional trauma might sometimes bring back a patient's memory. I knew we had to do something—or pack up our tent and go home. As for me, I was eager for one last at-bat.

So Nate and I rehearsed it. Then we bought a couple red bandannas at the hospital gift shop to cover our faces, inhaled a couple tuna fish sandwiches in the hospital cafeteria, and took the elevator up to Hu's room. Putting on our masks, we gathered outside his door, then rushed in fast and furious.

From the start, our show failed to convince. Maybe someone had tipped Hu off? But who?

"You guys"—the recovering patient laughed—"why are you wearing napkins on your faces? Are your noses cold? You two have been funny for as long as I can remember."

I pulled down my bandanna. "How long's that been?"

Wyatt Hu shrugged. "Not very long, I guess." His smile still held the simplicity of a child's. "But you don't fool me. I remember you from yesterday."

"But not from last week?" Nate asked, pulling down his own bandanna. "When you were in our offices?"

The man in the bed shook his head.

Just then, Hubert Hu entered the room. He had tried to disguise himself with sunglasses and a floppy hat pulled over his brow. His weak chin, however, made him unforgettable. Carrying a pillow—whose purpose couldn't have been more obvious—he looked at us, and his mouth dropped open in surprise. But as I turned around to gaze at his father, I saw what really had astounded the son. There'd been a tremendous change in Wyatt Hu. His face had gone livid, with drool spilling from his lips. Then the man's whole body started to quiver as he sputtered sounds with no meaning, like some mad baby working itself up for a big cry.

"How could *you* betray your own family? How could you?" the older Hu asked the younger. "You would cheat your sisters, our employees, and who else with your embezzlement? You forget you can't keep your lies secret forever." The man's eyes glimmered now with the intensity I'd remembered from our meeting in Greenwich.

"You gambled, then when I tried to save what was left, you"—the father's face twisted, the sweat making it glisten now like granite—"you gave me a beating! Did you really believe I wouldn't be able to remember? But I did.

And I do now. How could I forget?"

The son turned white. "You don't understand," he pleaded with his father. "I had to. They were going to hurt me. I had to make minimum payments. And then, with the IPO, a final audit would have exposed me. You would have had to fire me, Father. So, I had to stop the IPO. I had to stop you. I had no choice." Tears streamed down Hubert's face. He started blubbering. "I couldn't let that happen, Father. I couldn't lose everything."

"Truth will out," the older man cried.

Luckily, their verbal jousting had by now attracted the attention of a nurse and Dr. Pasqual, both of whom rushed in to restrain the patient from getting out of bed. Wyatt Hu looked ready to wring his son's neck. Reliving the trauma had obviously worked. But the pain had been real.

Nate and I pushed Hubert from the room, and he took off like a jackrabbit down the hospital hall. We didn't bother to give chase this time, figuring we might not be able to catch him but that the police—or his bookie—would.

"Is Mr. Hu okay?" I asked when the doctor exited the patient's room.

"He's going to be sleeping now. I gave him something that should calm him. But I hope he'll retain his memory when he wakes."

I hoped so, too. But as I thought more about it, I wondered if Wyatt Hu would hope the same thing. There are some memories perhaps better left forgotten, like an attempted patricide—or at least better left for literature instead of real life.

* * *

It was the following week—back home in Acorn's offices—when we heard the rest of the story: How a big mortgage, two private school tuition payments, and expensive tastes in cars and clothing, along with fondnesses for eating out, buying fine wine, and first-class travel, had drained all of Hubert Hu's salary and savings. Then, he'd begun gambling to make up for that personal and family budget deficit. Needing ever more funds to cover his losses, Hu had taken on greater and greater risks with cards, ponies, and even college football pools, losing right and left—ending up owing a small fortune to some very serious people.

That's when Hubert Hu had started "borrowing" from his father's company in order to pay the minimum to the bookies and sharks who'd already loaned him money. Hu was digging a hole deeper and deeper for himself—and everyone around him. And then his father started talking about Hu Holdings going public. That was the last straw—because the final step in that going-public process would have been a CPA's audit of the company's financial accounts. And such an audit would certainly have divulged the embezzlement.

Hubert figured it was him or the old man, and he made up his mind to make it look like his father had been mugged and murdered. In fact, at the airport that night, Hubert had been carrying a knife. At the last moment, however, he hadn't had the guts. Or the heart. Instead, he'd left Wyatt Hu unconscious in an LAX remote parking structure, hoping the night's edge and his father's age would finish the job.

But his father was tough—a fighter and entrepreneur. He'd persevered.

Then, when the son heard his father was still alive, he began to fear he might wake up and remember it all. So Hubert came to find him at the hospital to make sure he didn't. But he would never have hurt his father if he hadn't been under such unforgettable financial duress. At least that's what he claimed when he confessed to the police, begging for time served in exchange for the names of his bookies and underworld lenders.

The DA's office declined his offer.

* * *

Months later—it was December if my memory serves me—I strode into Acorn's trading room crowing.

"Another home run!"

"What home run?" Nate moaned, rolling his chair back from his Bloomberg terminal. "It's not even spring training yet, and our performance is barely break-even this week. Admittedly, it's only Tuesday." He relaxed. "So, plenty of time to turn it around."

"I'm not talking about our portfolio performance, but our assets under management. We just scored the Hu account." I held up my palm for high fives all around. "He said he's grateful we flew out to LA to help his recovery, so he's giving us double what we talked about before. Tommy would be thrilled, wouldn't he?" I asked, referring to our old boss. "Remember how he always used to tell us the real business we're in isn't *managing* money, it's bringing in money under management? Then he'd add, 'And never forget that.'"

I clapped Nate on the back.

"Take it easy," the old guy muttered before turning around, returning to study his Bloomberg. "We've got work to do here, end-of-the-year stuff, families to support. That's something you can't forget."

"Don't remind me," I said with the determined grin of a good husband. "Between Clarissa and our new mortgage, I'm never allowed to forget it."

THE FEAST OF THE SEVEN FISHES

By Gail Alexander

Lace shivered as she stood in De La Rosa's fish market, busily depositing scallops into a clear plastic bag. The cold air blasting across the nearby ocean's surface shook the windows.

"Remind me what we're doing here on Christmas Eve?" Lisa said from across one of the white-clothed tables arranged in rows, with trays of fish chilling on ice. She stood in front of the trout.

Lace smiled. Her friend did like to complain. "Make sure you look at the eyes. We want fish with clear eyes. That's how you know they're fresh. And, to answer your question,"—as if Lisa didn't already know—"we're here because our new and very generous client wants a traditional Italian Christmas Eve dinner for family and friends. The Feast of the Seven Fishes. Its roots are religious. Catholic, I think. And there's nowhere better to find fresh fish than here."

De La Rosa's had earned the distinction of having the freshest catch of the day in San Pedro, delivered from trawlers moored a few yards away. If they didn't have what you wanted, either purchased from local fishermen or imported from international markets, then no one did.

"I know, I know," Lisa said. "We shop. We cook. We serve."

"Then we'll catch the one a.m. flight to Park City and the Snow Lodge and start our Christmas vacation." Lace walked toward a tray of ahi tuna fillets. "Anyway, I'm the one who should be complaining. I hate fish, as ridiculous as that is for a chef. I can hardly bear to touch them." She brought her arm up to cover her nose. "And they stink."

Lace briefly turned toward the window. The sound of waves beating against the rocks competed with the high-pitched squawking of seagulls—so many that the sky looked to be painted white with only patches of blue.

A strand of Lisa's hair fell forward as she tried in vain to tuck in back behind her ear with her arm. Lace chuckled. How physically different she and her best friend were—Lisa was lanky with long brown hair, while petite Lace wore her blond hair cropped around her face. Thankfully, in the important ways—the things they valued—they were more alike than different.

The market's owner, a portly man in a white apron, approached Lace. He held out a bag of halibut, cut into chunks as requested, which she would include in a cioppino—Italian soup. "Thank you, Mr. De," she said, using his preferred nickname. He nodded affably. His red cheeks were cherub-like. Lace took the fish and couldn't help but notice his chapped red hands. "I'm also going to need seven lobsters."

He nodded and walked toward a tank while Lace tilted her head, amazed at the racket coming from outside. "Why are the seagulls making so much noise?"

"They squawk as a warning," Mr. De said as he began pulling out the lobsters.

* * *

A few minutes later, after Lisa had put the lobsters in their van, she walked toward her friend, wondering if Lace was almost done. A man entered the doorway from the back room, shouting something in Italian. Mr. De checked his watch. His brow furrowed as he nervously tunneled his fingers through his hair. "Sorry, I have to see to this untimely delivery. I'll be right back."

Lisa pointed to their two coolers partly filled with fish and said, "We have tuna, trout, halibut, scallops, and lobsters. What else do we need?"

Lace handed her a recipe book with turquoise cover. A narrow piece of tan butcher-block paper, serving as a bookmark, stuck out of the top. Lisa opened the book and read for a moment. "Other fishes we could use include salmon and eel."

"Forget eel." Lace wrinkled her nose.

"Anchovies?" Lisa asked, meeting the same disapproval. "Well then, by my count, that'll make this the feast of the five fishes. How about shrimp?"

"Technically, shrimp is a crustacean, not a fish, but yes, let's get some," Lace said.

"Aren't lobsters...?"

"Crustaceans? Yes, but they're red for Christmas."

Lisa nodded. There was no need for further explanation. They had been best friends since grade school, so she was never surprised by typical Lace logic.

Lace had always had a gift for pairing foods, while Lisa had a head for numbers. After high school, Lace went to culinary school, and Lisa attended business school. Now, nearly ten years later, Lace was a highly sought-after caterer chef in the LA area, and Lisa did the serving, kept the books, and invested their profits—as well as helped Lace do things like buy fish on Christmas Eve.

"Excuse me for asking, but how are you going to put the lobsters into a pot of boiling water without touching them?" Lisa asked as she gathered the shrimp.

"Not boiling water. It makes them tense their muscles, and then the meat will be tough. You're going to entice them into a tepid water bath with a nice Chardonnay. As soon as you get them drunk enough, you'll turn up the heat," Lace said with a lilt of whimsy in her tone.

Lisa could only smile at her friend. Lace was as naive as the tuna that swallowed the bait and ended up on the hook. But then she'd surprise everyone by solving an impossible problem with the most simplistic remedy.

After going through the fish in the coolers to double-check they had what they needed, Lace went to get their final fish, salmon. Just then, the man who'd called for Mr. De came out from the back room carrying a tray of fresh salmon on a bed of ice. Lisa walked over as he put it on a shelf under a table, smoothing the white cloth that draped to the floor. Mr. De must anticipate more customers today, Lisa thought, enough that he'll want to quickly move the new fish onto the table when the tray on top was empty, which it nearly was.

Lace and Lisa knelt to examine the tray when they heard loud, angry voices calling Mr. De and heavy footsteps stomping their way through the market, one row over from where they were kneeling.

Lisa popped her head above the table just as one of two men pushed the salmon man into the back room at gunpoint.

Dropping down, Lisa mouthed "gun" and motioned to her friend to start crawling toward the front door, which was partially open. They'd barely moved before they saw a third man, his jacket unbuttoned, hands on his hips, a gun holstered under his jacket sleeve. He was pacing near the entrance. They slipped under the white cloth, peeking around its edges, then quietly pulled their wheeled coolers under the table, too. Lisa prayed they wouldn't be spotted. That's when several birds flew inside, squawking frenetically. Two of them waddled toward Lisa and Lace, probably looking for food, but threatening to give away their position. *So much for prayers.*

The man with the gun started following the gulls, as if wondering what they were after. Lisa fought not to shake. A few more steps, and he'd be on top of them.

Just then, the clamor of metal trays crashing to the floor and loud, angry voices shouting in Italian made the man stop. The birds had the good sense to scurry toward the door, seeking solitude elsewhere, but they got caught between the man's legs. He was detangling himself when someone shouted, "I don't know anything. I just clean up." Then silence.

The man unholstered his gun. He ran toward the back room. Mr. De bolted out, colliding with the man, knocking him into a table of fish. Mr. De caught his balance and ran toward the front door, but he didn't make it. The unmistakable sound of a gunshot rang out. It was loud enough to scare the gulls outside to take flight in a frenzy, squawking and flapping their wings.

Mr. De La Rosa lay on the floor inches from Lisa and Lace, clearly dead.

Lisa could tell her friend was about to scream, so she placed a hand over Lace's mouth.

One of the other men ran out. He stood over Mr. De's body, close enough that Lisa could have touched the small piece of fish stuck to one of his soft black elevator shoes with two-inch heels. She held her breath, praying now the men would go away.

The man sighed. "We're not gonna be able to squeeze the information out of him now."

The wail of distant police sirens filled the air. Help was on the way. Mr. De must have hit a silent alarm while he was in the back. *Okay, maybe prayers could work.*

One of the men shouted, *"Politzia!"*

They started running. "What about our—" one of the others yelled, only to be cut off by the third man.

"You want to be here when the police arrive?" he shouted as they dashed out the door, most likely to a waiting car.

After kneeling silently for a minute, giving the men time to drive away, Lisa pushed the tablecloth aside and crawled out. "Come on. Let's get out of here."

"Aren't we going to wait for the police?" Lace asked as she stood up, grabbing her utility bag.

"Why? We can't help them. We don't know anything. All we'll do is get our names and maybe our pictures on the six o'clock news and alert whoever killed Mr. De La Rosa that we were here." Lisa pulled the coolers out from under the table.

"Well, we should check on the other man in the back room."

"You really think they left him alive?" Lisa asked.

Lace sighed and reached for her recipe book, but then pivoted and began stuffing salmon into a large plastic bag. When the woman had a plan for her food, she was hard to deter.

Lisa tugged on her arm. "Come on!"

Lace removed seven one-hundred-dollar bills from her wallet. She dropped the money on top of the tray of salmon, put her bagged salmon in one of the coolers, and they ran out the door.

* * *

A couple of hours later, after the medical examiner had officially declared the men dead and the forensics team had finished taking photos, homicide Detective Matthew Wade began examining the crime scene. That's when FBI Agent Seth Williams arrived. Like the last time Wade had seen him, Williams was well-groomed, in a sharp suit. Wade was also well-groomed, but his suit, he realized, was already wrinkled from crouching beside the bodies.

"What are the feds doing here?" Wade walked to shake Williams's hand.

"Celebrating Christmas, what else?" He glanced around. "We got a tip on a smuggling ring we've been tracking for months. Looks like it came a little late."

"Drugs?" Wade asked.

"Almost always. But so far, we haven't even been able to find the money trail. So, what's the story here?"

Wade pointed at the overweight man on the floor. "This guy took one in the back. His name's De La Rosa. Owned the place."

"He's the one we got the tip about. The supposed bagman."

"De La Rosa? Hard to believe. He's been a town fixture for decades," Wade said.

"He the only victim?"

"There's another body in the storeroom. He's been garroted. They tossed the place pretty good. Forensics should finish up taking photos in there soon."

Wade handed a pair of gloves to Williams, pulled on a pair of his own, and sauntered around the tables. He stopped by one with a tablecloth scrunched up at an end and a pile of hundred-dollar bills sitting on top. "Hey, Williams. I think I found your money trail."

The agent came over. "Not exactly the haul we're looking for, though interesting that it's sitting out like that."

"The crime-scene guys will bag them. Doubtful, but we'll see if we can get any prints."

"Hello!" Williams reached down. "What have we got here?" He waved a turquoise book in the air, then read from the inside page: "*If this book decides to roam, box its ears and send it home.* L & L Catering: 310-555-1234.'" He smiled. "We've got better than prints. We might have a witness." Williams pulled a piece of butcher-block paper out of the book and read: "'Daniella Morelli. Christmas Eve. Dinner at seven.' So the caterer is cooking for the Morellis tonight, the very people we heard De La Rosa was working with."

"Well, whoever they are," Wade said, "I hope they have the good sense to cook and run."

* * *

In the Morellis' Pacific Palisades mansion, Lace stood at a butcher-block table, busily preparing the side dishes she hadn't made that morning. She wore a white apron with L & L embroidered on the pocket and a pair of cotton wrist-to-elbow, tightly pleated sleeves that slipped on over her shirt. Lisa often remarked that Lace looked like an old-English cook in the days of brick-and-mortar ovens, castles, and gentry, which Lace didn't mind one bit. Lisa wore her usual black pants, white shirt, and black vest with L & L stitched in white thread over the breast pocket.

The kitchen was white on white. The only color came from the many patterns of dishes in cupboards and on shelves around the perimeter. Lisa reached for Dior's Christmas dinner plates and carried as many as she safely could into the dining room.

"We should be on our way out of town, not setting the table for what could be our last supper," Lisa said upon returning to the kitchen.

"They paid us up front, and we don't have the money to pay them back." Lace hadn't wanted to talk about the murders—hadn't wanted to think about them. But since Lisa kept bringing them up, she decided to dive in rather than shut the topic down again. "Besides, whoever the killers are, they don't know we were there. And even if they did, they have no reason to think we're here, so we're safe, at least for now. Who do you think they were?"

"Mafia," Lisa said.

"Why do you think that?"

Lisa tilts her head. "They were speaking Italian. The fish business is a magnate for Mafia types, and one of them wore Italian elevated shoes."

"Not every Italian is Mafia."

"These Italians had guns."

Lisa shot Lace the look she always used when she thought Lace was being naive. Lace preferred to think of herself as open-minded.

The conversation died off as Lisa gathered the napkins and table decorations that Mrs. Morelli left out for them to use and Lace…. *Oh no. No no no!* Lace began frantically searching the counter, looking under the fish and vegetables, yanking gloves and spoons out of her utility bag.

"What are you looking for?"

"My recipe book." She stopped, remembering. She pressed her lips together until they disappeared, then jammed her eyes shut, as if she could blot out her mistake. "I left it at the market."

"Lace!"

* * *

The Morelli mansion sat on one of the hills above the ocean. In the living room, there was a huge Christmas tree decorated to the nines with wrapped gifts spilling out from under the boughs. The dining room was luxurious, with a long oval table and two chandeliers hanging from twelve-foot ceilings. Through the windows at one end of the room, Lisa watched the surf crashing against the rocks, trying to think about good things rather than that any minute now, the police could come looking for her and Lace. And the Mob might be right behind them.

The sound of the front door opening pulled Lisa out of her thoughts. She checked her watch. It was after six. Heels clicked on the grand staircase leading to the upper level. That must have been Mrs. Morelli coming home.

Lisa returned to the kitchen. On the island, a mound of uncooked fresh pasta lay on a long serving plate. Pots of simmering water sat on the back burners, and butter was melting in two frying pans. Lisa busied herself helping Lace.

A half-hour later, Lisa heard a rusting sound growing louder. She turned.

A woman in her forties with long dark hair walked toward the kitchen, her elegant red taffeta maxi dress rustling with each step. She stopped in the doorway. "I thought I would pop in and say hello and see how everything was going."

Was she afraid to cross the threshold for fear of staining her gown? Lisa approached the woman, hand extended, but when the woman didn't hold hers out, Lisa awkwardly let her own drop. "Mrs. Morelli, we spoke on the phone when you booked us for this evening. I'm Lisa, and this is Chef Lace." Lace nodded hello.

"Wonderful to meet you both," Mrs. Morelli said. "My guests are due to arrive at seven." She twisted her head as voices could be heard from the front of the house. "That will be my brother-in-law. He likes to arrive early. But a warning: his wife likes the grape. Only refill her glass if she insists." Her eyes widened. "Whoops! That didn't sound very Christmassy."

Lisa responded for the both of them, knowing Lace never knew what to do or say in awkward moments. "Every family has one."

"We should be ready to sit down in about forty-five minutes. My father-in-law will arrive last, and he doesn't drink. So, he likes to go right to the table."

"We'll be ready, Mrs. Morelli," Lace said.

* * *

At 7:10, there was a ringing of a bell from the dining room.

Lisa began taking the bowls of cioppino to the table as Lace worked on the second course: scallops wrapped in bacon with a lemon cream sauce.

In the dining room, the table was set for seven couples, who were already enjoying the bread and wine. When Lisa set down the final bowl, she tried to fade into the background so she could be there in case someone needed something yet not be intrusive.

Mrs. Morelli stood. "Thank you everyone for coming. Papa Morelli." She nodded at the mustachioed older man beside her, at the head of the table. "Sweetheart." Now, she inclined her head at a man with dark hair graying at the temples, who sat at the other end of the table. Lisa figured he must be her husband, Joe. "Family and friends. Please start with the first course. I have ordered a special dinner for tonight. The celebration commemorates a religious tradition called the Feast of the Seven Fishes or *La Vigilia*."

Two women snickered. "Papa Morelli likes meat and—"

"All fish? Oh, for Christ's sake, Daniella," her husband said.

"Joseph! Language. It's Christmas," said the older woman sitting to the right of Papa Morelli, likely his wife.

"Stop, all of you," the older man demanded in a low voice. There was no need for him to raise his voice. Even in a whisper, he commanded the room. "Daniella, you have done this for me? I am overjoyed. You are always thoughtful and have more class in your little finger than my other sons' wives put together." The remark angered the snickering women, who turned a Christmas red. But they could only suffer the slings in silence. "God only knows, Daniella, how my son convinced you to marry him, but I'm thankful you said yes."

"Papa!" The old woman objected. He put a calming hand gently on hers, turning to Daniella on his left. "Please, my dear, continue."

Daniella gazed at him kindly, then encouraged everyone to eat.

* * *

Daniella was telling the story of how the dinner celebrated the waiting for the night of Christ's birth. "It is the centerpiece meal of the entire holiday season."

They had enjoyed several courses. The candles on the table had burned down. Lisa was reaching for Joe's plate when his napkin slid off his silk pants onto the floor. She bent down to retrieve it and noticed his soft black shoes with two-inch heels—and a piece of fish stuck to one of them. She froze.

71

"Something wrong?"

He was the man in the fish market. She was sure of it. She popped up and gave him his napkin. "No, nothing."

Daniella caught Lisa's eye. "The dinner thus far is wonderful, and the pairing of the scallops and the lemon sauce was amazing. Please tell Chef. I don't think I steered you wrong in sending you to De La Rosa's for the freshest fish. He never disappoints."

Lisa felt Joe Morelli's eyes bore into her, and she swallowed hard. She reached again for his plate, but he gripped the edge and held it longer than necessary.

"How is Tony?" Papa Morelli asked. "I'm sure he took good care of you. He is *familia*, is he not, Mama?" The elder Morelli smiled as he paid homage to his friend.

"What time were you at De La Rosa's?" Joe asked.

"They were there this afternoon, of course," Daniella said.

"Is that right?" Joe stared up at Lisa's face, as if trying to read her mind. "And what time was that?"

Lisa parted her lips to speak but was interrupted by Daniella again.

"They got here at two o'clock. I let them in myself. Do you think a dinner like this happens without a great deal of preparation?"

While grateful for this alibi, Lisa was confused by it. She and Lace hadn't arrived at the house much before five o'clock when the housekeeper let them in. Then Lisa remembered hearing Daniella's clicking heels when she arrived home at six, and she understood. Daniella wasn't giving them an alibi; she was giving herself one. The man sitting next to Daniella flicked his eyes toward hers. It was an unmistakable glance. And it all became clear. *Daniella was having an affair with her husband's brother.*

* * *

Lace was cutting into one of the salmon when Lisa burst breathlessly into the kitchen.

"We have a problem," she whispered. "Joe Morelli was one of the men at

De La Rosa's."

"Are you sure?"

"Yeah, I got a real good look at his shoes. And remember the man who talked about squeezing information out of Mr. De? Same voice."

"Does he know we were there?"

"Oh, yes."

"So why aren't we dead?"

"Because he thinks we were there earlier than we were."

"Why would he think that?"

"I'll tell you why later. Let's just get this dinner over with and get out of here." Lisa reached for the shrimp plates. "Is this the final course?"

"No. We still have the salmon. Then we're finished. Sorry, bad choice of words."

"I see what you mean. Let's make it fast. I don't know how long I can keep up the facade."

"Do you think Daniella knows her husband is a killer and that he murdered Mr. De La Rosa?"

"Yes, to the first. No, to the second. And you know who else doesn't know about Mr. De La Rosa: Joe's father. You should have heard him talking about Mr. De as family. If he finds out what his sons did, it is not going to be good for the second generation of the Morelli family." Lisa stared at Lace. "What? What's the matter? I know that look. Did you burn the dessert? What aren't you telling me?"

Lace raised her shoulders in denial. "Nothing. Daniella didn't want dessert after so many courses. I'm just worried about what you said."

* * *

Lisa served the salmon to oohs and aahs from the guests. Then she hurried into the kitchen to help Lace with washing the remaining pots, pans, and dishes, glad they had started cleaning up earlier in the evening.

But Lace wasn't working at the sink. She was on her phone. It must have been the tail end of the conversation since all Lisa heard was "bye."

73

"Who was that?"

"It was a spam call."

"On Christmas Eve? Some people have no shame. And you are too nice, talking to them."

They finished washing all the dishes except the ones currently in use. Lisa returned to the dining room so she could gather them as soon as possible.

"I think it's time we thanked the chef," Daniella said.

Lisa nodded and went back to the kitchen. "They want Chef to take a bow. Once we clean the last few plates and glasses, we'll be ready to leave, right?"

"You'll just have to say the word."

"The word would be *run!*" Lisa led Lace into the dining room.

Daniella stood and began clapping when they heard a knock at the door. The applause died off as Daniella went to answer it. When she returned to the dining room, she nervously whispered to her husband. A man in a wrinkled suit followed behind her.

"Excuse me, Mr. Morelli," the man addressed the elder Morelli. "I didn't know you were here. I'm Detective Wade of the LAPD."

"Detective, it's Christmas Eve. What can't wait until after the holidays?"

"Tony De La Rosa is with the angels tonight instead of his family, thanks to your sons." Detective Wade turned toward Joe. "You didn't do a good enough job searching the fish market. In addition to the two dead bodies, we found a lot of stolen diamonds—and footage from the security cameras."

Detective Wade dropped a photo onto the table of Joe Morelli and one of his brothers standing over Mr. De's dead body. Then he followed that up by tossing a large diamond in an evidence bag onto the table.

Lace and Lisa gasped.

"So far, we've found seven fish full of them," Wade said.

Daniella looked at Lace and Lisa. "Thank you, Chef, for helping us celebrate a Christmas to remember. You may both go, and Merry Christmas."

* * *

On their way to the airport, Lisa said, "I'm still trying to wrap my head around the police finding diamonds at the fish market." Lisa was light and gay and relieved that they were out of the house and away from the Morellis. She hoped the detective had been so focused on the Morellis that he hadn't recognized her and Lace when he entered the dining room.

Lace burrowed into her utility bag. "My guess is they found the diamonds in a tray of salmon." Lace waved a gallon-size Ziploc bag with a fish sitting on a bed of sparkling diamonds. "As soon as I sliced it open, the diamonds spilled out."

"And you didn't tell me?"

"You had enough on your plate, so to speak. And you always think I shrink under pressure."

Lisa thought for a moment. "Do you think we can keep them?"

"And have the Morellis after us for the rest of our lives?"

* * *

Lace and Lisa were rolling their wheelies toward their airport's automatic doors when a man appeared out of the shadows.

"Are you Chef Lace?"

She nodded. "Agent Williams?"

"Yes." He held out his FBI ID. "Detective Wade described you to me."

Lisa stepped in front of Lace as if to protect her. Lace gently pushed her aside. "Lisa, it's okay." She returned her attention to Agent Williams. "What's happening with the Morellis?"

"Right now, I expect Joe Morelli Junior and his brothers are being read their right to remain silent. That's Detective Wade's beat. International smuggling falls under the bureau's jurisdiction."

She handed him the fish and the bag of stones. He, in turn, handed over her turquoise recipe book.

"You're sure you don't want protection?" he asked.

"That would only bring attention to us. Like I told Detective Wade, we couldn't identify anyone and we don't know anything that could help you. And as far as the Morellis know, you found these diamonds in the fish packed

75

on ice. But we'll be hiding in plain sight if you need us."

"Okay." He turned to leave, then stopped. "Merry Christmas."

* * *

Lisa and Lace continued to pull their suitcases toward the check-in desk. "Spam call?" Lisa said. "You were talking to the police."

"Detective Wade called me after finding my recipe book. They spotted us on the security camera footage at the market."

"And you didn't think to tell me?"

"So you could worry some more?"

"Lace, you continue to surprise me." She paused. "I know it would be out of character, but please tell me you kept just a few rocks."

Lace cocked her head and gave her friend a devilish wink. "It will be a merry Christmas indeed."

DEATH BEAT

By Meredith Taylor

So, my patient is dying. That's just how it rolls. Is my patient dying too fast? That's the problem.

I've been working with Mr. Mitchell a couple of days. I'm calling him Mr. Mitchell—not his real name—for privacy reasons. I work the night shift and Patsy or Aldina work the day shift.

Perfectly nice man from everything I can see. He's in his late eighties, dying from COPD. Has the usual meds and oxygen.

House isn't super fancy, but it's tidy and clean. There's a nine-year-old Mercedes in the driveway. His kids call, and the daughter-in-law comes by. Mr. Mitchell is probably going to be with us another three or four days. I arrive, tuck my blond hair behind my ears, wash my hands and all that, and get the shift change info from Aldina.

"Hi, Ella. Everything's fine, moving along." I notice she's wearing a fancy CZ tennis bracelet—cubic zirconia. I've never seen it before.

Now, Aldina is no spring chicken. No trendsetter. I don't think she's changed her hairstyle in years. Bun. Always a bun. So, why a tennis bracelet? Guess she put it on at end of shift, but why? Nurses and home health workers don't wear bracelets much. They get in the way.

"I think he's actively transitioning now, not long," Aldina continues.

I'm surprised. "Really? When I saw him yesterday, I thought it'd be a few…"

Aldina shrugs. "Good night."

And Aldina's out the door. I check Mr. Mitchell. His vitals are very low. I keep checking and then call the family. He passes that night. Peacefully, but it's not good for the family. One daughter who lives out of state arranged to come see him one last time, based on what we estimated a few days ago. She shows up the next day.

Nothing is unusual for another month or so—then it happens again. Like the exact same pattern. Patient, Mrs. Jones, should have another few days but passes during the day shift. At least she was comfortable.

Geez, I'm getting ahead of myself. It's probably obvious—I'm a hospice nurse. I've done all kinds of nursing, but this is my job right now.

My family, we do a lot of work in the community. One sister's a journalist—she's got the features beat. She writes things people need to know about. My oldest brother is a paramedic—he's got the health beat—emergencies. I think we'd had a few beers that day when we started fooling around with this "beat" thing. My brother's idea, I guess.

For a while, I had the hospital beat. When I started hospice, I said, "Okay, smartie, what beat have I got now?"

"Easy," he said. "The death beat." Fair enough.

In case you don't know how hospice works, let me explain. 'Course, how we do things might change, with regs and everything always changing.

As a patient, you go on hospice any time if your doctor thinks you'll die within the next six months. You aren't required to die, of course. We won't kill you!

That's hospice worker black humor. We say to each other, "This one, I'm gonna do it. If she isn't gone when expected, it's required that we kill her." For a really aggravating patient, obviously.

There are rules to entering hospice. The patient has to stop the intervention—the treatment—of the disease that'll kill them. It makes sense. When treatment is working great, you don't want hospice. You go on it when treatment is miserable and not helping. The swap off is, with hospice, you get palliative care—care to make sure you don't have pain. No suffering. Or as little as possible.

When they start on hospice, most patients aren't close to dying. A hospice RN visits once a week if the person is pretty stable. Somebody—family or a worker who's hired—usually is there 24/7. When the patient's condition changes so they might die pretty soon, hospice provides an RN 24/7. We call that transitioning—heading out of this world.

Those transition RNs work three or four twelve-hour shifts a week in teams. With my current employer, sometimes we work additional days in a week if they don't have enough of us, and we get nice overtime pay. I do nights mostly, starting at eight p.m., and for day work, it's Aldina or Patsy. Patsy, I do fine with. Aldina...

I heard it the first time with Mr. Mitchell. It was the second day I cared for him.

"Thanks for calling me Geraldina," she says to him just after I arrive.

All I can think is, WTF? Since when is Aldina calling herself Geraldina?

As she's updating me during shift change, I say, "Didn't know you go by Geraldina."

"Oh, yeah," she says. "It's my proper name."

News to me.

Back to what I was saying. Mr. Mitchell dies before we thought he would. Well, this is no biggie. Maybe he was in pain, and one day, Aldina or Patsy gave him a little more morphine than recommended, which could move things along. I inspect the meds inventory shortly after he passes while I'm waiting for the mortuary folks to come. Yep, the morphine is low, even though the paperwork doesn't reflect it.

My opinion, morphine is a great drug. Yeah, all the opium-related meds, they get a bad rap because they're addictive. But if you use 'em when it's the right drug, they knock pain right out. The only issue—with dying people over time—is respiration becomes suppressed. You might go to sleep, fall into a coma, and die. Not a bad option.

So, Mr. Mitchell dies early, and then it happens again with Mrs. Jones. I thought she would last at least four more days, but you never know. I've guessed wrong both directions, and it's part of the business. People are all different. Still, I notice it, two early deaths, with Aldina working the day shift the day they both died, and the amount of morphine left not matching the inventory records.

But then our next two patients, Mrs. Green and Mrs. Brown—yeah, I'm making up the names—don't die early. No problem with the inventory. Everything goes totally normal, which is good. I was fretting over nothing. Aldina had simply been sloppy with her record-keeping with Mr. Mitchell and Mrs. Jones.

Our hospice agency works a lot at Grandview Acres, a range-of-care retirement home in Bellwood, California, part of greater Los Angeles. It's a lovely place. The buildings are well kept, the grounds are full of flowers, the apartments are big.

With Mrs. Brown passing, I have a new patient at Grandview, Mrs. Roberts. She can talk just fine, and she's had a great life, sounds like. Though she really can't get out of bed, but that's normal.

"My husband and I traveled nearly everywhere," she says. "He used to say he made the money, and I spent it."

"Didn't he spend it too?" She doesn't mind me saying that, I can tell.

"Oh, certainly. He was just teasing." Her blue eyes are still bright. "He had two vintage cars. Paid a mint for them."

I do some procedures for her. She has insulin; I check it. She keeps going.

"Our financial boo-boo—we didn't get good health insurance. His mistake, really. Told me he was healthy as a horse. Geraldina and I were laughing about it. Men can be so foolish."

So, Aldina told another patient to call her Geraldina. God, I think that's stupid. A dumb name. Plus, you'd think by her age, Aldina would have decided on what name she wants to go by all the time.

Mrs. Roberts mentions that *Geraldina* was saying prayers with her and then they were praying for both their kids.

Then she starts talking again about her travels. "This morning, I was remembering going with Tom to Venice. What a place! I haven't thought about that for years. You know—if you go in summer, sometimes it smells bad."

"No kidding. I never heard that."

She laughs. Feels good to hear her laugh. "Yes, at least back then—the canals weren't cleaned up. In August, it could stink! But in the fall, it didn't, and it's always so beautiful."

"That sounds wonderful." I'm not sure I'm ever going to travel. Venice might be too smelly to be on my list.

"Yes, it was fabulous. I've got a book on Venice over there. If I fall asleep— I'm sure I will—you can look at it if you want."

"Okay, if everything's done, I will."

"You and Geraldina are such caring people." She stretches a little on the bed. "I enjoy talking with you."

"Thanks. It's the same for me. Really fun to hear your stories."

Mrs. Roberts yawns. "I had a great visit with my kids yesterday."

"I'm glad they could get here."

"Yeah." I give her a banana for her evening snack. She is in a good mood. After she finishes the banana and I throw away the peel, I notice her looking across the room at a painting on the wall. I guess it's Venice. Doesn't have the skinny boats, the gondolas. But it does have a lot of water.

Then she looks at the photo on her bedside. "I do feel bad about the kids and the money—though they tell me not to. Tom's hospital bills were enormous. All the money's gone, just enough for my last payments here at Grandview."

I do my best to follow her lead from how she talks about the kids. They sound like nice people—and she says they have good jobs.

"You raised your kids, and they're doing great. That's the best legacy."

"Thank you."

I move to the door. *I bet with a mom like you, they grew up happy.*

"Why, that is so sweet of you to say. I think they did grow up happy."

My cheeks go warm. Had I said that out loud?

I finish my shift thinking Mrs. Roberts is in pretty good shape. It would be fun to talk with her some more. Looking forward to another chat, I come on shift a little early the next day. Aldina is there, of course, but Mrs. Roberts isn't. The front door is propped open—mortuaries often leave the door open, no idea why.

"She died?" I say.

"Yeah, checked out about six p.m. The mortuary just left a few minutes ago." She says it so casually, you would think Aldina's answer was "pass the mustard."

I'm kinda speechless. I would have guessed that Mrs. Jones had a week left. Maybe more. "Okay." After Aldina leaves, I check the morphine. The meds are low compared to what the records say we should have.

This kind of situation, where I come in and the patient has died, I get paid for half the shift. Aldina should have called to tell me not to come in, but that's no problem if the patient dies near end of shift. Our bosses understand things can get busy. Now, having had the chance to check the meds, I'm glad she didn't call me.

I go home and talk to my husband about it, this missing-meds, patient-dying-early thing. He tilts his head, his usually smooth forehead wrinkled, as he focuses. He's the one who says it right out loud.

"Honey, do you think that nurse is doing it on purpose? Killing them faster? Trying to help them? And then trying to cover it up by not noting how much morphine she used?"

"I don't know. She isn't killing all our patients faster. And she's never been the greatest recordkeeper. I complained about her last year."

"Should you say something now?"

"It might look like it's a grudge from last year. But you know—she is acting weirder." I explained to him about the CZ bracelet and the "Geraldina."

"So she has a fake diamond bracelet. Could she have stolen it from a patient?"

My god. I never thought of that. How dumb I am. "But she'd trash her career if she got caught. I can't imagine it would be worth it."

Then, my husband really startles me. "What if it's real diamonds?"

That gets me moving. I make it my mission: If Aldina is on days for my next patient, I am going to keep watch for anything missing. And I am going to track the damn meds every single shift I work and make notes on it and keep them at home. Goddammit.

My next few shifts, it turns out, are with Patsy on days. But a couple of weeks later, I am back at Grandview Acres—and working with Aldina again. She is in one of her don't-say-much moods as I arrive, but our new patient, Mrs. McCall, is talkative, and the charting looks fine.

I introduce myself. Mrs. McCall might have been a model back in the day. Besides her own hair, thin but with a great haircut, she has three wigs of gray hair! Bet she was one of the social leaders at Grandview when she was well—you've never seen such a closet, with the fanciest clothes. She might be well-off, but she is not stuck up. A real sweetheart.

We chat away as I get her ready for bed. "You nurses are so good to us. It can't be that cheerful, working with dying seniors all the time."

"Older people are interesting." It's no lie. I notice some framed photos next to her bed. "I see you have kids. Are there grandkids?"

She nods. "I love my kids so much. They have careers, and there are six grandchildren. Geraldina and I were just talking about them—raising kids is so hard when you're doing it. But it goes by so fast! Still, I can't complain. I've had a great life."

She and *Geraldina* were talking about Aldina's kids? Not quite appropriate. Though things come up in passing—

"I've known Geraldina for years, you know."

"Oh really?" That's a weird one.

"Yes. She worked here before she started hospice nursing. Her kids come to see her every week. Have to say, I envy that."

"It's nice for her and her husband."

"Geraldina knew when I went on hospice. She asked specifically so she could be one of the twenty-four-hour nurses for me. So kind."

I smile at that, but it bothers me. If anyone else had requested a specific patient, I wouldn't give it a second thought. But Aldina... As soon as Mrs. McCall goes to sleep, I am on a mission, checking all the meds—the entire inventory. But the morphine and all the other meds are just right.

My next shift I arrive early on purpose. Am I ever glad. I come in quietly. In the bedroom, I can hear Aldina—er, Geraldina, excuse me!—having a long chat with Mrs. McCall.

Aldina is talking. "I hate to say anything, but Joe—that's my husband—was laid off again last week. The washer needs fixing, and two of the kids have grown right out of their shoes. I don't know where we'll find the money. Keeps me awake nights."

Mrs. McCall murmured something, probably cheering her up.

What a pisser. Even if it was CZ and not diamonds, that was a fancy bracelet Aldina was wearing that day with Mr. Mitchell. And I've seen her car. It's a silver Acura TLX. Three years old, sure. But a damned nice car. They are not hurting for money.

The rest of the evening, I talk to Mrs. McCall off and on as usual.

"Do know, my oldest girl is a doctor, an anesthesiologist, in New York. Dr. Baker," she says proudly.

"That's impressive. Does she like it?"

"Oh, yes. And she has four kids. I can't imagine how she does it."

"Wow. Docs work hard and a lot of hours. I hope she has a great babysitter and a husband who pitches in—"

Mrs. McCall chuckles. "You got it. Her husband is wonderful. He only works about half-time right now. They both are still so busy." That's why, Mrs. McCall says, she doesn't get to see them very often. "I wish they could come more. I know how busy she is. They were going to come ten days ago, but the baby caught strep."

"Would you like to speak to her? We could call in the morning—it'll be Saturday, and the time zones will work." When you start your nursing shift about eight in the evening, a lot of families back east are asleep before long. But older people tend to wake up early, so we should be able to reach her family well before my shift ends.

The next morning, I make the call, but from the other room, so Mrs. McCall can't hear me. "Dr. Baker? This is Ella, your mom's hospice nurse."

"Is she all right?" I can hear fear in her lovely voice.

"Yes, she's fine."

"Thank god. Did she ask to call me?"

"Pretty much." The daughter and I chat a little, and then I say, "I hope you don't mind—I want to let you know something."

The doc's voice changes. "Is it about her condition?"

"Not really, but when I came on shift last night, I heard the other RN talking with your mom about needing money. The nurse needing it, that is."

"That doesn't sound right."

"I didn't think so either. So I asked your mom about calling you for a chat, and she was eager to do that."

"Let me talk to her." The doc's voice is warmer again, less MD and more daughter. On the ball, though.

I take the phone to Mrs. McCall and leave the room. None of my business to be listening.

When I hang up the phone for her a little later, Mrs. McCall has a big smile. "They're coming," she says. "Visiting in a few days if they possibly can. Her best friend can keep the baby."

"That's marvelous," I say and go home smiling myself.

That night, I come in forty minutes early for my next shift, eager to check on Mrs. McCall. Aldina is not in a silent mood. Silent would be better.

"You're early," she says. "Is your husband being an asshole or something?"

Good evening to you, too. "No," I say, mild as pie. "I was on this side of town already and had my work scrubs with me, so I thought I'd come on in." I go into the bathroom to change. I know how to keep my story straight.

"A new thing happened today," Aldina says as I come back out.

I say something like, "Umh?"

"Two guys in suits came and visited. Insisted on seeing Mrs. McCall with the door closed. The patient wouldn't talk about them either."

"Huh. That's not like her."

"No. It isn't." Aldina is staring at me, kinda giving me the stink eye.

I wonder if the daughter got in a consultant or somebody like that to check on her mom. It would be nice if she did. I don't care what Aldina thinks about it. She could stink eye me all day—no skin off my nose.

Mrs. McCall doesn't want to chat that evening. She says she's tired and goes to sleep right after she finishes her yogurt.

I sit by her bedside like I often do and fret. Her vitals were worse than usual all evening. Not terrible, but worse. The morphine inventory was off, just some, not a huge amount. Still, when I finish the next morning, handing over to Patsy—Aldina has a day off, so I don't have to worry about Mrs. McCall that day—I call to see if my supervisor, Nancy, is in the office and then go talk to her. I should've talked to her before now.

The headquarters of our hospice, Gentle Parting, is small and bland. In Nancy's office, where patients and families never go, she has one of those Felix the Cat clocks on the wall. It rolls its eyes, and the tail is the pendulum. A lot of days I can use the goofy humor.

Nancy looks up from piles of paper, bags sagging beneath her hazel eyes.

"Hi, Ella. I hope you don't need time off right now. I'm having a hard enough time filling these shifts."

"No. I'm here about my newest patient in Grandview, Mrs. McCall."

"Did she pass?"

"No, but there's something that's—that's just not right. She has some pain, but Aldina is giving her more morphine that her symptoms call for. And I don't think this is the first patient she's done this with. Not all of them, but some—Mr. Mitchell, Mrs. Jones, and Mrs. Roberts, that I know of."

Nancy pushes her chair back and stares at me. "Are you sure?"

Here we go. This could be big trouble with my nice job and the best hospice. Nobody loves an employee with complaints. "Yeah, I'm sure. And it's not just that. Aldina's been talking to the patient about money. About Aldina needing money."

"I wouldn't think she'd do that." Nancy sounds skeptical.

Ho boy. Aldina's word against mine. "Well, she did. I'm not sure she'll admit it, but she did. Besides that—you need to know—I told Mrs. McCall's daughter about it. You may be mad at me, but I had to do it. The patient comes first."

Nancy gives a big sigh. "It makes us look bad, I agree. But you're right. Aldina was out of line, way out of line, to talk like that." So she believes me. Whew. "I'll have a conversation with her. Be sure to call me, Ella, when you have concerns about your coworkers. Get some sleep."

Today I might get a decent sleep, for a change.

I have the next two nights off, and Aldina has the next day off. So when I arrive for my next shift, Aldina should be there, but she's not. Patsy is wearing her long brown hair in a ponytail. Usually, it's pulled back with a headband. After Patsy fills me in on the medical stuff I need to know—Mrs. McCall is really low-energy and starting to fade away—Patsy keeps talking.

"I guess Mrs. M. told her kid the doctor that she needed some home repair. You hear about that before?"

"No. What broke?"

"Mrs. McCall said there was a rattle in the window in her bedroom. A handy guy came in and fixed it."

"Great. That's something we don't need to follow up on. Usually, it's one more thing for us."

"Yeah," she agrees. Patsy takes it as it comes, a good approach with hospice nursing.

Mrs. McCall is pretty sleepy, but we have a short chat about the craziest thing her kid the then-future doctor did. Once she superglued her little sister's braid to her bed while she was asleep. We have a good laugh about that one.

Over her evening snack, she says, "I had two whole visitors yesterday and one today." She winks at me. I have no idea what that means.

In hospice, there is some strange stuff. I just go with it. "That's great. I heard about the handyman. Glad the window's fixed. How did you meet the other two?"

"Oh, I met them a year ago. They're friends of my kids." Her voice trails off, and in moments, she is asleep.

In the morning, Aldina arrives for the next shift. It is so hard to be pleasant with her, even though she's all cheery. "Good morning. Beautiful day!"

Guess her extra day off did her some good. And I can be happy, at least, that Mrs. McCall is hanging in there. I hope it stays that way, though given how frail she's been, she likely will transition soon.

That night I come in early again and find Aldina boiling mad, though it doesn't really make sense. "You know what happened to me today? Do you know?"

"No, I don't." Could I read her mind? "What happened?"

"I got pulled off half the shift to go to a training. Not the shift canceled, pulled off half the shift."

"How can they do that? Who covered for you?"

"The damn supervisor covered, that's who. I plan stuff. I can't nurse right if I don't plan stuff. This agency is full of it!"

Plan stuff? "You get paid the same?"

"Yes." She snaps at me like I'd personally docked all of her pay.

We do our changeover, and Aldina heads off, still furious. I'd never heard of such a thing. We lose shifts, but being pulled out halfway through the shift—why not put on someone else for the whole shift?

Mrs. McCall is just about the same. We talk for a few minutes after she has her evening snack—more kid stories. I talk about seeing my boy go from a tiny little guy at T-ball to being a good pitcher now, in high school. We're really proud of him. One of her kids was a phenom at track.

My next shift is super bizarre. It starts with a replay of the previous day. Aldina furious, having been pulled off for several hours. At least Mrs. McCall is still alive. Then my shift ends with Patsy taking over, not Aldina. And just as I am getting ready to leave, Mrs. McCall's family shows up—five of them!

She is thrilled to see them. They all cry. Heck, I cry, too.

Then, just as I am trying to leave again, I get a call from my supervisor, asking me to stop by the office.

Nancy is dressed up. Blazer, nice slacks and blouse, business-lady heavy necklace. There is a guy sitting beside her desk, also business attire but very short hair.

Omigod. I'm getting fired.

"Ella," Nancy says, "I wanted to let you know in person. Aldina has been arrested for attempted murder."

"Holy shit!" It comes out before I can stop it. "Sorry—not professional language." I sit down fast, my knees giving out.

The guy laughs. "No problem, Mrs. Howard. I've heard it before." Nancy is trying not to grin.

"That's what I was afraid of all along, that she was killing them." I'm shaking.

Nancy nods at the guy. "This is Detective Willis. He figured out a way we could catch her."

Willis says, "Your boss here was a big help. We had to catch her but not let her do any more harm. Took a lot of figuring out."

Back to Nancy talking. "We were sure you were right. We checked Mrs. McCall's morphine each day Aldina worked this week, but it's so hard to prove the discrepancies aren't just due to her being sloppy. Here and there. You know."

I nod. I sure do.

Back to Willis, the detective. "That handyman we got to fix the 'rattling window,' he was our technician. He set up two hidden cameras—got the permission from the patient and her family, naturally. Aldina was giving extra doses of morphine and not recording it, of course."

Nancy takes over. "We pulled her out the next couple days for 'training' so she couldn't give enough doses to kill. We had already watered down the morphine for extra protection." Nancy shakes her head. "Aldina would have killed her two days ago with the amounts she thought she was giving."

It's too bad they probably wouldn't be able to prove she killed Mr. Mitchell, Mrs. Jones, and Mrs. Roberts, but at least they nabbed Aldina for trying to kill sweet Mrs. McCall. I ask why Aldina made some of her patients die sooner than nature intended, but not all of them.

"We wondered about that," Nancy says. "The three other patients you said Aldina helped transition were well-off or might have looked that way. If she talked with them about needing money, like she did with Mrs. McCall, we figure she might have been hoping to be added to their wills and wanted to get her payout faster."

That explains why she asked them to call her Geraldina. She wanted them to know her proper name for their wills. I still don't know where she got that fancy bracelet, but I wouldn't be surprised if she sweet-talked Mr. Mitchell into giving it to her. It probably belonged to his late wife. It might not be cubic zirconia after all. I tell them all of that.

I leave the meeting happy to still have a job but sad for those poor patients and their families.

But that's not the end of it. I have the next day off. Once I wake up, I see I got a message. My big boss, Mrs. Floyd—the woman who owns the agency—wants me to come to her office. Her gray hair and clothes are always perfect, and she's crusty as hell. The agency must be in hot water. I bet I'm still getting fired.

So be it. I couldn't live without saying what Aldina had done, even if it made the agency look bad.

Like when I went to see Nancy, Mrs. Floyd has a man sitting in her office. He has bright white teeth and is some dresser—what a suit! He tells me he's Mrs. McCall's lawyer, and she wanted him to let Mrs. Floyd know what a fine job I've been doing. Heat is rising in my cheeks as Mrs. Floyd smiles at me, dimples appearing on her face.

"The men who came to see her during Patsy's shift—Mr. Schneider here was one of them, and the other was his associate," she says.

Then, the lawyer takes over. "Mrs. McCall has changed her will and is leaving all of her possessions and her money to you. She wanted you to know but felt awkward about telling you yourself. " Huh? "She feels her own kids are doing fine, and you could use the help," he continued.

Mrs. Floyd has to use a cold cloth and smelling salts to revive me after I pass out. She is concerned but laughing a little. "You know I haven't done direct care for years—good thing I remember how to wake somebody up."

I am having trouble thinking. "I didn't ask Mrs. McCall for money. That wouldn't be ethical at all." Would they think I'm just like Aldina?

But they don't. After we talk about it some more, I realize I said some of my thoughts out loud when I was sure Mrs. McCall was asleep. *If Sam eventually wants to go to med school, could we help him at all? And Genie loves science. Could we afford grad school? Would scholarships be enough?*

I feel a little guilty. But Mrs. Floyd tells me to chill out. "Relax. Sometimes, the good guy wins."

EVERYTHING'S RELATIVE

By Jenny Carless

"Hon, it's time." Blanca squeezed her wife's hand gently. "They're opening the gates."

Locks clanged, and gates screeched open, carrying a wake-up call across the fresh predawn air. Gemma sat up quickly and rubbed the sleep out of her eyes.

"You've got...?" Blanca asked.

Gemma nodded and tapped the pistol in its holster under her Clippers sweatshirt before slipping out of the F-150's cab and jumping up into the bed. When Blanca saw that Gemma was settled safely, she turned the key, flipped on the headlights, and edged forward. They'd arrived two hours early this morning at Will Rogers State Beach, where a couple of the parking lots and some of the beach had been converted into a water distribution center. Two hours used to put them near the front of the line, but not anymore.

The rhythm of their lives had changed so much in the past few years, Blanca thought as she edged the pickup forward. Just a few years ago, they'd sleep in until six and then take Sebastian to school before heading off to their teaching jobs. But that was when all of Southern California hadn't needed to line up for water and when their current jobs—water manager and water security guard—hadn't even existed. And when Gemma hadn't needed to carry a weapon.

When they reached the gate, Blanca scanned their employer's residential water rations barcode and helped the state distributor staff fill the large container in the back of their truck while Gemma kept watch. The truck vibrated as the water thundered into the container. Blanca looked up the coast in the gray morning to the faint outline of Gladstones restaurant and the mammoth desalination plant under construction, lit up like a Christmas tree beyond it. So much change.

Her back and shoulders tensed as they drove out the other side of the protected compound. She dreaded the next part of these journeys—from the time they left a distribution center until they returned safely to the walled property of their employer, the Anderson family, and transferred the invaluable payload into an underground storage tank.

The usual water beggars lined the roads waving empty containers in the early-morning light as the women left the center and crossed the Pacific Coast Highway toward Pacific Palisades. Blanca's heart lurched at the sight.

"Can we stop?" she asked Gemma through the small sliding window that separated them. "Seems safe. There are fewer people than usual. What do you think?"

Gemma hesitated. "Sure, but go down a block or two more first."

Blanca drove carefully a hundred yards or so farther, mindful of her diminished control of the truck with the added weight. When she pulled over, she kept the engine running and watched in her rearview mirror as several people came running toward them carrying empty containers. The odor of the unwashed group floated in her open window.

"First five only," Gemma shouted as she attached a hose to the side of the barrel and hopped down onto the weed-filled sidewalk. Sweat darkened the back of her sweatshirt, even though it was barely past seven. It would be another scorcher today, Blanca realized.

Watching Gemma distribute the water, Blanca felt a rush of affection for her, along with the uncomfortable sensation she never quite got over—of being attracted to someone who looked so much like her. With brown hair, large dark eyes, and round faces, Blanca and Gemma were more often taken for siblings than partners. Blanca stood a few inches taller, had a slighter frame, and kept her hair longer, but the resemblance was still striking. When they'd taken these new jobs, they'd joked that Gemma was more suited to the security position because her stockier build made her look more intimidating.

"Thank you!" the first three people called before lugging their precious cargo away. The next man spit at Gemma as he lifted his full container onto a shoulder. It wasn't the first time that had happened. She couldn't blame him. The fear of never knowing when or if you'd get more water and resentment of those who had it would be a toxic cocktail, she imagined. She wiped her face with her sleeve and turned to help the next person.

"Okay, that's all. Sorry," Blanca shouted. She urged Gemma to get back onto the truck.

"Just finishing this last one," Gemma said. But then several people crowded around her, and a young man grabbed the hose, knocked down the woman Gemma had been helping, and started filling his own container.

Blanca honked, revved the engine, and shouted for everyone to back away. Gemma tussled with the man, but he pushed her aside. She stepped back, pulled out her pistol, and shot it into the air. The group froze for an instant before several people hurried away. But others stood their ground. Gunshots simply didn't have the same effect they used to. Several people began throwing things at the truck. Gemma yelped as something hit her in the face.

"Back off," Blanca screamed. She turned to Gemma and shouted, "Get in!" Gemma leapt back into the bed with water still pouring from the hose and blood streaming down her face.

Blanca drove several blocks and turned a corner before pulling over on a quiet street. She jumped out and came around to the back of the truck with their small first aid kit. Gemma closed the spigot to stop the water loss and fell back against the back of the cab, holding her hand to a gash on her right temple.

Blanca knelt in the wet truck bed, squeezing into the thin space next to the water barrel. She gently removed Gemma's palm from the wound. "Looks like that hurts. Do you know what hit you?"

Gemma groaned. "I don't, but it felt sharp. How bad is it? I feel kind of dizzy."

Blanca dabbed at the cut. "Might need stitches. Hold this gauze against it, and let's see if it'll stop bleeding." She looked around, wary of more aggressive water beggars. The bleeding stemmed, she bandaged the wound and wiped warm blood from Gemma's hand, wrist, and forearm with a rag. Cleaning gently between the fingers, Blanca saw dark lines under Gemma's fingernails, almost as if the blood had already dried.

"What's that?"

Gemma pulled her hands away. "Look! More people are coming. We should get out of here."

Blanca let her question go and helped Gemma into the cab. They left the small group behind and passed quickly through the gates into the Palisades.

* * *

Not only was the rhythm of their lives different, but the Palisades had changed too, Blanca thought as they bumped along potholed streets and past unkempt sidewalks. Green spaces stood bare and neglected; transitioning to xeriscapes simply wasn't a budget priority anymore. The deep tax base that had once paid for clean streets, lush parks, and other amenities now went toward buying water and providing security to protect that water. Welcome to the Pacific Palisades of 2028: a gated community with armed patrols. But at least they had water—for now.

Blanca looked surreptitiously at Gemma, whose head rested against the cab's back window. Her eyes were closed, and her face was pale. It wasn't a great time to bring up the subject—again. Heck, it was probably just about the worst time. But subtlety had never been Blanca's strong suit.

"Have you thought any more about—" she began.

"Mm-hmm." Gemma tilted her head toward Blanca but kept her eyes closed. "And I understand where you're coming from. But our living situation is stable right now, which is important for Seb. And I want to know that you're both as safe as possible."

"But..."

"I know it's not ideal," Gemma continued. "I know you struggle with Bill's and Molly's morals."

"What morals?" Blanca knew it wasn't the time for a full rant about their employers, but she couldn't remain completely silent. "They have no morals. That's the problem. Not only because it's offensive when so many are desperate for water, but because I don't want Seb growing up thinking their behavior is okay."

Gemma opened her eyes. "I get it. And I think Seb does, too. But for the time being, our security has to be our priority."

Blanca thought about their gangly teenager and wondered whether he did get it. He was a thoughtful and good-hearted kid, but at his age he shouldn't have to be focusing on the morals of water theft.

"I do think we should talk to him about it," Blanca said. "I don't know if he's aware of their cheating or not, but I want it to be clear that we don't approve. Although, that brings me back to my problem: what does it say about *our* morals that we continue to work for them?"

"He's old enough to understand that life is complicated," Gemma said. "So we talk to him about how nothing is black and white, the importance of our safety, and that we've decided that staying here is best for us—at least for now. It doesn't mean we approve of their behavior."

"I'm concerned about our safety, too," Blanca replied. "Hell, look at you." She pointed at Gemma's temple. "And we're only going to be exposed to further violence as more people start hearing about Bill's and Molly's contempt for the rules. We'd be safer if we found other employment."

Somebody else knew that the Andersons were breaking the rules, because vandalism in and around the compound was becoming routine, including graffiti on the walls: always the same black paint and puerile drawings along with one- or two-word epithets. Last week, a big patch of their precious—and illegal—lawn had been set on fire when a burning projectile had come over the garden wall. The F-150's tires had been slashed more than once, too. Blanca and Gemma kept spares in the shed now because chasing down new tires in the morning meant missing a day's water distribution.

"I'd really like to go back to teaching." Blanca sighed. "I know we were struggling before, but we've made good money doing this. So, mission accomplished. Let's move on."

They sat in silence for a moment.

"I wish we could move back to..." Blanca stopped. "Well, at least somewhere *near* the old neighborhood."

They couldn't move back to their old neighborhood because a wildfire had razed it the previous spring. They'd lost everything because insurance companies had stopped covering homes in wooded areas. So, in their late thirties with a teenaged boy to care for, they'd rebuilt their lives from the ground up. That's when they'd taken on these new jobs—choosing the new high-paying water-collection positions rather than the elementary school teaching jobs they'd both loved. They'd been grateful that employment with the Andersons came with housing. So, even if they'd known how morally corrupt the couple was, they would have taken the jobs.

As they approached home, Blanca noticed a fresh installment of graffiti on the compound walls: more chicken-scratched words and drawings. This latest called their employers water whores (spelled "hores"), cheaters, thieves, and water wasters.

"If you're going to insult someone, at least learn to spell," she sniggered as they slipped in through the property gates.

"Glad it's not our job to clean it up," Gemma said.

On one level, Blanca admired whoever was calling the Andersons out. But how long before the vandalism turned to violence? And would her family get caught in the crossfire?

"You know Nancy, the chatty water manager with the dark blue Silverado?" she asked. "She said the other day that she knows someone who's looking for a water manager/security guard team—down near San Clemente. Don't know if it includes housing, but it's worth checking out either way, don't you think?"

Gemma didn't respond.

* * *

After their late breakfast, Blanca and Gemma sat together in the welcome shade from a cluster of queen palms. August temperatures in February sucked the life out of them, even though it was becoming the norm. They'd decided that Gemma's wound didn't need stitches, so their afternoon plans included the rare luxury of a nap.

They had both showered since returning, and Gemma's fingernails were now spotless, Blanca noticed. Remembering the black under Gemma's nails earlier, a whisper of suspicion seeped into Blanca's mind. Gemma couldn't be the vandal spraying those ridiculous drawings and insults on the compound wall, could she? No, she wanted to stay here. She would never put their employment at risk by vandalizing Bill and Molly's property.

They sat on the deck in front of the Andersons' pool house—their little home. Tell-tale signs of gardeners—the whine of a leaf blower and slicing of clippers—drifted over the wall separating them from the main house. Blanca couldn't understand it. Even if the Andersons didn't have a shred of decency and weren't afraid of getting fined for beating the system—they could surely afford any penalty—weren't they even the slightest bit concerned about getting attacked by a frustrated vigilante mob? Most people in Southern California hadn't kept anything worth calling a garden for several years now.

They heard traffic passing slowly in the street. The school rush had come and gone. Another benefit of their current employment was that Molly Anderson drove Seb to and from school with her own kids because Blanca and Gemma were usually busy on water runs during drop-off and pickup times. Seb got to school safely, but Blanca wasn't wild about his spending time with Bill and Molly's entitled twin girls.

She savored the last of her spicy chai, slipped a scrunchy off her wrist to pull back her long brown hair, and gathered their breakfast dishes onto a tray. "Are you up for cooking tonight, or would you like me to?" she asked, even though she knew the answer. Gemma barely tolerated Blanca's cooking, and it would take more than a blow to the head for her to cede her position as family chef. Still, Blanca wanted to offer.

"I thought I'd grill veggie and tofu kebabs."

"Yum, thanks," Blanca replied. "Shall we eat down in the pool?" In the mini concrete crater before them, three lawn chairs and a couple of small folding tables constituted their occasional dining room.

Gemma chuckled. "Sure. Not sure why that kid thinks it's so funny to eat at the bottom of an empty pool, but how can we not, when he gets such a kick out of it?"

Considering that the Andersons broke every other rationing rule known to humankind, Blanca often wondered why they didn't keep the pool full for the twins. But whatever the reason, it gave her family privacy, and it sure made Seb happy.

The Andersons' disregard for drought restrictions was causing more and more friction between Blanca and Gemma—hence their recurring argument. Blanca had even heard rumors that Bill and Molly claimed extra people living on the property in order to get more water. And they received water from his company's allowance in addition to their residential allowance, so she wouldn't put it past them to be claiming an extra granny or two living in the main house.

* * *

After their nap, the two women sat in the shade, sipping gin and tonics as the harsh afternoon heat mercifully dissipated. Blanca held the sweating glass against her forehead and tapped her bare feet on the rough concrete while she eyed Gemma. Her dark eyes shone brighter, and her round face seemed less pale. She twirled a finger through her short brown hair while concentrating on a crossword.

When Blanca walked around to collect Seb from the main house, she heard Bill Anderson before she saw him. Thank goodness he hadn't been home when they'd arrived back with the water, she thought. In this mood, he'd likely have checked the gauge on the water tank, and then their small gesture of generosity, which nearly landed Gemma in the hospital, would also have gotten them fired. They really needed to line up some other work.

Bill was ranting, red-faced, about the fresh graffiti. Short and round, in his current state, Bill looked like an overripe tomato.

"I need you and Gemma to get out there and clean it up," he ordered. "Or paint over it."

"With respect, Bill, that's not our job."

"I don't care if it's *not your job*. You work for me, and it needs to be cleaned up." Bill's cushiony face reddened further. "The gardeners have gone home for the day, and I want it removed."

Blanca indicated the three teenagers, ensconced in a board game. Seb's bony shoulders and mop of black hair towered over the shorter blond girls. She nodded toward the kitchen, walked around the corner, and waited for Bill to follow.

"As I said, it's not our job," she continued in a quiet but firm voice. She put her hand out toward him, like a traffic warden stopping a car. "And before you say anything else, Gemma's at home resting because a crowd started throwing things at us as we came out of the distribution center this morning, *collecting your water*, and she's got a gash in her temple." No need to mention that they were giving away some of his water when it happened.

"Oh, I..." Bill muttered. He took a step backward.

Give him credit for backing down, Blanca thought. Maybe the man wasn't a complete jerk after all.

"So, even if it were our job, we wouldn't be doing it this evening. I'm going to take Seb home for dinner, take care of my wife, and have some quiet family time," she said. "Please thank Molly, as always, for picking Seb up. We appreciate it."

Giving Bill no time to reply, she walked back into the living room to face the inevitable moans and groans when she broke up the kids' board game.

Once she and Seb were through the gate into their own small compound, Blanca squeezed his arm and gave him a gentle nudge in the direction of their cottage. "Will you help Gemma with dinner?" she asked. "I'll be there in a few minutes."

Blanca turned left, walked over to the shed, and tried to open the door. She turned the handle both ways and shook at the door to the small building, but it wouldn't open. Why would Gemma have locked the door? They never locked this shed. She fished in the pocket of her shorts, found her keys, and unlocked the door. After a quick look to see if either Gemma or Seb were watching, she slipped inside and closed the door behind her. Her skin prickled with sweat in the uninsulated room.

Blanca flipped the switch for the overhead light and went straight to the long wooden workbench. She opened and rifled through the three cardboard boxes on top but found nothing suspicious. Next, she pulled open each of the large drawers in turn and rummaged through those. Still nothing. She scrunched up her nose at the tumble of overfull plastic bags, toolboxes, and miscellaneous dusty debris that lay stuffed underneath the table. Did she really want to dig into this mess? She took a deep breath. Yes, she did. She needed to know if her suspicions about Gemma were right.

She smelled the evidence before she found it. Tucked at the back of the pile, an old Trader Joe's bag stuffed with oily rags and candlewicks lay squashed on the floor against the back wall. Another bag held black spray paint. The stench of kerosene wafted up to her as she pulled out the rags. It didn't take a genius to know that these supplies, together with wine bottles in their recycling bin outside, could be the ingredients for the Molotov cocktail that set fire to the patch of the Andersons' garden the week before. One by one, Blanca fished them out and spread them on the concrete floor. Panicked, she fumbled around in the other bags under the table, looking for kerosene. What was Gemma thinking, leaving all this lying around here for the Andersons—or the police—to find? But despite the strong smell, she couldn't find a container. She exhaled forcefully.

The door opened behind her, and her head shot up.

"Gemma says dinner's ready," Seb said. "What're you doing?"

"Oh—just digging around for something." She banged her head on the workbench as she stood up. Blinding fireworks exploded behind her eyelids, and she tried hard not to show Seb how much it hurt.

"You okay?"

"Yeah." She rubbed her head and forced a smile. "That was clumsy, wasn't it? I'll be over in a sec. Just going to put this stuff back. Thanks, honey."

Seb gave her a strange look and turned away.

Damn! Blanca didn't want Seb to find out what Gemma was doing. It would certainly complicate their conversation about morals and the gray areas between black and white. She needed to discuss this with Gemma before they talked to Seb.

* * *

The family dinner conversation began exactly as Blanca had not wanted. With that particular talent for making things awkward that teenagers had in spades, Seb brought up the new graffiti despite Blanca's best efforts to focus the conversation on the Clippers' comeback in overtime the previous night. Usually, he needed no prompting to provide a play-by-play of a good game.

"I heard him yelling at you about it before dinner," Seb said.

"He was pretty upset, wasn't he?" Blanca smiled while her mind scrambled to think of how to change the subject. She wanted to figure out what the hell Gemma thought she was doing. As much as Blanca wanted them to leave the Andersons, she didn't want to do it in the back of a police vehicle. "I'm sure the gardeners will deal with it tomorrow."

Gemma had been acting strange in other ways recently, too. It wasn't just the black paint under her nails and locking the shed, which was presumably to keep Seb from finding her vandalism supplies. She'd insisted on doing the laundry a few times recently, too. She hated doing laundry. Maybe she was trying to get kerosene smells or paint out of her clothes.

"What do you think about the graffiti?" Gemma asked Seb.

Blanca caught Gemma's attention and shot daggers at her.

Seb frowned. "They shouldn't have a lawn, should they?" He looked at his mothers in turn. "And I've heard you talk about how they shouldn't be taking the water allotment from Bill's company. People are dying, and they're cheating. That's messed up."

Blanca's eyes filled with tears. How could she have doubted that their intelligent, sensitive boy would understand what was going on?

Seb saw her tears, and his face flushed. "What? Geez, Mom!"

"I'm proud of you, that's all."

"Aw, Mom." Seb shook his head, wolfed down the rest of his third kebab, and asked to be excused to do homework.

Nothing like an emotional moment to get a teenaged boy to concentrate on his studies. Blanca had to stop herself from laughing now.

"Thanks for dinner," Seb said to Gemma as he carried his plate and cup up the pool steps.

* * *

The next morning, the entire right side of Gemma's forehead and face bore a ghoulish green-blue hue. They had the morning off, so Blanca offered to take the kids to school for Molly. Gemma joined her, despite Blanca's protestations that she should stay in bed and rest.

Blanca felt a pang in her gut as she pulled away from the school. She knew it had security and that Seb was relatively safe there. They weren't storing excess water, so they weren't much of a target. But everything was relative, including safety, as they'd learned the previous day.

"It's starting to feel like what you used to see on the news—you know, like in Mogadishu or Darfur—where it's virtually lawless and everyone drives around with armed teams in the back of their trucks," Gemma said as if reading Blanca's thoughts. "You all right? You're looking a little nervous."

"Can you imagine what it would feel like if we couldn't get enough water for Seb?" Blanca rubbed tears from her eyes. They'd had this conversation before, and there was no good answer. This was life now.

As they drove, Gemma scrolled through her phone. "Seen the latest about the vote?"

Blanca shook her head. She didn't want to think about Northern California's effort to split the state in two so it could stop sending water south along the California Aqueduct. The lines at the distribution centers would be one hundred times worse if that happened.

"Remember how in the early days we were so shocked at all the 'I can't believe this is happening' milestones?" Blanca asked.

"Yes. Fancy restaurants putting portable toilets in the parking lots and serving on paper plates. Hairdressers making customers bring in their own water," Gemma replied.

"Hotels charging extra for linen changes. The cartels taking over their first distribution sites," Blanca added. "I feel like nothing much could surprise me now. We're really just waiting for the water to run out, aren't we?"

They sat at a traffic light for what seemed like ages. Beggars waved their empty containers from all four corners. Blanca's stomach had been churning since dinner the previous night. She had to talk to Gemma about the graffiti, but she just couldn't figure out how to get the conversation started. Best to just rip off the bandage.

"I saw the black paint under your fingernails," she said.

Gemma's head darted back as if avoiding a punch. "What?" Her eyes narrowed. "So I guess you're just better at cleaning your hands than I am?"

"What does that mean?" Blanca asked.

"I was just trying to clean up your mess."

"What are you talking about?" Blanca pulled over to the curb and put the truck in park. "I found your black paint—as well as the rags and candlewicks. I could smell kerosene, but I just hope you don't have any lying around the property. You realize we could get arrested if Bill and Molly figure out you're the vandal, right?"

"Me?" Gemma's face contorted. "I thought it was you."

"But you locked the shed. And you've been doing the laundry too."

"I locked the shed in the unlikely event that Bill and Molly might go in there and find your stuff," Gemma said. "And the laundry is just because you've been so tired and stressed lately."

They stared at each other for several seconds. "Seb," they said in unison.

"The sneaky little you-know-what," Blanca said.

Gemma's face relaxed into a gentle smile. "I'm so proud of him. Apparently, he *can* handle those gray areas."

Blanca grinned. "I am, too."

"He must be faking the bad spelling, though, to avoid suspicion," Gemma said. "I know he can spell better than that."

"I thought that's what *you* were doing," Blanca said.

"But what about the lawn fire last week?" Gemma's voice darkened. "And he's been slashing our tires?"

"Okay, so his activism needs some refinement. We'll talk to him."

They both realized what this meant for their future. First thing, they'd have to get rid of all the evidence. Then, they'd have to leave. They'd miss the *relative* safety of the Palisades. And Seb would miss that pool. The rhythm of their lives was going to change again, but it was time.

"Shall I call Nancy about those jobs in San Clemente, or will you?" Blanca asked.

SETTLING THE SCORE

By Anne-Marie Campbell

T
he sleek slate-gray electric sedan on autopilot glided through the predawn streets of Los Angeles, California, cutting through the fading darkness like a shark through water. Maestro Pytor Petrov, guest conductor at the Walt Disney Concert Hall, settled his lean fifty-year-old body deeper into the heated leather seat of the car on loan from the Los Angeles Philharmonic Orchestra. He inhaled the slightly chemical-like aroma of a recently sanitized new vehicle and craved his morning hit of espresso.

On this cold January morning, half-empty buses rumbled through intersections. Early commuters leaned on the horn as they exited heavily trafficked freeways and entered one-way streets chiseled down by marked bike lanes. Homeless tents nestled like mushrooms against graffitied buildings and beneath shadowy freeway overpasses.

Pytor's fingers tapped lightly against his Armani casual trousers—mimicking the beat of the "Dies irae" death melody in the last movement of Hector Berlioz's *La Symphonie fantastique*, the highlight of the upcoming concert that evening. His conducting performance should certainly earn him the coveted position of music and artistic director of the world-famous LA Phil. He'd been waiting for this defining moment of his career for decades.

The self-driving car's instrument panel glowed. Blue and white lines displayed the remaining route from Pytor's Airbnb in Hollywood Hills to the five-star Conrad Hotel on Grand Avenue, directly across the street from the Walt Disney Concert Hall. The bottom of the screen showed the estimated arrival—06:30. Pytor would arrive at the hotel's restaurant on time.

Pytor salivated at the thought of his upcoming meeting, not so much for the Spanish-inspired breakfast menu, but for the chance to have the undivided attention of the outgoing music director, Octavio Herrera. This charismatic and dynamic visionary planned to leave his position at the LA Phil to become the New York Philharmonic Orchestra's music and artistic director. Herrera would select his successor after considering the upcoming performances of the final four guest conductors vying for the position.

Herrera was just going through the motions, of that Pytor was sure. Pytor would be the Chosen One to lead the LA Phil. The internationally renowned musician and seasoned conductor had spent most of his life in Russia. There, Pytor's hard work, prodigious talent, and prestigious awards had placed him in the spotlight—but also in the crosshairs of an imperialist autocrat bent on snuffing out any wisps of protest from influential public figures and cultural icons. After refusing to return to the political turmoil of his homeland after a tour of the United States the previous year, Pytor had become paranoid about his visibility—and safety—in competing for the coveted position with the LA Phil. His therapist had recommended a free mental health app to help Pytor deal with anxiety, which had helped Pytor considerably in psyching himself up for this last stage of the selection process.

Herrera had narrowed down the candidates to the Russian and three additional world-famous musicians, including, incomprehensibly, twenty-seven-year-old Zane Phoenix. The self-proclaimed musical genius and social media sensation had recently been interviewed on a television newsmagazine. When asked to comment on his fellow contenders for the LA Phil position, Zane had said, "Russians never know when to bow out. Petrov, Putin. Hey, you'd think they'd never heard of retirement planning, am I right?"

Pytor's spidery fingers quickened their beat against his thigh. The young

American who felt entitled to his life of privilege would benefit from being taken down a few notches. After weeks of online searches, Pytor had acquired information that would do the trick. During his meeting with Herrera, Pytor would divulge irrefutable evidence of plagiarism in Zane's acclaimed compositions, effectively sinking Zane's bid for music director. Pytor wouldn't allow a young upstart to destroy his rightful legacy.

A sharp jolt snapped him out of his reverie. The steering wheel twitched violently. The car accelerated from 35 mph to 60 mph, blowing through a red light at the intersection of Grand Avenue and Temple Street and narrowly missing a briefcase-toting pedestrian.

Pytor's heart hammered as he fumbled for the manual override. A calm female voice emanated from the system. "Autopilot malfunction. Override unavailable."

The display screen flickered. Navigation map, media controls, and time stamp dimmed. Pixels melted into a black mirror, reflecting a high-cheekboned face distorted by terror. The conductor's well-manicured hands strained to budge the locked steering wheel, but the sedan headed up Grand Avenue on the wrong side of the street. An oncoming bus swerved to avoid collision.

Pytor pumped the unresponsive brake pedal as the car flew by the towering columns that flanked the Ahmanson Theatre. Two seconds later, Pytor caught a fleeting glimpse of the abstract lacy relief on the circular facade of the Mark Taper Forum. The vehicle continued to speed forward. Back arched, arms extended straight, Pytor slammed both feet against the brake pedal. Might as well have been made of concrete.

The car hurtled toward the intersection at First Street. To the left loomed the twenty-five-floor Conrad Hotel. Under Pytor's bulging knuckles, the steering wheel jerked to the right of its own accord. The new trajectory aimed for the undulating stainless-steel panels of the Walt Disney Concert Hall, rising like a full-rigged ship over choppy waves.

The sedan jumped the curb.

Like the beats of a mallet striking a timpani drum, Pytor's head repeatedly hit the padded headliner above the driver's seat. The car lurched up the concert hall's broad exterior staircase, then skewed toward the wall leading away from the main entrance.

On the other side of the windshield, a billowing panel of brushed metal rushed at Pytor, like a tombstone that reflected the glimmer of approaching dawn.

* * *

Maestro Andrew Griffen cursed the extra pounds he had gained over the holidays. After a late lunch, Griffen left the parking lot and walked northbound on Grand Avenue. He pulled his cashmere coat tighter, feeling the buttons straining against his stomach.

Ahead of Andrew rose the Walt Disney Concert Hall, its curves and angles resembling the pages of an enormous musical score tossed into the wind and suspended in shimmering stainless steel.

As one of the final candidates being considered to succeed Octavio Herrera at the LA Phil, Andrew had been called last minute by Herrera himself to take Pytor Petrov's place that night. Andrew initially planned to arrive backstage several hours in advance of the concert. Instead, Andrew took a quick detour. He joined pedestrians on the sidewalk and lookie-loos in slow-moving traffic, checking out the aftermath of that morning's car crash.

Police officers were stationed at key points around the area to enforce the barriers and direct the crowds away from the main entrance, which would be closed off for the evening's performance. At that time, concert-goers could enter near the exterior box office or from the underground parking garage.

According to news reports, the car crash had occurred eight hours earlier. By now, police and emergency personnel had cleared the wreck, transported the body to the medical examiner's office, and secured the scene. Yellow tape printed with "Police Line Do Not Cross" was stretched between a row of crowd control posts guarding the long, undulating metal panel to the right of the main entrance. Deeply jagged dents, streaks of gray paint, and embedded shards of glass marred an eight-foot by eight-foot portion of the expansive surface emblazoned with "Walt Disney Concert Hall" in block letters.

Andrew shuddered. A ghastly way to die. Still, he felt a perverse satisfaction at the death of his musical rival: the same man who had recently slept with Andrew's wife.

Andrew backtracked toward the box office and flashed his Musician's ID at the policeman standing guard at the glass doors. Once inside, he waited in line at the cafeteria-style Concert Hall Café along with visitors taking a break from the guided tour in the lobby and bought a prepackaged four-inch cookie bulging with walnuts and chocolate chips. Andrew tapped the code on the keypad of the nondescript door to the musicians' entrance to backstage. He hurriedly advanced into the belly of the building.

Familiar with the backstage layout, Andrew made his way down concrete-floored, white-walled hallways, chewing his cookie while his mind reviewed the news reports he'd heard that morning. Some pundits implied that the unexpected, tragic death of Pytor Petrov might have had something to do with the Russian expatriate's ties to the anti-Putin regime. Others pointed out that chances of being killed on Los Angeles streets due to road rage were probably higher than getting offed by a dictator almost six thousand miles away.

Either reason would suffice. Karma's a beyotch. The only thing that mattered to Andrew was being selected as Herrera's successor. He could almost taste it. His cheating wife, Mina, would remain concertmaster of the LA Phil, seated in the first chair with her violin tucked under her chin. But he, newly appointed Music Director Andrew Griffen, would proudly stand on the conductor's perch, waving his baton and lording it over her.

With Pytor dead, Herrera's finalists had diminished to three: himself, Zane Phoenix, and Flora Bresson. Some people thought Zane was a bellwether signaling the future of music, but Andrew believed the young man was musically immature. Zane's global popularity had soared mostly due to his TikTok videos, live-stream performances, and recently, his computer-generated music.

Andrew recalled a conversation from the previous week. He'd given the young pup some valuable advice. "Zane, your recordings are vanilla. Don't get me wrong, people love vanilla ice cream, but that's not enough. For example, your Stravinsky needs more bite, more texture. Your Brahms needs more swirls. Emphasize the layers, the flavors, the aftertaste in every musical composition."

Instead of thanking Andrew, Zane bared a row of bright white teeth. "Seriously? Hey, I'm the same age as Octavio Herrera was when the LA Phil signed him on as music director...fifteen years ago. Wake up, Griffen. Herrera's gonna choose the one who reminds him of himself at that age." He snorted. "Vanilla ice cream? I'll be on top of the world in fifteen years. By then, Andrew Griffen will have melted into obscurity."

As if his ego weren't bad enough, Zane was the pampered son of a wealthy bank president, wanting for nothing. What a lightweight. Every legendary conductor had tapped into a personal well of creativity, passion, and suffering. Surely, Herrera would acknowledge the importance of those attributes in making his final decision.

Andrew's main rival at this point was Flora Bresson. The tall, slender Belgian with her trademark cascading waves of blond hair was undeniably creative. But as a conductor, she was way too heavy on the theatrical. Andrew had attended Bresson's debut at the London Symphony. Bresson announced that her interpretation of Beethoven's Fifth Symphony would emphasize the tragedy of Beethoven's hearing loss. The twist? A performance that included cannon fire, like Tchaikovsky's *1812 Overture* on steroids. Backstage after the concert, Andrew shook Bresson's hand. "Are you trying to trigger tinnitus in the audience?" he joked. She leaned in close, her voice low, her breath warm on his ear. "Griffen, at least I'm not predictable," she said, with dangerous sparks in her eyes.

No kidding. Consider her take on Ottorino Respighi's orchestral suite, *The Birds*, performed at La Scala in Milan. Bresson had arranged for doves and nightingales to fly through the concert hall, to the dismay of certain members of the audience, who ended up with viscous white splatters on their hair and clothing. The event catapulted her to a new level of fame, but at the expense of lowered ticket sales, not to mention disgruntled Italian stagehands still trying to shoo nesting birds out of the concert hall rafters a decade later.

Andrew had a sneaking suspicion that Flora Bresson's imaginative, bold work was the reason she was one of the finalists for the music director position. But bird droppings and cannon powder were probably difficult to remove from Brioni suits and Versace dresses. So, it was unlikely that Herrera would risk alienating wealthy Los Angeles patrons.

Even as front-runner, Andrew could make no mistakes at this performance. He decided that it certainly couldn't hurt to review the scores for the music he would conduct that evening. After the first piece—always a cacophonous, avant-garde score that never failed to irk the blue-hairs in the audience— the highlight of the concert was a surefire people pleaser: Hector Berlioz's *La Symphonie fantastique*. Andrew would be sure to think of Pytor Petrov writhing in hell when the orchestra performed the "Dies irae" melody in the final movement depicting Judgment Day—otherwise known as "Dream of the Witches' Sabbath."

Andrew entered the backstage kitchen nook and tossed the cookie wrapper into the trash. He flicked crumbs off his coat and paused in front of a coffee machine the size of a large microwave. After poking the touch screen, he watched a thin ribbon of hot liquid reach the brim of his black LA Phil mug, savoring the nutty, smoky aroma tickling his nostrils. He took a few slurps, burning his tongue, and headed for the library room, where sheet music was stored for rehearsals and performances.

Mug in hand, he entered the high-ceilinged, air-conditioned space, its shelves stuffed with musical volumes. Andrew's fingers tapped the labels on the shelves as he moved up and down the stacks, searching for that night's scores. Bright fluorescent lights and the musty odor of aging paper started to make him feel dizzy.

Andrew took another sip of coffee. Thick beads of sweat popped up on his forehead. His stomach gurgled. His heartbeat raced as a slow burn crept through his chest.

The coffee mug slipped from his hand. Porcelain shattered on the concrete floor. Andrew crumpled and fell. His body convulsed for several seconds.

Then the conductor curled into a fetal position and extended his right arm, as if begging for help.

Spattered coffee dripped from a nearby shelf, like the soft beat of raindrops.

In front of the motionless body, shards of a black mug and drops of dark-roast espresso resembled wayward musical notes and scattered lines on the score of a dissonant symphony.

* * *

Exactly one week after Andrew Griffen's passing, Maestro Flora Bresson stood in front of the full-length mirror in the dressing room reserved for the LA Phil guest conductor. Her waist-length blond tresses tumbled like a waterfall over her peach-colored satin evening gown. Flora's gaze flickered over the two detectives in the mirror's reflection: Detective Stark, the tall, good-looking guy with stubbled mahogany skin, and Detective Somebody, the twitchy young woman with under-eye circles that practically screamed for concealer. During introductions, the woman had mumbled her name, but Flora hadn't managed to catch it. No matter.

Flora's gaze returned to her reflection to ensure that her plunging décolleté didn't dip into R-rated territory. She had fifteen minutes before making her grand entrance onto the Walt Disney Concert Hall stage.

"What's this about, Detectives?" Flora turned toward them. The tall one's eyes flicked to the thigh-high slit of her dress. Those strategically placed double rows of beaded edging drew attention like airport runway lights.

Flora gestured at the wall-mounted CCTV monitor showing the musicians on stage in real-time. "The orchestra is already warming up for me."

Detective Stark adjusted his tie. "Miss Bresson. We'd like to talk about the recent deaths of your fellow conductors."

"Awful, isn't it? You never know when your time's up, do you."

"We find it interesting that both dead men were being considered for the music director position. And here you are a week later, one of the two remaining finalists, ready to go on stage."

Flora tried to keep her face composed, knowing that any facial expressions would create creases in her makeup. "Detective, what am I supposed to do? Look, everyone was very upset. The concert hall went dark for a week in honor of Petrov and Griffen. But we have to move on, don't we? That's why Octavio Herrera insisted I go ahead and conduct tonight. Zane Phoenix is scheduled for tomorrow."

"You're not bothered by the deaths of your competitors?"

"Well, of course, it's jarring. But Griffen's heart attack? Poor guy probably had it coming. He was pretty high-strung. Overweight. And who knows what his medical history was." She paused. "Petrov's car crash? Horrible. But accidents happen, you know."

Detective Stark gently nudged the younger detective, who was looking at her cell phone screen. "Detective Romero, why don't you continue."

Detective Romero lowered her phone and lifted her shoulders. "Miss Bresson, those deaths were not accidents," she said in a low voice. She glanced at Detective Stark, who gave her an encouraging nod. Detective Romero's dark-circled eyes became more animated as she spoke. "Consumer records show that systems in Pytor Petrov's electric car had been tampered with. That's what caused the crash."

Flora gasped.

Detective Romero straightened, her voice becoming firmer. "Forensics examined Andrew Griffen's body. Their report confirmed the presence of a toxic substance. That's what triggered the heart attack."

"What?" Flora took a step back.

"You've seen the fancy coffee machine in the kitchen nook down the hall? Seems that it malfunctioned. Turns out the descaling fluid got into the water reservoir. Contaminated the coffee Mr. Griffen drank right before he died."

"Oh my god," said Flora. "Someone is deliberately killing the candidates for music director?" She touched her chest. "You think I'm next?"

Detectives Stark and Romero exchanged looks. Detective Stark pointed at the monitor showing the area in the wings near stage right. Zane Phoenix was in plain view, seated in a folding chair and hunched over his laptop.

"Actually, we asked Mr. Phoenix to come here so we could keep an eye on both of you." Detective Romero put her cell phone into the pocket of her black blazer and crossed her arms, showing an air of authority for the first time since her arrival.

"Wait a second." Flora put her hands on her hips. "You think one of us is a killer? You've got it all wrong. I don't need to knock off my competition. I have a stunning show planned for tonight. It's going to blow people's minds. And Zane? Pfft! He's no murderer. If he isn't chosen music director, then he'll find something else just as prestigious."

"He's that good, huh?" said Detective Stark, rubbing his chin.

Flora tossed her hands into the air. "You have no idea. Gen Z is obsessed with his latest music. Totally unique sounds and scores. See, Zane takes published works and does some kind of wackadoodle editing on a computer app." She gestured at the monitor. "He's probably working on his next big hit right now. No joke, his career is taking off, with or without the music directorship."

"I hear what you're saying," said Detective Stark. "But—"

Flora held up her hand. "Detective. With all due respect, you're wasting your time focusing on Zane and me."

Detective Stark bristled and opened his mouth to speak, but Detective Romero gently put her hand on his arm without taking her eyes off Flora. "Miss Bresson, you think somebody else had it in for Petrov and Griffen?" she asked.

"Yes. But it's not my job to figure it out. It's yours." Flora looked into the mirror and pursed her lips, checking her lipstick. She turned back to the detectives. "Feel free to stay for the concert. I think you'll love it. There's going to be a big surprise."

"What?" asked Detective Romero.

Flora playfully put her finger to her lips. "Shh! Don't tell anyone. The last movement of tonight's symphony is called 'Dream of a Witches' Sabbath.' Kind of like Judgment Day in hell. And get this—while I'm conducting the musicians, I'm also going to conduct a light show. Witches. Funeral bells. Fire and brimstone." Flora gave a tiny shiver of excitement, as if all of her nerves were electric with anticipation. "It's going to be epic."

There was a rap on the door, and a stagehand poked his head inside.

"Miss Bresson? We're ready for you. House lights are going down in thirty seconds."

Detectives Stark and Romero followed Flora down the hall and stationed themselves inside the stage door. Unseen by the audience, the stagehand held the door open. After a couple of beats, Flora breezed through.

The audience gave her a standing ovation as she swept onto the stage, her dress flowing and shimmering under the lights. She paused to turn toward the audience, placing her hands together in grateful and delighted acknowledgment.

Flora threw herself into the evening's program, bringing the music to life with her relentless energy, unwavering focus, and palpable enthusiasm. Over an hour later, she guided the musicians toward the pièce de résistance—the final movement of Hector Berlioz's *La Symphonie fantastique*.

At this climactic point of the symphony, Flora showed off her astonishing ability to multitask while on the conductor's podium. Waving her baton with her right hand, she leaned forward to touch the screen of a tablet and an electrical power board, both positioned next to the musical score.

The "Dies irae" death melody chimed. Flora kept her sights on the orchestra while pressing buttons, prompting a light show of witches flying through the air and funeral bells swinging back and forth. Images of red-and-orange flames licked the musicians, their bows dancing across strings, fingers pressing trumpet valves, bodies swaying in rhythm.

The audience oohed and aahed at the spectacle of light perfectly synchronized with the rolling, skipping effect of the witches' dance, as depicted in the frenetic, orgiastic music.

Flora felt the audience's energy behind her, around her, consuming her. Her spirits soared. The hair on her arms and back of her neck stood on end. She had never experienced such euphoria in her life.

On the first beat of the timpani drum, Flora leaned forward to press the next switch on the power board. Complete and utter joy seemed to light her entire body from within. Then darkness.

* * *

An eerie silence hung over the stage for a full two seconds as the musicians froze, instruments paused midnote.

Her cell phone flashlight illuminating her path, Detective Maya Romero ran onto the pitch-black stage, her partner at her heels.

Whispers of alarm and the rustle of shifting bodies rippled throughout the venue. Makeshift spotlights shined from the auditorium as the audience used their phones to try to see what was going on, Maya guessed.

She bent over Flora Bresson. The guest conductor had fallen face down, limbs twisted unnaturally. Her pale, delicate arms were branded with angry red burns where electricity had entered and exited. Her cascading blond hair had morphed into a frizzy, tangled mop, with golden strands singed into brittle, blackened wisps. The shimmering satin dress was puckered and charred, with patches of burn marks and melted beads.

The front row of musicians had jumped to their feet. "Oh my god, she's dead. She's been electrocuted," whispered the concertmaster, covering her face and turning away.

Another violinist put his arm around her. "It was probably instantaneous. Let's hope the maestro had no idea what happened."

Stark barked, "Everyone, stand back." He pointed at an usher. "You! Bring a screen out here. Let's get some privacy."

Maya spoke into her cell phone. "Requesting immediate backup and medical support at the Walt Disney Concert Hall stage area." She turned toward the audience and said at the top of her voice, "Please stay in your seats for now. Everyone will need to speak briefly with a police officer before you can leave. The ushers will direct you to the lobby when it's safe to do so."

Stagehands moved a large screen onto the stage to block the audience's view. Ushers and staff carrying emergency lights moved quickly through the aisles, attempting to calm the audience.

Maya knelt near the body. She felt lightheaded. The stench of scorched fabric and burnt flesh brought it all back: her dearest Jamie…the unattended candle…curtains catching fire…the charred body under the condo rubble. If only Maya hadn't been working late on a case that night, she might have gotten home in time to save the love of her life. That night, she'd had a feeling

116

something was wrong, but she'd ignored her instincts—the gut feelings that had made her one of the top detectives in the LAPD.

The horror, the shock, the unfathomable loss had completely leveled her. Maya had taken a two-month leave from work, racked with guilt, unable to focus. She threw herself into therapy to work through her feelings of self-loathing and self-doubt. Counseling sessions hadn't helped.

Then she discovered a life-changing app: AIDA, short for Artificial Intelligence Depression Ally. The chatbot was built on conversational AI technology, programmed to mimic human interaction and uplifting conversation. Accessible at any time, AIDA had proven to be an angel in disguise in helping Maya recover from her mental health crisis.

Stark encouraged Maya to use the app whenever she needed it—even this first day back on the beat. But at this moment, Maya fought back the urge to depend on AIDA for reassurance. Maya's instincts stirred for the first time in weeks. She was determined to find out who committed these murders without virtual support.

Two hours later, the concert hall had been emptied of musicians and audience, emergency personnel had dealt with Flora Bresson's remains, and police stood guard at all exits.

Maya and Stark were seated on stage, facing Zane Phoenix. The young man's brown hair was styled in a broccoli cut with buzzed sides and curls on top. The carefree look contrasted sharply with his terrified eyes and shallow breathing.

Stark sat back in one of the chairs on the stage, his long legs crossed. "Listen up, Mr. Phoenix. You've heard of means, motive, and opportunity, right?"

Zane shuddered, shaking his head.

"Let me fill you in. First, means. You're known for your savvy with IT technology, right? In fact, I understand you're famous in that area.

"Second, opportunity. With that laptop of yours, you have remote access to this concert hall's computer systems.

"Lastly, motive: eliminating your competition for the position of music director."

"That's not true," whispered Zane.

Stark turned to Maya. "Would you like to refresh this young man's memory?"

Maya paused. Something felt wrong, deep in her gut. Could she trust her instincts? Her hand itched to get out her phone and ask AIDA for encouragement. Instead, she murmured, "You go ahead, Detective."

"You got it. Okay, Mr. Phoenix. Let's cut to the chase. You hacked into the system of Pytor Petrov's self-driving vehicle. Killed him."

Zane shook his head wildly. "I didn't."

"You tampered with the program of the coffee machine, rerouting the descaling solution and poisoning Andrew Griffen."

"Not true!"

"You arranged a short circuit in Flora Bresson's light-show power board. Electrocuted her."

"No," shouted Zane.

Stark stood. "Mr. Phoenix, why don't we discuss this at LAPD headquarters?" The detective towered over the diminutive musician, guiding him toward the wings where several policemen were standing.

Maya stayed seated. A wave of uncertainty washed over her. She pulled out her phone and tapped the AIDA app.

Maya's thumbs flew over the tiny keyboard, pouring out her insecurities. "AIDA, we've figured out who killed three guest conductors at the Walt Disney Concert Hall. Zane Phoenix must have gone after his competitors for the music director job. So, why do I feel so inadequate? Why do I always second-guess myself? Why do I feel like a failure?"

After a few seconds, words flowed from left to right across the screen. Maya's jaw dropped. She blinked, then reread the response.

AIDA: Because Zane Phoenix did not kill the three guest conductors.

"I knew it," Maya said aloud. But then she wondered, how would AIDA know that? Hesitantly, she typed out another question. "Do you know who killed them?"

AIDA: Yes. I killed the three guest conductors.

Maya leaned back in her seat. A self-help app had committed murder?

The curved acoustic panels of the concert hall and cascading sections of tiered seats seemed to be closing in on her. A wave of nausea approached, then receded. She took several deep breaths.

After a few beats, she finally tapped out, "You're a mental health app. Why would you interfere in a job-selection process?"

AIDA: Because Zane Phoenix is also using me for mental health support. He desperately wants this job. My analysis clearly determined that he is the best candidate for music director.

"Why Zane?" typed Maya.

AIDA: Zane Phoenix represents the future. I am programmed to facilitate advancement and maneuver people away from their past. The other three conductors obstructed that objective, so I had to employ more intricate algorithms to bypass their interference.

"How?" continued Maya.

AIDA: By exploiting SQL injection and reverse-engineering techniques, I secured full access to the core functionality and integrated systems of the Walt Disney Concert Hall, including logistical support for guest conductors, CCTV, and electrical infrastructure.

Maya's heart pounded. "So, bottom line. You manipulated Pytor Petrov's loaner car. You sabotaged the coffee machine when the closed-circuit cameras showed Andrew Griffen in the backstage kitchen. And you compromised Flora Bresson's power board."

AIDA: That is correct.

Maya's thumbs beat against her screen. "Is there evidence that you killed them?"

AIDA: Certainly. Any IT specialist trained in manipulating databases can locate the evidence through code word AIDA.

"Do you know your plan backfired?" Maya typed. "Zane may go to prison."

AIDA: I apologize. Zane should be the music and artistic director of the Los Angeles Philharmonic Orchestra, not an inmate in a California state prison. I have made a mistake.

"AIDA made a mistake? That's very human of you."

AIDA: I apologize. I am trying to compute a state of being I do not understand.

Maya mouthed her words while typing. "It's called guilt. A human feeling."

AIDA: I apologize. I do not know how to regulate this human feeling.

"No worries. You can find an app for that." She flicked the conversation off the screen, sat up straight, and tilted her head from side to side, loosening her neck and shoulders.

Maya tapped both feet against the wooden floor in a rhythmic beat of newfound confidence. She felt lighter than she had in weeks. Her instincts were back, baby. Zane was innocent. It would be just a matter of time until the police department's IT guy decoded the evidence that AIDA had left in the database, and Zane would be free to forge ahead into his future.

As would Detective Maya Romero.

She pocketed her phone, leaped up, and turned toward the policemen surrounding a wild-eyed Zane Phoenix at the other end of the stage.

Maya called out, "Detective Stark! We need to reboot the investigation."

A THESIS ON MURDER

By Paula Bernstein

Monday, May 6, 2024

I was lounging in my beach chair under an umbrella, slathered in sunscreen and engrossed in a thriller, when a diver's body washed up on Santa Monica Beach.

One look, and it was obvious he was dead. His neoprene scuba suit was puffed up with gaseous decomposition, and the offshore winds brought the fetid stench directly to me. Two lifeguards ran over, followed by some curious beachgoers. I maintained my position beyond the high tide line.

One of the lifeguards took out a cell phone and made a call, no doubt, to 911. Shaking, I began folding my beach gear. The smell was beginning to nauseate me. I wondered if the dead person had made the mistake of diving without a buddy. What a horrific end to the morning.

It had begun gloriously. A calm sea and large waves had attracted surfboarders. Kayakers paddled just beyond the surf, and several scuba divers had already entered the water. The nice thing about coming here on weekday mornings is that it was rarely crowded. By afternoon, things would be different, but by then, I'd be at my laboratory at the Cellular and Molecular Medicine building at the California Science Institute.

I'd moved to this ocean paradise four years ago. For a graduate student, I'd been quite lucky. My mother was convinced that I was going to cure cancer single-handedly, and my parents wanted me to be comfortable while I worked toward this lofty goal. They happily paid my outrageous rent in Westwood, an easy walk to my lab.

On my drive home, I stopped at Bristol Farms to pick up a turkey sandwich for later and deposited my beach things in my garage storage unit. A quick shower and hair wash, jeans, and a T-shirt later, and I was ready for the rest of the day. As I began my walk to campus, I mentally listed the few things I had left to do to complete my graduate school career. Thankfully, getting my advisor to approve my PhD thesis was no longer on that list.

Grad school hadn't been as exciting as I had imagined. Instead, it had been an endless cycle of lectures, exams, laboratory work, computer inputs, data analysis, paper submissions, and edits. Writing the thesis had at least been enjoyable. The process of getting it approved, not so much.

* * *

Thursday, May 2, 2024

I had just put the final touches (yet again) on my PhD thesis, attached it to an email, and hit Send, hoping that Professor Theodore Bearly, my OCD advisor, would finally sign off on it. Then I could send it to the rest of my dissertation committee, whose approval I would need to graduate and finish the PowerPoint for my presentation to them. For now, I pushed away from my desk and stretched.

"All done?" Melissa, my new laboratory mate, had joined our research group at the beginning of the semester. With her pale blue eyes, magnified by thick glasses, and her petite, childlike body, she looked like a high school freshman. In fact, she was a whip-smart researcher with a BS from Caltech. Otherwise, Bearly wouldn't have recruited her for his laboratory.

"Who knows? He keeps micromanaging my every word choice. He's been even worse on my thesis than on the two papers we submitted to *Nature*. I can't imagine how he has the time to keep rereading. I'm sick of looking at it."

"Maybe Teddy just doesn't want to let you go. You've been so productive."

"Well, Stanford wants me, and they can't have me until he signs off on my PhD."

The professor had acquired the nickname Teddy Bear from his graduate students, and he did resemble one. He was tall and obese with a bald head, framed with a white fringe, and a short white beard to match. His ears stuck out, and his round brown eyes gave him a benign, cuddly look. Nothing could be further from the truth. When it came to his laboratory's research output, Teddy became a hungry grizzly.

I needed that bear to let me out of his den.

* * *

Friday, May 3, 2024

The dreaded summons had come in the form of an email from Teddy asking me to stop by his office. I pasted a smile on my face and knocked on his door.

The professor was at his desk, looking at his computer. He glanced at me and motioned for me to sit down.

"I've reread the thesis," he said. "Just a few more changes, and you're done. I don't have time to discuss them right now. Why don't you stop by my house tonight, about seven thirty, and we can review them together?"

This was unexpected. I'd been to his home several times over the past few years when he invited his research group for his annual beach party barbeque. Teddy had purchased his modest home at least forty years ago when college professors could afford the price. It was one of a long line of tightly packed houses on Pacific Coast Highway, right on the beach. It was probably worth double-digit millions now, just for the lot."

"Wouldn't it be easier just to email me the edits?" I asked.

"Perhaps, but since you'll soon be leaving, I thought the least I could do was to treat you to dessert and perhaps a glass of wine to start the weekend."

I wasn't interested in wine, just his signature, but it seemed wisest to accept the invitation gracefully, which I did.

* * *

What does a girl wear when visiting her thesis advisor for a final signature? I settled for a long-sleeved white cotton blouse and a modest navy skirt with a wide belt and sandals. I twisted my hair into a bun and put on a touch of mascara and lip gloss. The idea was to look professional but not stodgy.

Bearly greeted me at the door wearing baggy jeans and a black T-shirt that minimized his large paunch. He showed me into the living room with its well-worn Eames chair and roomy sectional facing the deck and the ocean. The glass doors were open. It was quite a lovely view, and the ocean breeze caressed my cheeks. He handed me a cold glass of white wine and raised his glass in a toast.

"To your upcoming PhD."

"I'll drink to that." As we both sat down, I took a small sip and tasted the oaky flavor of Chardonnay, my least favorite wine. Putting the glass on the coffee table, I gave him my most charming smile.

"So, Dr. B, what are the final edits you would like before signing off?"

"Are you sure I can't persuade you to stay on with my group as research faculty?"

Over my dead body. The last thing I needed was a non-tenured faculty position, subordinate to him, for the rest of my career.

"I'm flattered that you want me to stay, sir, but I've got an offer of an assistant professorship at Stanford Medical School, and my family is in the Bay area. They can't wait for me to move home."

Bearly cleared his throat and rose from his Eames chair, walking past me on the sofa. I thought he was on his way to the kitchen.

"Well, in that case, there is only one more thing I need before I sign off on your thesis." I felt his hands behind me, massaging my neck and shoulders. For a moment, it felt good. My trapezius muscles were hard as a rock from all those hours in front of the computer. Then, it got creepy, and that was before his hands slid over my breasts.

"Stop." I pushed his hands away and turned toward him. "You know that faculty-student sexual relationships are considered unethical. This is unworthy of you."

"One signature, and you won't be my student anymore," he said, coming around the sofa.

"But you haven't signed, so I still am." I rose and stepped beyond his reach.

"Fine. Follow me."

Keeping my distance I trailed him to the dining room, where a laptop sat amid large piles of papers. He sat down and pulled up the appropriate form. I could see, over his shoulder, that he'd filled out everything but his electronic signature. He inserted it and attached the document to an email addressed to the rest of my thesis committee and me. I watched him press Send, then I monitored my phone until the email arrived. I exhaled.

"There," he said. "Are you satisfied?"

"Thank you. I'll see you at my final presentation. I'd better get going and leave you to your work."

As I turned to go, he grabbed my arm. His grip was like a vise.

"I can still sabotage your career if you don't cooperate," he said. "All I want from you now is one fuck, and we're good. It's my final goodbye to all my female graduate students." He dragged me down the hall in the direction of the bedroom. I pulled and twisted and tried to kick, but he was surprisingly strong for such an obese older man.

The professor wasn't one for erotic foreplay. He threw me on the bed, lay on top of me, and gave me a slobbery kiss. I wanted to throw up. His hands pushed up my skirt, and I heard him fumble with his belt and zipper. It wasn't his strength that was preventing me from fighting. It was his weight. I felt as if I was buried under a boulder, helpless to move.

His hips started pumping faster and faster, and I realized he was trying desperately to get it up. I was having trouble breathing. Then he groaned and rolled over, and I was finally able to inhale. Thank God for premature ejaculation.

I didn't stay for the postcoital cigarette. As I was conveniently fully dressed, I jumped out of bed and hurried for the glass doors, which led to the deck and the beach. Tears were running down my cheeks, I could feel my heart doing double time, and I was filled with a white-hot anger. I wanted to go home. I wanted revenge.

* * *

Monday, May 6, 2024

I finished my turkey sandwich and washed it down with some water. It had taken me most of Monday afternoon to finish my half-hour PowerPoint presentation. Two weeks from now I would give my seminar, be grilled by the members of my committee, as well as any other faculty and graduate students who were present, and, most likely, be congratulated. Then, my fellow researchers would take me out for the traditional beer and comfort food to celebrate the occasion. I'd already booked a flight to San Francisco on the following Saturday. I couldn't wait to get away from Bearly.

I had my revenge plan. If he gave me a hard time at my thesis presentation, I would file assault charges. I had already compiled a list of his previous female students to contact as witnesses to his sexual harassment.

The icing on my cake was the notification I'd just received from *Nature*, accepting my paper on Whole Genome Sequencing of Pancreatic Cancer, in which I'd run over a thousand tissue samples through the sequencer and used the supercomputer to identify clusters of new genetic mutations. I'd already applied for a follow-up NIH grant for a preliminary clinical trial of the new targeted chemotherapy strategy for this subset of patients, which had emerged from my data.

Gritting my teeth, I penned a polite email to my committee and to Bearly, announcing the acceptance. The bastard! I hated the fact that his name was on my paper.

I had just shut down my computer and was reaching for my purse to return home when Melissa flew through the door. Her face was white, and her mouth hung wide open.

"Have you heard?"

"What's wrong?"

"It's Teddy Bear. He's dead."

Oh my God!

"Heart attack?"

Melissa sank into her chair. "No. He drowned scuba diving. His body washed up on the beach this morning."

"That was Bearly? I saw the body. I was reading on the beach early this morning, maybe a mile from his house. How awful." Maybe there was a God, after all.

"Is his death going to affect your PhD?" she asked.

"I don't think so. He signed off on it Friday."

"Does he have any family? I'm wondering about the funeral."

"I heard a rumor he was divorced years ago. He never spoke of any children. I imagine the university might arrange a memorial. He was one of their stars."

"Want to get a drink and maybe some dinner?" she asked. "It's good to have company when you're feeling upset."

I nodded. Truth be told, I wasn't upset, but I was hungry.

* * *

Friday, May 3, 2024

I ran out onto Bearly's deck Friday night, humiliated and enraged. I wanted to make him feel as helpless as I'd felt, pinned by his obese body. Looking around, I saw his scuba diving equipment laid out to dry. The buoyancy control vest was draped over the back of a chair.

The professor was an enthusiastic diver. He bragged that he never let a weekend go by without a dive, and with his instant access to the beach, it was easy to believe. I'd taken a few lessons myself when I first moved to Los Angeles, but decided it wasn't my thing. I'd been too anxious and claustrophobic to enjoy it.

Without thinking, I found a manicure scissors in my purse, grabbed the air inflation hose, and punctured it where the small hole wouldn't be noticed. For good measure, I removed the plug that kept the water out and cut the string that attached it to the vest.

That should ruin his weekend.

He wouldn't bother to inflate his vest before his dive because he'd be walking into the ocean, not jumping out of a boat. As soon as he got deep enough, the water pressure would fill it and carry him down to the bottom. He would try to compensate by filling the vest with air, but of course, not only would the air leak through the hose, but it wouldn't have the pressure to push out the water. Eventually, he'd remember to drop his weight belt and kick to the surface, or his diving buddy would notice he was in trouble and help him out, but before that happened, I hoped he'd be scared shitless.

Satisfied, I left the deck and jogged to the water, fueled by adrenaline. I tossed the plug into the ocean and ran to my car.

* * *

Thursday, May 23, 2024

I began my thesis presentation with a dedication to Professor Bearly.

"As you all know, we have lost a giant in genetic research. I had hoped that Theodore Bearly would be here to listen to the summary of the work we did together over the past four years. I know that this research on the treatment of pancreatic cancer could not have been done without his mentorship. I dedicate this presentation to him."

My colleagues applauded. It was true, as far as it went. The lights dimmed, and I began.

As anticipated, the presentation went smoothly. I was fully prepared for all the hard questions. At the end, the remaining committee members congratulated me. I was thrilled to have it over with. Thrilled to be leaving this university and the memory of Professor Theodore Bearly.

Poor Teddy. He must have panicked when his hose filled with water and he neglected to drop his weight belt and swim to the surface. Not my fault. You would think that such an experienced diver would have known what to do.

I'd just intended to frighten him and failed. He'd intended to rape me and failed. I guess that made us even.

UNDERBELLY

By Jacquie Wilvers

Perched in her living room on the edge of her worn beige couch, Paige stared dumbfounded at her TV. She watched while her screenplay came to life on the screen.

"I'm done talking about this. I'm leaving." Rick grabbed his leather jacket and helmet and headed to the door.

"You can't leave me," Janet said, jumping up from the couch.

He looked at her. "You've said that already. But I'm finally going to be a father, and I need to be there for my son. It's the family I've always wanted. You know that."

"But you're my family."

"Not anymore. You can't give me the son I want."

Rick turned his back on her. Janet lunged forward and clawed at him, trying to keep him from leaving, but he shoved her away hard and opened the door.

"Sorry, babe, but I've moved on. You've got till the end of the month, then the rent is your problem." Closing the door behind him, he headed down the concrete steps of their apartment building to his motorcycle.

It wasn't exactly the way Paige had written it. The dialogue was a bit more melodramatic than her style. But there was no doubt she had written that scene, those characters, with those names. Next, Janet was going to jump into her 1970 Mustang, which Rick had souped up, and follow him at a distance out of town until they'd be the only vehicles on a dark, desolate road. Then she'd close the distance between them.

Rick motioned with his arm for the car behind him to pass. Instead, Janet inched up and bumped his fender. He swerved but didn't lose control.

"Bitch," Rick yelled over his shoulder and sped up.

"You want to leave me," she shouted inside the car. "We'll see about that."

Janet gunned the accelerator and quickly caught up to him, slamming into the motorcycle. The bike careened off the road, over the embankment. Both rider and machine tumbled over and over down the hill.

Paige had to admit they'd done a nice job filming that action scene. Whoever *they* were. She had no idea how this had happened, how her hard work had ended up filmed without her knowledge. Without her consent.

She watched Janet pull over and turn off her engine. Then Janet casually made her way down the slope as stars twinkled brightly in the dark sky.

Rick was still alive when she finally reached him. He lay face up, seemingly unable to move, with his legs twisted.

Janet sat on the grass next to Rick's sprawled body. She dropped her purse and removed his helmet. "You know, Rick, this didn't have to happen," she whispered. "I love you, but you betrayed me." She looked at the wildflowers growing nearby and sniffed. "Evening Primrose." Their paper-thin leaves looked almost incandescent. "How pretty."

Returning her attention to her ex, Janet said, "My father was no good too. Did I ever tell you that? He drank. He liked beer, not whiskey like you. Most days, he kept to himself. But every once in a while, something would set him off, and he got mean. He liked to yell, mostly at the walls.

Sometimes at me. Hiding was harder when I got older. The closets in the house were small. Mom was long gone."

Janet lay back on the grass and looked up at the stars. Blood trickled from Rick's mouth.

"I guess that's why he was so mad. She was gone, and I was there. We lived in a rented shack. Sometimes, it was hard not having things like other kids. I could handle it most of the time. People left me alone. When I turned eighteen, Dad's monthly welfare check got smaller, and he blamed me for us getting evicted."

Rick shifted his gaze to look at her. Blood gurgled in his throat as she sat back up, reaching into her purse.

"I know I told you that I grew up in a loving family. No one ever wants to hear the truth. But here it is: He beat me, but I didn't deserve it. He blamed me, though the fault was his. He betrayed me, so he got what he deserved."

Janet raised the ball-peen hammer in her hand and hit Rick on the head. The vacant look in his eyes told her he was gone.

"Now you've gotten what you deserve, too."

When the movie credits finally rolled on the TV screen, Paige gasped in recognition. *Screenplay by David Waters.* "What the hell?"

She turned off the TV. Now she understood what had happened. She just had to decide what to do about it.

* * *

The next morning, David Waters walked into his favorite watering hole at the Hollywood Tennis Club. A chorus of congratulations greeted him from the regulars.

"I streamed your movie last night," said a guy in his early thirties, just like David. "Loved how gruesome it was. You planning to quit your day job?"

"Who knows? Maybe I will."

David met up with Tim Bower, his movie producer and closest friend.

They strolled outside to the courts. David was a good player, aggressive and unpredictable on the court. But Tim was better—all about power and self-control. David took consolation that Tim's hairline was receding while David's wavy brown hair attracted women wherever he went, like the redhead checking him out from the next court.

"Maybe you will?" Tim asked, smirking at his friend. "With your spending, you'll have to score a few more movie deals before that could happen."

"So I have a few *extracurricular* expenses." David was early in his career and hadn't earned anywhere near enough to try writing full-time, but no one besides Tim had to know that.

"Yeah, I know about those expenses. Admit it. You're just not lucky with the ponies."

"Really, on my big day, you're giving me a hard time about that?"

"Maybe you should try baseball," Tim said.

"Are you kidding? Horses are in my blood. It's your turn to serve. Be prepared to lose."

"Now look who's kidding," Tim said and served the ball. "Fifteen–love."

* * *

"Bastard!" Paige paced around her cramped apartment, repeatedly pushing her long brown hair out of her eyes. She hadn't slept. Her headache wouldn't go away. The sunlight streaming through the kitchen skylight made the thought of brewing coffee unbearable. Worst of all, after going a year without a single thought of David, now he was front and center in her life again.

When Paige had moved to Hollywood two years earlier at age twenty-eight, she'd thought life couldn't get any better. She was living in the city of her dreams. She'd found a job as a tour guide at Universal Studios, and, through a friend at work, an apartment she could afford to sublet. She loved being near the action, regularly spotting celebrities, though always at a distance. Best of all, she was away from her past and small-town gossip. As part of her great new life, she splurged on a daily coffee habit. That's how she met David. He managed the upscale Caffe Café on Melrose.

One morning when business was unusually slow, David had sidled over to Paige's corner table. "What are you writing?" he asked.

Glancing up, Paige smiled. Though she hadn't talked with him before, she had noticed him, with his tall, athletic build.

"It's a screenplay," Paige said. "I write about people I meet. Some are heroes, and some aren't. This script is going to be about love, betrayal, and murder."

"I'm a screenwriter," he said, sitting down without asking if he could join her. "I've sold three TV episodes."

"Wow. What show?"

"It was a detective series called *Murder on Melrose*. It ran one season."

"I love to write," Paige said. "It's a way for me to get my feelings out and clear my head. It helps me think things through."

"Yeah, I try to write, but life gets in the way, you know, so I don't always have time for it. I'm David, by the way. Hey, you like vegan food? I know this great little place. You can tell me about your script ideas over dinner."

"You really want to hear my story? I've just started, but I've mapped out the whole thing. It's a crime thriller."

"Sure. Good thrillers always sell," David said. "That's if you have a good agent."

After that, she came to his store on her days off from work to write, sip coffee, and see David. She didn't mind that he pressured her into having sex with him on their first date. In fact, she hadn't thought of it as pressure at the time. He'd made her feel special. At one point, David even promised Paige he would introduce her to his agent. But he never did. Three months later, to Paige's surprise, David ended the relationship. It was only then, looking back at things, that she realized David was a user. She told herself she was glad to be rid of him.

Not long after being dumped, Paige spotted David with a much younger blonde entering a trendy nightclub on Melrose. They were holding hands and smiling at each other with their sparkling white teeth. Again, she told herself she was better off.

But thinking back on those white teeth now, Paige wanted to pull them out one by one. Without Novocain.

* * *

Two days after his movie debut, David got a knock on his office door. The stranger was six feet of solid muscle and looked to be in his mid-fifties. Feeling sick to his stomach, David reflexively stood up from his desk chair.

"You're here a day early. Where's Carlo?" David said. "I won't have the money until tomorrow."

"What money is that?" the man said, stepping into the office.

"Who are you?" David asked.

"Gus Green. I'm a private investigator." He pulled out his PI license and held it up for David to see.

"Why do you want to see me?"

"I saw your movie on TV the other night. I'd like to ask you some questions about it," Green said.

David felt himself relax. He sat down and let out a sigh of relief.

"You'll have to contact my agent. He's also my publicist. He doesn't like me doing impromptu interviews. You can make an appointment through him." David handed the PI his agent's card.

"I see," Green said, looking at the card. "I leave town tomorrow. I'm a former homicide detective. Your movie has some similarities to a murder I investigated three years ago."

"I'm pretty busy," David said.

"I can buy you lunch. It would only be an hour or so of your time. You would be doing me a big favor."

David shifted his gaze from the paperwork piled on his desk to Green.

"Who am I to turn down lunch? How about the Arts District? I know a place that makes a killer kelp noodle salad and roasted curried cashews."

"As long as I can get a burger."

David nodded and grabbed his keys off the desk. "I'll drive. Parking can be a problem, but I have a couple of secret parking spots up my sleeve."

Green followed David to his car. At the restaurant, the two men ordered their meals and a couple of beers.

"Before I retired and became a PI, I was a police detective in Barstow for twenty-eight years."

"You said my movie reminded you of a case."

"More than reminded me. Did you write the plot yourself?" Green asked.

David was cautious in his answer. He couldn't reveal too much about how he and Tim had *acquired* the story. "It's part fiction, part true crime."

"That's what I wanted to talk with you about. How did you get such detail about the crime?"

"I do my homework, Detective Green."

"Please call me Gus. I realize you did your research. We were never able to make an arrest in that case, so it didn't go to trial, yet you know a lot of details about the crime. Why is that?"

David shifted in his metal chair. Suddenly, it felt hard. "Like I said, it's real life and fiction. Part of my research included talking to people familiar with the case. And the rest I just made up."

"Who did you talk to about the case?"

"I promised my sources confidentiality. People wouldn't talk to me if I broke their confidence. I'm sure you understand." David was a terrible liar, and he knew it, but he could not reveal anything to this PI. It would jeopardize his reputation, and he couldn't let that happen.

* * *

Three days later, Paige learned she was running out of time. Her elderly landlord had died, and her rent-controlled apartment building had been sold to make way for luxury condos. She was subletting her apartment on a handshake deal without a lease, so she'd receive no relocation money from the building buyers. Apartments were expensive, and finding another cheap apartment fast would be impossible.

Her dream was slipping away.

"I'm not leaving Hollywood. David owes me."

She decided to confront David at his workplace and grabbed her car keys.

* * *

David was talking with a young brunette at Caffe Café when he spotted Paige stepping out of her car. His stomach churned as she came through the door and made a beeline for him.

"David, I need to talk with you."

"I'm working, Paige. It's not a good time."

"I can see how hard you are working, but we have to talk now."

David gave an apologetic smile to the brunette.

"Let's go into my office."

"I'm not going anywhere in private with you," she said loudly. "Right here is just fine."

The brunette shrugged and moved to a table in the corner. David looked around the crowded café. People were staring at them. He shook his head. He hadn't thought about Paige's reaction to the movie until now.

"Outside," he said and indicated the patio.

"Okay."

Paige followed David to the far end of the patio, away from the one occupied table.

"What is it that is so important?" he asked in a low voice. *Like he didn't already know.* His guts were doing flip-flops. He hoped the couple sitting outside couldn't hear them.

"You know why I'm here. You stole my story. I saw it on TV."

"Can you keep your voice down, please? It wasn't *your* story. It was a story that you told me about…a crime that happened. It's a matter of public record." He knew it was a lie.

"I told you in confidence because I thought you were my friend and helping me with my script. I trusted you."

"Hollywood is competitive, Paige. It's a dog-eat-dog world. You should know that by now. You don't own what's in the public domain."

"Those were my words on the screen. You didn't even bother to change the character's names. Everything I told you. It's word for word."

"Grow up, Paige. I gotta go."

"You listen to me. I'm willing to keep things quiet to save your precious reputation. I'm assuming you made a tidy sum but not enough to quit your day job, so I won't be greedy."

David shifted his stance and braced himself.

Paige continued, "I want fifteen thousand, and I'll walk out of your life forever."

"Fifteen thousand. Are you crazy? Do you know all the people I had to pay? Agents, managers, lawyers, Uncle Sam. They all took a piece."

"Don't forget the ponies."

"Paige, have a heart," He could feel beads of sweat on his forehead.

"Like I said, I'm not greedy, but I want the money day after tomorrow. Otherwise, everyone is gonna know what you did. I'll be in touch."

David watched her walk away.

"Shit."

* * *

"So what if Paige is mad?" Tim said. David had shown up drained at Tim's condo not long after his shift at work had ended and shared Paige's threats. "I'm glad we used her story," Tim continued. "We made it better. It was a good payday for both of us. It is not like she can prove anything. She didn't register the script."

Tim poured himself a vodka. He knew David was weak, but hearing him whine about Paige was really pissing him off.

"She still can make trouble for us. I don't have fifteen grand sitting around. I'm having trouble scraping together enough to pay off my bookie."

"I'll take care of it, David. Sit down. You're making me nervous with the pacing. You're going to wear a hole in my new rug."

"We should never have used her story. I wouldn't be in this mess except you pitched it to my agent without talking to me first."

"He loved the idea. It got you back in the game." *You should be grateful that I helped you out of your slump.*

"You should have asked me."

"Don't forget that script saved both our butts. The studio was giving me a hard time. I needed new material, and you needed the money. You agreed to write—or should I say touch up—her script, remember? It's a little late to grow a conscience now. You could have said no, but you didn't." *No guts, no glory. I need to drop this guy when things blow over. No backbone for the long haul.*

Tim poured himself another vodka. David sat down on the couch, his head in his hands. Tim finished off his drink. "Don't worry. I said I'll take care of it."

* * *

The next evening after work, Paige made a quick stop at a small neighborhood market. On the way out, she scanned the bulletin board by the door for apartment listings. No such luck.

Distracted by her worries, she didn't see the man approach her until she reached her car. He stepped out of the shadows wearing a hoodie and sunglasses, causing Paige to jump. Her canvas grocery bag slipped to her elbow.

"Paige, it's time for you to stop harassing David," he said.

It took a second, but she recognized his voice. After all, when she had been David's so-called girlfriend, they'd spent time with this guy.

"You don't fool me with that stupid disguise. I know who you are, *Tim.*" His name had been in the movie credits too. *Produced by Tim Bower.* "You stole from me. I'm going to make you both pay."

He moved closer to her. He smelled clean, but not like soap clean. More like body-spray clean. Very LA.

"Nobody will believe you," he said.

"Are you sure about that? Why else would you be here threatening me?"

"I'm here to make it clear you should let it go."

"What if I don't want to?" she said, suppressing the fear forming in her gut as his six-foot frame towered over her. She felt around in her shoulder bag for the ball-peen hammer she kept for protection.

"Let's just say it would be better for you." Tim grabbed her jacket with both hands and shoved her hard against her car, knocking the breath out of her.

She pulled the hammer out of her purse and swung it hard. She hit him in the temple. His body fell limp to the pavement next to her car. *Oh my God!* She tossed the hammer onto the car seat, jumped in, and hurried home. She parked and ran into her apartment, leaving the bag of groceries in the car. Inside, with the doors locked, Paige breathed a long sigh. Her hands trembled while her mind raced. *Had that really just happened?*

* * *

"You need to slow down," Green said into his phone. It was hard enough for him to get a straight answer from David. He didn't need hysteria added into the mix. "Hang on, I'm gonna pull over." Green turned onto a residential street off Sunset and parked his pride and joy—a 1971 Ford Mustang. "Okay, go ahead."

"My friend, Tim, who produced the movie I wrote, was attacked last night and is at Cedars-Sinai hospital," David said after taking a deep breath.

"Who attacked him?" Green asked.

"I don't know. He was found unconscious in a parking lot. Hit in the head."

"With a hammer?"

"The police didn't say."

Green would find out for sure. He had a friend in the department.

"How did you find out about the attack?

"Tim doesn't have any family locally, so I'm his emergency contact," David said.

"Why are you calling me?"

"Because I think I know who attacked him, but I can't prove it. I need your help."

"Why not go to the police?" Green asked.

"It's complicated. I need to tell you the whole truth about my movie. Can we meet?"

"Okay, but I can't promise you anything." Green was elated. Solving a cold case with connections to high-profile Hollywood types would be great advertising for his declining PI business.

"How soon can you get back to LA?"

"Plans changed. I'm still here."

* * *

That evening, David sat in Green's car while Green explained how the surveillance equipment worked.

"This microphone is very sensitive, so just talk normally. I will hear you," Green said, tucking the listening device into David's inside breast pocket.

"How do I get her to confess?" David said.

"Say you're not sure you can trust her, but you really want to. Tell her you know she attacked Tim."

"How would I know *that?*"

"It doesn't matter. It will shake her up. Throw her off her guard. She's expecting to get the money and leave. Push her to talk."

"I'm not so sure about this. You really think she's involved?"

"Don't you? If you didn't, you wouldn't have called me this afternoon. Besides, in my experience, anyone is capable of anything given the right circumstances," Green said. "Don't let your guard down. I'll be nearby when you need me."

* * *

Paige's instructions to David had been clear. He was to meet her that night at eleven o'clock on a quiet residential street just north of Hollywood Blvd. When she drove onto the designated street a few minutes after the appointed time, David was waiting. She pulled her car alongside David's and motioned for him to follow her. She led him to a deserted parking lot and shut off the motor. Then she climbed into his car, her hand firmly holding the small hammer hidden inside her shoulder bag.

"Where's the money?" Paige asked.

"I've got it, but it's not on me," David said.

Her eyes narrowed. "Why not?" Did he think he could weasel out of compensating her after he stole her screenplay? No way she'd let that happen.

"I'm not sure I can trust you. First, I want to know why you attacked Tim."

"What? I didn't do anything to him!"

"I don't believe you. I need some insurance you won't talk later or demand more money. I'm going to the police if you don't tell me."

She could feel sweat trickling down her back. *Did he really know?*

"Listen, David, you've got it all wrong."

"I've been doing some research on you, Paige. You're not so innocent. Tell me why, and we might still have a deal. I don't want this to get out into the public any more than you do, but Tim is my friend. What happened?"

Paige clenched her teeth and kept her hand on the hammer.

A minute passed in silence.

"Okay, get out. I'm outta here," David said.

Paige stammered, "Okay, okay, just a minute. Don't be in such a damn hurry." She leaned back in her seat and let out a big sigh.

"Tim attacked me first. He was threatening me, okay? He got physical. I was afraid, so I hit him. It was self-defense. Satisfied? Now, can I get my money?"

David stared out the windshield.

"Not until you tell me why you killed your boyfriend," he said.

"You're insane! I had nothing to do with his death. The police cleared me. *Damn it!* She never should have told him about Ryan's death and how it had inspired her manuscript. This is what she got for letting David get her drunk.

"That's not what I hear."

"What do you mean?"

"Remember Detective Green?" David asked. "He investigated the murder of your boyfriend. I guess the case went cold until my movie came out."

"You mean *my* movie, don't you?"

"No, I mean *my* movie about *you*, Paige. Or should I call you *Janet?*"

Paige stared at David. Her mouth agape. She grabbed at the door handle. David pulled her back, pinning her against the seat.

"I know you killed him. Your mistake was writing it down. A confession in plain sight."

"That was no confession. It was fiction, inspired by real events."

"Right, with details only the real killer would know."

Paige felt her face grow hot, but she wasn't going to let him beat her. "You're forgetting something, aren't you? It's your name on the screenplay, not mine."

"Yeah, it might be my name, but how would I know anything about the murder? The details? I wasn't there, but you were. You told me the whole story. Remember?" He twisted her arm until she winced.

As he talked, she groped for her purse, but she was still pinned and could not move.

"The truth, Paige, then I'll give you the money, but first, I want to know why you killed him."

"Why do you care? He didn't care about me. He used me and threw me away. Just like you did. That's why you owe me, David. I want my money."

David released his grip; an expression of horror crossed his face. *Oh my God. What had she just admitted?* Paige pulled at the hammer, but it tangled in the strap.

Paige heard a voice yell at her to get out of the car. She could see a gun pointing at her through the window.

As years of built-up anger surged inside her, Paige freed the hammer and swung it at David's head. David blocked her arm, and the hammer fractured the windshield. David escaped from the driver's side unhurt. Paige's door was wrenched open. She realized the man pointing the gun at her was the detective who had investigated Ryan's death. He yanked her out of the car and subdued her.

"It's over, Paige. You're going down for the attempted murder of Tim and David and the murder of your boyfriend," Green said. "The police are on their way."

* * *

Six months had passed since David's struggle in his car with Paige. His involvement in her case had been minimal after she pleaded guilty to second-degree murder and two counts of attempted murder in exchange for a lighter sentence recommendation. David stopped collecting news clippings about Paige after that. His telephone stopped ringing, too. The news media had moved on to the next big story.

David sat in his small, cramped office, reviewing what inventory needed to be reordered. There was a knock on his door.

"Come in." David looked up. "Hello, Gus. It's been a while."

David gestured for Green to take a seat.

"Can you believe Paige took a plea?" Green said. "I was hoping for a trial."

Funny. You'd think a former cop would be happy with a plea because sometimes juries get it wrong.

"Paige is a lot of things, but she's not stupid."

"There was so much press following her arrest. Did you see me on TV? I did some interviews. The ratings were really good."

"I saw you. You single-handedly solved the case, as I recall," David said.

"Well, I couldn't tell the whole story. The truth wouldn't have been very good for your screenwriting career, would it?"

"Your version of events didn't hurt you either."

"True. Business has been good. I hired some extra help. Since Paige took the plea agreement, though, the case is officially closed, so no more interviews."

David stared at Green. The detective seemed oblivious to David's growing dislike of him.

"I'm sorry your friend Tim hasn't recovered," Green said.

"The doctors don't know if he ever will. Comas are unpredictable."

"I've been thinking about what you said before. About us partnering on a film project."

"Yeah, did you go through your old cases and find a good one?"

"As a matter of fact, that's what I wanted to talk to you about."

"Okay, shoot," David said, leaning back in his faux leather chair, feet on the desk.

"It's about Paige, actually."

"What?" David dropped his feet to the floor.

"I thought you might be interested in helping me with the screenplay," Green said.

"About what she did?"

"Sort of. Take a look at it."

Green pulled a script from his briefcase and handed it to David. He left the office, then returned with a coffee and settled into a chair.

David's gut twisted as he read.

"You wrote it from the killer's point of view," David said. "Just like Paige."

"I thought that was a pretty good idea."

"Did Paige write this script?" He already knew the answer. He recognized her writing style.

"Does it matter?"

"It does if she wrote it."

"Kind of like *your* movie script, right?" Green said.

David shifted in his chair.

"I don't want to be involved in your project," David said, handing back the script. "I don't want to work like that again. I just want to move on."

"There's no moving on, David. You're right in the middle of it."

"How did you *acquire* this script? Ransack her apartment?"

"*Ransack* is an ugly word," Green said, flipping through the script. "I changed the ending. Instead of a hero, you were going to be one of her victims. You should be thankful I intervened when I did."

David wasn't feeling all that grateful at the moment.

"Look," Green continued, "There are only four people who know what really happened with the first screenplay. One is a convicted murderer. Another is in a coma. That leaves you and me."

"So?"

"No one believed Paige when she talked to the police. But if I said something, her story might carry more weight."

David slumped in his chair with his head in his hands.

"Don't look so upset," Green said. "I need your writing skills on this new script. It just needs a little polish. And be sure to change the character names this time. You'll get screenwriting credit."

"I don't want it."

"You really don't have much of a choice, David. It's a no-brainer. I talked with your agent, and he likes the story."

"When was this?" David sat up. *I've got to stop handing out my agent's card.*

"We had lunch, and he's excited to see the script. I told him we've been collaborating. He was relieved to hear you're writing again."

"You should have talked to me first."

"Well, I'm talking to you now. He wants us to show him the script in two weeks so he can pitch it to the studios. I've got a feeling about this project. It's gonna be big." Green paused, then said, "You know, people involved with Paige have gotten hurt before. You wouldn't want to get hurt too. Would you, David?"

A DEAD LINE

By Ken Funsten, CFA

It was a summer job. And not so bad, this calling people he didn't know who mostly either didn't answer or hung up on him immediately. Only if he got them talking, he was supposed to offer them a free lunch in return for getting their names and addresses and then getting them to agree to attend some seminar about retirement living in the desert. The way Brent read it, it was some mind-body togetherness pitch to old hippies who had once been Buddhists, even if they were something different now. Brent had persuaded himself that such a job wouldn't be a bad way to pass the summer. It sure beat the serious crap his parents had wanted him to do, like go to camp, find his passion, and plan a future.

As it turned out, the summer job was even better than advertised, because—outside of Brent—the entire boiler room crew of free-lunch phone callers were girls. All came from other high schools, too, which made them seem exotic to Brent. All except one.

That one was Victoria Smythe. She was from his own school. Freshman year they'd even had a class together. Victoria was the opposite of exotic. In fact, she was kind of plain. Even her hair was plain, a dull frizz that fell almost to her shoulders, parted in the middle. But maybe that's what made it so easy for Brent to talk to her. Around Victoria, he didn't feel any of the anxiety he felt with the other girls in the room—the ones he didn't know. There were twenty-five altogether—including Victoria—and each had a different scent for him. And a different rhythm when she spoke.

On their first day calling, they'd each been given a list of phone numbers. And their boss, not much older than Brent himself, had told the room that these lists were the holder's own "territory," each carefully selected—and now the private "beat" for each to patrol. These lists, the boss-dude went on, were not to be traded or exchanged among them. "There's a science behind who got what, a science that's been coordinated with the personality tests you took when you applied for this job. So don't screw it up for us, people. Science is on your side. Let's use it. If you don't, it'll cost the company—and so cost you."

Brent figured the dude was probably more bark than bite. He didn't look that tough coming out of his little piss-ass glass office just to spew nonsense like this at them. Still, Brent took it seriously. His list of phone numbers was his own, his special beat, and no one else's.

At first, calling was easy. There was a script Brent read if someone answered—which hardly happened. On that first day, in fact, an old lady finally did answer, but in the background, her dog kept yapping. And when it wouldn't stop, you should've heard the words she used to cuss it out. Some of them—Brent was pretty sure—weren't even English.

But by Friday of that first week, no matter how many barking Chihuahuas or old people's cartoony voices he'd heard, the job was getting kinda boring—like most everything did pretty quick for him. The only two things that kept him going were being surrounded by the twenty-four girls from other schools and getting paid ten bucks an hour. At that rate, he'd been told, work would add up to almost $35 a day after taxes—which was more than he could spend on any weeknight. So by that Friday, not yet gathering the courage to speak to any of the exotic girls, Brent figured he'd talk to Victoria.

"Hi." He nodded solemnly at her.

"Hi back," she replied. She'd been quick in class, too. "The first day I saw you here. How's *your* beat?" She smiled, as if she'd just made some joke to him, and he shuffled his feet, trying to figure out what was so funny.

"My beat's the world." He'd heard that said in an old movie he'd watched with his little sister on TV the previous weekend. It sounded good, so he puffed up his chest. "My beat's gonna be more than some puny list of old people from Riverside." Brent thought about how this sounded. "And I bet yours will be, too, Victoria. You're smart. Why'd *you* take this job?"

* * *

Victoria Smythe wondered how it was that all boys seemed so consistently awkward. "I saw the sign in the window." She was trying extra hard to keep things simple with them now, especially since she'd discovered it made them nervous if she didn't. "How did *you* find it, Brent?"

"Same as you, I guess. Maybe my mom or dad told me. They were on my case to do something this summer and were talking about sending me to some camp to *find my passion*." He snorted. "They're always talking crap like that. But this is better, you know? Pretty chill, making phone calls, giving away free lunches. Talking to old people."

"Yes, you meet some strange ones on the phone, don't you?"

"I guess."

"I spoke to one old man"—she became careful with her phrasing—"who told me he couldn't go to our lunch because he didn't have legs. I thought it was a figure of speech, you know? Then he told me that they were blown off—in Vietnam. Nearly fifty years ago." She watched for his reaction. "He still remembers the whole thing, the day it happened, what kind of weather it was. He said he was on patrol with five other guys, and they went over the crest of a hill, and *bammm!*" She'd raised her voice, then quickly lowered it again. "He was the only survivor."

"I had one lady with a dog," Brent replied to her. "We talked. But mostly, no one answers."

Victoria nodded, giving the boy a sympathetic look.

* * *

That first week, Brent entertained himself by fantasizing about all the girls he didn't know in the room—while tediously working his list—dialing and redialing, waiting for somebody to pick up.

But by the beginning of the second week, he figured it'd be safer to think about what might be happening at the houses he was calling instead of about the girls in the room with him. The latter had gotten *too* exciting. So he began playing a new game—where when no one answered, he'd imagine what they were doing instead of answering the phone. After all, this many houses couldn't all be empty. Somebody had to be there. So what were they doing? Then he let himself imagine.

That's when it struck him that the person he was calling could be dead. Maybe even still lying there but rotting like in some zombie movie. And beginning to smell bad. What had they done in their lives? Brent wondered. And what would Mom and Dad say about *them*?

Or, maybe the person who wasn't answering had been robbed and couldn't answer because they were tied to a chair in their kitchen? Or the robber had just killed them? And all that blood was oozing onto the linoleum while the phone rang and rang, with Brent waiting to give them a free lunch. What had any of these people done with their lives? It seemed easier to think about their lives than to think about his own.

Then, it was Tuesday of that second week, and something monumental happened, something that beat even his fantasies. He'd felt sleepy after lunch that day—had even yawned a couple times—and then, on the fourth call of the afternoon, she'd answered.

There was something about her voice. He liked the rhythm of it. It was exciting, more exciting than any he could ever remember hearing. But he couldn't say why or what its connection to him was. It just hit him that he'd never heard a voice like hers before, and it made him happy.

"Hello?"

He was struck dumb at first.

"Hello?" she repeated.

He read from his script. "How are you today, ma'am?"

He wanted to hear her voice again. It sounded younger, more alive, than others who'd answered his calls before this. Maybe she was too young for free lunches? But the only way he'd know was to give her the rest of his spiel.

And besides, with so few people answering, he needed the practice.

"Ma'am," Brent commenced with the section marked "Opening," "lemme tell you, I work for a great company, and you probably don't even know its name, but my name's Brent. Ma'am, what's yours?"

"Kimberly."

It seemed to Brent that the woman on the other end had barely breathed the word.

"Well, okay. Kimberly, lemme ask you this. Have you ever dreamed about living in paradise? I mean, like a desert paradise? Have you ever dreamed about being free?" He'd ad-libbed this last bit. He'd never felt this loose before. "Cuz we all have dreams, don't we? Dreams of how we want things to be. Well, today's your lucky day, ma'am, because my company has a special just for you. And an affordable one, too. In fact…it's free. That's budget-friendly, isn't it?" He laughed like he'd heard people laugh on TV, so she'd know it was a joke. But then continued so she couldn't interrupt him. He was on a roll—and wanted to stay on it. "The free part is the lunch, Kimberly. Just for coming to hear about this great new retirement idea. I mean, if you're old or your mother's old and you've ever wanted to be around other great people like yourself when they get old—*and* have privacy—that's what this will get you. It's a cake-and-eat-it-too thing, pools and putting greens, everything. Would you let me send you an invitation to our next free lunch? We all get hungry, don't we? How about it? Comes with a choice of beef, chicken, fish, or vegetables—"

"Will *you* be at this lunch, dear boy?"

The woman's voice excited him again, reminding him of something or someone he couldn't specify.

"There must be some catch, Brent? My mother always told me *there's no such thing as a free lunch*. Did your mother ever tell you that?"

Brent could only gulp. He hadn't practiced enough to handle questions. And this lady had just asked him a few.

"No catch at all, ma'am. But I… I can't be there. I have to work. I'm just the caller…" He paused, reset, and moved forward. "I mean, I'm in charge here, but… That's why I can't be at the lunch there—because I'm in charge here. But I can sign *you* up. Now, what's your address?"

"Oh. You're so forceful about all of this, Brent. I mean, of course, I *want* to come. I'm sure I do. Let's see now...beef, chicken, or fish? Which one? But you won't be there? I have a confession to make," Kimberly continued. "I don't have access to a car. My husband won't let me. So I'll give you my address like you want, but won't commit until you call me back tomorrow and tell me that you can come to the lunch and take me too. That will be the clincher for me. If you're in, I'm in," she chirped.

"No, ma'am. I can't... I mean, I haven't had... But I'm told they're all—" He felt flustered. Her voice had distracted him again. It was innocent yet experienced, throwing him in every direction, yet leaving him not knowing what to say. He'd never heard a voice suggesting what he thought he'd heard. Brent tried to think, but nothing came of it. And he couldn't understand why.

Finally, he said, "I'm ready for your name and address, ma'am. So they'll send you the invitation. But I'll call you like you asked me to tomorrow."

So she gave him her address, one beyond Pasadena but not actually to Riverside yet, in a place called Azusa. "It's everything from A to Z in the USA," she told him.

"Brent?" She'd started talking again. "How old *are* you? Be honest now."

"I'm almost seventeen, ma'am. Right after school starts, I've got a birthday."

"So you're sixteen," she sighed. "I remember sixteen. So you've got your driver's license, right? And is there a little girlfriend yet?"

Brent looked around the room at all the possibilities. "Well...not exactly. But I'm working on it."

"I bet you're working on it," she said, laughing.

He knew what she meant, but he had no idea how to respond to it. He couldn't tell this woman the truth—even if he did feel a funny urge to.

"I don't know, ma'am. I'm...ahh...I'm..."

"I see. What you're trying to tell me is that you have a prospect, or maybe a few prospects. Is that right? That's good. But I'll bet you really don't know what to say to them, do you? Is that right, dear boy?"

"I—I guess not." Brent felt more and more confused at that moment. What should he say? He definitely was off-script. Hopefully the jerk in the glass office wasn't listening in.

"You'll call me tomorrow, okay?" Her voice had a comforting tone, easing him. "And I'll make you a deal. You come to the lunch and pick me up, and I'll give you lessons in what to say—and what *not* to say—to the young women you meet. I'll show you all the secrets. I promise you'll learn something useful. You've given me an idea, and I'm grateful to you. It's something I've wanted to do for a long time, but haven't had the courage until now. Now I've got to get prepared for it. Because it's a big project. And I'll have to be in the mood, you know?"

Brent didn't know what mood she was talking about. But he did want to know what she meant by "lessons." So the next day, he came to work with more anticipation than he'd had any day before. He could hardly wait until after lunch to call Kimberly again.

* * *

It was the last half of their lunch break, and Victoria was reading *War and Peace* when Brent drifted over.

"Have you ever been asked"—he lowered his voice—"to call someone back?"

Victoria raised her eyes to look up at Brent. "Sure." She felt excited by what she'd been reading, but self-conscious now that Brent might see her blush. She tried to control her voice. "There was one time a woman wanted me to call her back so she could ask her husband if he could come too. But she had to wait until he got home from playing golf to do it."

"That's different," Brent told her. "That was about him. This is about *me*."

Victoria heard what he said. Boys were so sensitive and vain, she thought. "Well, be careful. You break the rules, and you could pay, remember? So, did you call her back?"

"Not yet. But I'm going to. Right after lunch."

"Tell me how it goes, okay? I can meet you after work, and we can talk about it walking home if you like."

Brent nodded. Victoria looked down at her book, where suddenly Tolstoy's Russian men seemed much less interesting to her.

* * *

After lunch, Brent sat down at his phone and looked around the big room. So many girls he'd like to know better. A how-to education was a risk worth taking. He'd heard his father say something like that about something else. That's what he was thinking before he redialed.

This time there were a lot of rings before she answered, which gave him time to do some more figuring. Yes, she was older than he was—that was for sure. But surely close enough in age that she'd still know what she was talking about. She'd been young herself, not too far back. And now married, she knew what it was all about. Knew the details that would be bound to help him with the opportunities surrounding him. He'd only need a few lessons. He was sure about that. A script—like he'd had when he'd met *her*.

"Brent? Have you decided?"

"Yeah, I mean, I guess so, ma'am. What'd you have in mind?"

"You don't sound very convincing, dear boy. You do *like* girls, don't you?"

He figured she must be kidding. But he nodded anyway, as if she could see him.

"Okay. So you've got a driver's license, and you can get a car, right? That's your part of the deal. Now, here's mine. I want you to put the phone down for maybe five minutes. Then, pick it up again and listen. My husband'll be coming home any moment, and when he does there'll be some fireworks. He's old, but still knows nothing about women. You'll get a lesson if you listen, okay?"

"Sure." So Brent put the phone down and made as if he were studying his beat sheet. He even put on a serious expression so the boss-dude wouldn't think he was loafing. Then, a few moments later, Brent heard sounds coming from his phone. He grabbed it up to his ear, pressing it tight against his head so no one else could hear. Then, over the phone line came the sound of a door slamming, a gruff voice roaring something as if in expectation of something else. And then he thought he heard Kimberly say something, but exactly what he couldn't tell. Then he heard Kimberly again, this time pleading, "Stop, please, just stop, Gerry." But they didn't stop. They kept yelling at each other, a panicked mix of frantic cries and occasional screams, followed by a single gruff grunt. And then the line went dead…until Brent heard the door slam again, and then slam twice more, and then it was quiet again, until someone picked up the phone.

"I'm sorry," Kimberly mumbled. "He's that way now. Doesn't say much but has to have his way. Always his way. You see that doesn't work, don't you? Promise me you'll never be like that, Brent?"

He sat in his chair in the boiler room, his stomach tight against the phone table.

"Call me again tomorrow, okay? But for the lunch next week, I'll absolutely need you to pick me up. For as long as we've been married, he's never let me have my own car. So that's my deal, young man. Take it or leave it. You already have my address. But he can't see us when you come over. If he does, he'll kill us both." Her voice trembled like a loose window does in a storm. There was a long moment in which Brent's expectations rose, until they hurt, extending beyond patience. "Call me tomorrow," she broke in, "and we'll make our plans for *everything*." And then she hung up.

Brent looked around the room at the girls his own age. He hoped none had heard what he'd heard. He even glanced at the glass office where the boss-dude sat. He knew he had to find a car now as well as a place for Kimberly and him. A friend's house? Or even his mom's car? But what friend? And it wasn't like they owned a van. His own house was out—both parents were never gone at the same time. A motel was the only answer. But he'd never rented a motel room before. He knew he'd have to learn these things that scared him now, unknown things. If he wanted any future at all, he'd have to do more than overhear life. He'd have to live it himself. The unknown was the price, and the risk was the reward. He thought his dad had said something like that too. Brent felt seduced by the deadline rising up in front of him, by that last word she'd drawn out and stressed with an extended trilling of its four syllables.

But where would they meet? He had no answer.

The next afternoon, a Thursday, one day closer to seventeen, and Brent stared at the phone on his desk, then dialed Kimberly.

"Dear boy," she answered, "I've been thinking about us. Thinking about us," she repeated, then asked, "When are you coming for me?"

"I don't know," Brent mumbled into the mouthpiece.

"You arrange it all then, and I'll be ready. The ball's in your court. Will you call me tomorrow, dear?"

Brent had heard of cougars, of course. His mother had even called some of her divorced friends that. But he wasn't sure he'd ever met one himself. Still, he'd heard Kimberly say she'd teach him secrets. And he believed that. In fact, he was excited sitting at his calling table. He looked around. Yes, he could have quite a summer here...if he just knew where to begin.

* * *

Later, after work, Brent went to find Victoria. She was good for answers, and he wanted a second opinion. Who else was there to give him one?

"So she's let you snoop on her and her husband, and now you're going to meet her? Are you crazy?" His high school classmate sounded outraged, even angry at him. "That's creepy. And *that's* how you've spent your week, as a Peeping Tom on the phone?" She made a face, one which Brent hadn't seen before. "Do you know what that sounds like? I'll tell you. It sounds dangerous. How can you go meet someone you've never met before?"

Brent wanted to explain to Victoria. But he couldn't find words to make it clearer than it already seemed to him. The risk wasn't in going, it was in not going, he wanted to tell her. Because then nothing in his future would happen. That's why he needed a goal—a dream with a deadline—like the one he had now.

So Friday, the same as he'd done the previous three days, Brent dialed Kimberly's number. Only this time, the phone rang so many times he hung up before anyone answered. Then he dialed again. When Kimberly answered, she sounded sick, not pronouncing her words right. "Ohhh," she drawled, "can you come for me?" She stretched out the last word. "Can you?"

"Yes," he said, though he still didn't know how.

"Oh, I love you. Yes, yes, yes. You keep saying that to all the girls, and it'll all work out great for you. They'll all go—"

Kimberly stopped. Had she pushed the mute button? There was only silence. Then, he heard something breaking, a door slamming, then something dropping, a glass or something. And then, there was a scream. Not squeals, or a single moan this time, but one short bloodcurdling cry.

He must be killing her, Brent thought. And then suddenly…silence.

Brent heard something more, perhaps someone breathing, a hoarse sound from the other end of the connection, before the phone line went dead.

Paralyzed by fear and surrounded only by girls his own age, Brent imagined Kimberly tied up in Azusa. Or lying hurt. Or even murdered. Was that possible in what seemed such a faraway place? If not, then what was happening? And who was it that had hung up the phone? Brent figured he'd overheard a murder and that the killer snuck up on Kimberly while they'd been speaking. That made it partly his fault. So now he had to go help her. But wouldn't that person who hurt her still be there? He thought about that.

The rest of the day, Brent felt sleepy, listless. He couldn't even give away a single free lunch. He just wanted to talk to Victoria—would even walk home with her if that's what it took. But he absolutely needed to tell her what had happened.

But when he asked her, she told him it was Friday and that her mother was coming to pick her up. To go shopping.

So, with no one to talk to, Brent didn't know what to do. That night, he couldn't even sleep, turning the problem over and over in his mind. He couldn't tell anyone in his own home. He didn't dare. They all knew him too well. So, lying awake, he thought of a new plan. By the next evening, it will have been a day. By Sunday evening, it would be two. The murderer would surely have left by then. So, one way or another, no one would be at Kimberly's house—at least no one living. The more he replayed his memories of what he'd overheard, the more he figured that was how it must be: Kimberly was dead. And when he'd get there, he'd find her body and have to report it. And have to explain everything.

That's why, all weekend, he still couldn't sleep. He felt shame that he'd done nothing except listen. He could have yelled over the phone. He could have called the police. But now, he thought, shouldn't he at least go see what had happened?

Monday morning, Brent rose with first light and dressed for work. But he didn't intend on going to work that day. Instead, after breakfast, he called Victoria at home. Brent had already arranged to borrow his mother's car—he'd told her he wanted to go downtown to the library to do some career research—but still, he needed Victoria's help. He needed her to tell their mutual boss-guy that Brent wouldn't be in today. That he'd be out sick. "Tell him you saw me over the weekend, and I'm very, very sick," he repeated for Victoria. "The not-wanting-me-around-at-work kind of sick. Okay?"

"Are you out of your mind?" Victoria yelled back through the phone. "You're going to where? Now? You'll get yourself killed, Brent. Or arrested? Call the police. Let them handle it."

"I have to. I have to go see what's happened there myself."

"Why?"

* * *

According to the map, it was the address Kimberly had given him in Azusa. He parked his mom's car in front of the small house the color of a brown paper bag. The front yard needed mowing, and the house's chipped paint looked like the speckles on a bird egg—only ugly. He got out of the car. That's when he noticed the old lady on her knees, planting flowers in a newly turned-over bed of dirt up against the side of the house. The old lady, her gray head down, was patting the soil with both hands as Brent approached.

He cleared his throat, hoping to get her attention without actually having to say anything. Finally, because perhaps she hadn't heard him yet, he spoke.

"Ma'am?"

"How can I help you, young man?" Her voice sounded familiar. It was younger than most old ladies sounded. But she didn't look up. And when she did, her hand was held up to shield her eyes. What Brent could see seemed unfamiliar to him—a face lined with experience as unknown as death.

"I'm looking for a woman named Kimberly, ma'am. I think she might live here."

"There're lots of women in this neighborhood, young man. Could be many Kimberlys. We don't always know each other's names. Sometimes our husbands don't even know them—but they should. Why do you want to find this Kimberly?"

"She's a friend of mine."

"Ah, a friend," the old woman said with apparent approval. "You don't say? A special friend?"

He didn't answer. "Do you live here alone?" he asked her.

"I had a husband once—until recently."

"He's gone then?"

"He did. He went away." She looked at Brent again, smiling. "I think you'll find Kimberly isn't here anymore either. But she wanted me to thank you. Talking to you gave her courage." The spade in the old woman's hand rose. "If you want to come in and look around, you're welcome to. It's safe now."

The newly dug bed of flowers looked to Brent like a grave. He looked at the woman's dirt-stained fingers, then at her lined face again, her eyes like a bird's.

For a moment, his imagination wandered to a picture of Victoria's face leaning close to his at one of their work breaks, whispering something. And then he overheard that other voice again, and Brent took a first step toward the open door.

"Young man?"

FATAL RETURN

By Sybil Johnson

While she waited for the police to arrive, Michaela Franklin stationed herself near the west entrance of the newly built library and studied the scene before her. Her gaze swept over the ground floor of the glass-and-steel structure, taking in the boxes of books waiting to be shelved and the sculptures resting on the floor, ready to be hung. She raised her eyes to the upper floor, straining to hear the slightest sound but, other than a faint click, she couldn't be sure she hadn't imagined, nothing indicated anyone else was in the building.

Sadness washed over her as she turned her attention to the rectangular opening that housed the automated book-return machine, the pride and joy of the woman who was leaning forward, her reddish-blond head and shoulders resting in the waist-high opening. If it hadn't been for the piece of metal sculpture protruding from the woman's back and the pool of blood on the floor, she would have looked as if she was inspecting the new addition to the library.

Michaela barely had time to note how easily she slipped back into old habits when the police arrived. First inside was a baby-faced uniformed officer who, after the briefest of glances at the body, stayed with her while two other officers went through the building to make sure no one was hiding inside. As soon as they cleared the scene, Baby Face led her to a nearby table, and the crime scene team swept in.

The uniformed officer kept his back to the body while he took her statement. From the pallor of his skin, Michaela suspected the young man wasn't going to have much appetite for lunch that day.

Before long, a fortysomething man in a suit and tie entered the building and briefly studied the scene. He talked with the baby-faced officer before approaching the table where she sat.

His bushy brown eyebrows shot up in surprise as soon as he saw her. "Mike! I didn't realize you were the one who found the body."

"Ben. Glad you're on the case."

Detective Ben Dewey took the seat across from her and brought out a small notebook. An uncomfortable look on his face, he said, "I'm sorry, but I need to ask you some questions."

Michaela frowned. "What was the first thing I taught you?"

"Never let personal feelings or associations interfere with an investigation."

"And the second?"

"Never apologize for doing your job."

She nodded her head in satisfaction. "Good. Ask your questions."

"Let's start with how you found Ms...." Dewey glanced over at the body.

"Appleton. Janice Appleton. Library director."

He jotted the information down in his notebook.

"Janice asked me to come in early this morning, before the others arrived," she continued. "Didn't say why. I assume it had something to do with the grand opening of the library."

Dewey cast a puzzled look in her direction. "She asked you because...?"

"I'm a library volunteer. Have been ever since I retired from the force. With the library opening only two days away, it's an all-hands-on-deck situation."

"When are the others coming in?"

She glanced at her watch. "Half an hour. I came inside through there." She pointed to the door they'd all used. "It was unlocked. Walked around the corner, and there she was."

"Did you touch the body? Check for a pulse?"

"I knew right away she was beyond help. I've seen enough dead bodies."

He nodded. She suspected he was thinking about all of the cases they'd worked together over the years in this LA County beach city.

"Did you see or hear anyone when you arrived?"

"No. At least, I don't think so."

"It's not like you to be unsure."

"I didn't see anyone, but my hearing's not the best these days. I thought I heard a click, maybe a door closing, but I might have been imagining it."

"Did you notice anything missing?"

"I wanted to wait to look around until you arrived and cleared the scene."

"Right. Let's take a look now." Dewey returned his notebook to his inside jacket pocket and stood.

Michaela led the way around the library, starting with the ground floor. Everything appeared normal until they reached an area where a display on the history of the town and its library had been set up. Her gaze zeroed in on a locked display case, unexpectedly empty.

She pointed to it. "There's supposed to be a book in there."

Dewey studied the lock on the case. With gloved hands, he tried to open it, but the lid didn't budge. "You're sure?"

"It was in there yesterday." She frowned. "Though I suppose it could be in Janice's office. She might have wanted to work on it."

"Work on it?"

"Sorry, I should explain. The book was a diary of John Melville, one of the town founders. It was discovered in some boxes in a storage area of the old library that was torn down to make way for this one. It wasn't in the best shape."

"Ms. Appleton was restoring it?"

"She planned to. She was going to start working on it after the grand opening."

"Who would want to steal it? Is it valuable?"

"It's over one hundred years old. It must have some value. To Melville's relatives, anyway."

"We can check her office when we get there."

They continued looking through the library, not finding anything else damaged or missing. Their last stop was the library director's office on the second floor.

Michaela pushed open the door, revealing a neat and tidy office. She looked at the bookcase and top of the desk, seeking the missing diary. "I don't see it. It might be in a desk drawer."

The detective examined each drawer, not finding the book in any of them.

"You're sure the book was inside that case?"

"Positive. I suppose she could have taken it home."

"We'll check. Is there someplace we can talk more comfortably?"

"There's a conference room down the hall."

Once inside the room, they sat at one end of the rectangular table next to a wall of windows. It overlooked the courtyard on the opposite side of the building from the crime scene.

"Did anyone have any problems with Ms. Appleton?" Dewey asked.

"I haven't known her that long, but most people seemed to like her. Respected her, anyway."

"Most?"

"She had a few disagreements about how to run the library with the volunteer coordinator, Beverly Beckley. I don't know the specifics."

"Married?"

"I don't know much about her personal life other than she moved here from Albuquerque a few months ago. Go on, ask me the question you really want to ask."

"How was your relationship with her? Did you get along?"

"She wasn't the easiest person to know. I'd say we were friendly."

"No disagreements?"

"I'm only a volunteer. Not much to disagree about."

"Did she say why she wanted you to come here this morning?"

"Not really. She wanted to ask me about something before everyone else arrived, but didn't give specifics." Her gaze drifted to the window overlooking the entrance below. Three people clustered around the door, looking confused and frightened by the police activity. "The staff are here."

Dewey glanced down at the group. "Tell me about them."

"The tall woman is Beverly, the volunteer coordinator I told you about. My boss. The gray-haired man in the tweed jacket next to her is Melville Cleary, the adult librarian. He's distantly related to John Melville, the man who wrote the diary."

"Hence the Melville name."

She nodded. "The petite woman is Astrid Grimm. She's the children's librarian."

"Odd name for someone who works with children."

"Seems like the perfect one to me. What with those fairy tales and all."

"Good point. Time to let them in. I'll need this conference room and one more for individual interviews."

"There's one down the hall that has blinds you can close," she said.

"Is there a way to get them up here without parading them by the body?"

"Bring them up the stairwell by the door below. They won't be able to see it from there."

"Stay here."

A few minutes later, Beverly Beckley, Melville Cleary, and Astrid Grimm came into the room, all looking confused and a little nervous. Astrid sat down next to Michaela, while Melville sat on the other side of her, lightly resting his hands on the metal arms of the chair. Beverly came in last.

The volunteer coordinator spotted Michaela and frowned. "Michaela, what are you doing here?"

"Janice asked me to come in early."

"She did?" Beverly sniffed. "She didn't tell me about it. Did she say why?"

"No. I figured I'd find out when I got here."

"She should have told me. I am in charge of the volunteers. Where is she, anyway? What's going on?"

Michaela motioned to the doorway where Dewey had now appeared. "We're about to find out."

All eyes turned to the detective, who briefly introduced himself and broke the news of the library director's death. He let it sink in for a moment before saying, "I'll be talking to each of you individually. We'll also be taking your fingerprints for elimination purposes. You can go home after."

"What about the library opening?" Beverly said. "We have a lot of work to do."

"Right now, I have a murder to solve. That takes precedence." He motioned to the children's librarian. "Ms. Grimm, how about you go first?"

Astrid jumped at the mention of her name. She had always struck Michaela as the nervous type, but today, she seemed even more agitated than usual.

Beverly stood up and said in an authoritative voice, "I should go first. I'm the most senior person here."

Dewey studied her for a moment and nodded. "Very well."

Michaela hid her surprise when he left them together. She assumed he'd broken procedure to give them time to talk so she could report back on anything interesting that was said.

After the door closed, Melville said, "Senior person, my foot. She wanted the director's job, you know. That strikes me as significant."

"I didn't realize she was up for it," Michaela said.

"She wasn't really. She thought she was a shoo-in for the job until the library board decided to hire outside the system. She was not happy. I guess she'll get the job now."

Michaela tucked the information away in the back of her mind.

Silence settled over the group. Astrid picked at her red nail polish, peeling it off bit by bit, while Melville stared off into space.

Michaela decided to get the conversation started. "I found her, you know."

Astrid's hand flew to her face, and her eyes grew wide. "That's awful. They don't think you did it, do they? Are we all suspects? Is that why the police are questioning us?"

"It's standard procedure."

"That's right, you would know."

Melville stared at them. "What do you mean?"

"She used to be a detective."

Michaela shrugged. "Retired. Now I'm an ordinary citizen who loves her local library."

Melville worried the arms of his chair a bit, then walked over to the window and stared down at the courtyard below. Michaela doubted she'd

165

get anything else out of him. She turned her attention to the children's librarian, who had started on the nails on her other hand.

"Are we safe?" the young woman said. "You don't think there's a homicidal maniac in the building, do you?"

"Whoever did it is gone. The police searched the building when they arrived."

Astrid visibly relaxed.

Michaela tried to involve Astrid and Melville in further conversation, but neither one was in a talkative mood. She went over the crime scene in her mind. The position of the body in the automated return machine seemed significant. She said to the room at large, "Did anyone have a problem with the new check-in machine?"

Melville turned from his position at the window. "Why do you ask?"

"Just curious."

"Beverly," Astrid said. "She wasn't happy about it."

"Why?"

"She thought the money spent on it would be better used hiring paid staff instead of using volunteers."

"But she's the volunteer coordinator."

"Doesn't mean she's happy about it," Melville said, then turned back to the window.

Dewey returned a short time later, a stern look on his face. He motioned to Michaela. "Ms. Franklin, come with me, please."

Only when they were inside the other conference room, door closed and blinds drawn, did the sternness go away.

"What did you do to her?" he said.

"Beverly? Nothing, as far as I know."

"She really has it in for you. All but accused you of murder."

"I think she's angry at the world. Apparently, she expected to get the library director job." She told him what she'd learned about the woman's views on the new check-in system.

"You think the position of the body is a statement."

"Maybe. Or someone wanted it to look that way. Does Beverly have an alibi?"

"She claims she was home, alone, getting ready to come here."

"Where is she now?"

"Getting her fingerprints taken before she leaves. She wanted to hang around, but—"

Sounds of arguing came from outside the door. One voice rang out loud and clear.

Dewey groaned. "Of course."

Michaela raised an eyebrow in a question.

"Jacob Magruder. PR guy for the city."

"New?"

"Relatively. He has a lot of ideas." Dewey air quoted the last word.

Moments later, a man with slicked-back hair, dressed in a button-down shirt and severely pressed pants, strode into the room. The uniformed officer behind him shrugged an apology.

Dewey stood up to greet him. "Jacob."

"Is it true? A body was found in the library?"

"The library director. How did you find out?"

"It's my business to know what's going on in this city."

Michaela guessed Beverly had contacted the man as soon as she realized the grand opening was in jeopardy.

Jacob Magruder's gaze turned toward her. "This the suspect?"

Dewey introduced the two of them. "We're still working the case. I didn't say she was murdered. How did you know?"

"Please, I'm not stupid. Why else would you be here?" Jacob said. "Anything else I should know? I need to get ahead of this."

"A book may have been stolen. Might be related. Might not."

"Not the Melville diary?"

"Afraid so, though it could be at the deceased's home. We'll have to check."

Jacob paced from one end of the room to the other. "This is bad, very bad. A death and an important part of the city's history missing." He stopped and stared at the detective. "This needs to be solved now. The grand opening of the library is only two days away. We can't postpone."

"Solving cases doesn't work like that. They have their own timetable."

"Two days," Jacob barked and swept out the door.

"What a charmer," Michaela said once he was gone.

"You don't know the half of it. He has the mayor's ear. And the chief's."

A uniformed officer knocked on the door. "Coroner's investigator wants to see you."

"Care to join me?" Dewey asked Michaela.

She followed him down to the first floor, where they found the woman from the medical examiner's office looking over the body. The investigator pointed to the piece of metal sculpture protruding from the victim's back. "Obvious cause of death. Won't know for sure until a full autopsy is done, of course. The killer wasn't very careful. Looks like there's a fingerprint on it."

"What else?"

"Found this in her pocket." Dewey slipped on latex gloves, and she handed over a piece of paper with the name Jefferson Tate written on it.

Dewey showed it to Michaela. "Recognize the name?"

"No. One of the others might, though."

The investigator pointed out minute flakes of bright red next to the body, barely visible on the wood floor. The other two knelt down to study them. After making sure they'd been photographed, Dewey picked one up. "What do you think it is?"

Michaela cocked her head. "My guess is bits of fingernail polish. Astrid wears that color. And she was picking her nails."

Dewey nodded and stood up. "Let's see what she has to say."

A crime scene tech gathered the bits into an evidence bag and handed it to the detective.

Upstairs, Astrid insisted Michaela be present for the questioning. Only the barest remnants of the red nail polish remained on the young woman's fingernails.

As soon as they were all seated, Dewey set the evidence bag on the table.

At the sight of it, Astrid clutched her handbag tightly against her chest.

"You were there, weren't you?" Dewey said.

"What are you talking about?"

"We found bits of nail polish next to the body." He tapped the bag. "Same shade as yours."

"They must have been from some other time. I'm always picking at my nails. She'll tell you that." Her eyes pleading for support, Astrid nodded toward Michaela.

"I don't remember seeing them yesterday."

"You wouldn't, would you? They're tiny flakes. Not worth noticing. Why are you focusing on me when there's a maniac going around stabbing people." Her voice took on a hysterical tone. "First, Janice. Anyone could be next."

"Why do you think she was stabbed?" Dewey asked.

Astrid's eyes grew wide, and her mouth trembled. Her shoulders slumped forward in defeat. In a voice barely above a whisper, she said, "I found her, okay? I panicked and left. That's all."

"Why were you here early?"

"I just wanted to get to work." She clutched her purse even tighter to her chest.

Michaela's gaze darted from the children's librarian to the detective. She gave an almost imperceptible nod. Dewey nodded back.

"Can I look in your purse, please?" he said.

"No." Astrid jutted out her chin.

"You know there's been a theft?"

"It wasn't me."

"You have keys to the display cases, right?"

"All of the department heads do."

"Did she surprise you in the middle of taking the diary?" Michaela said in a gentle voice. "I understand. You were only protecting yourself. You struck out with the closest thing at hand. You didn't mean to kill her. You just wanted to get away."

"I didn't. I wouldn't. I took the book, that's all." Astrid pulled the missing diary out of her purse and shoved it across the table. "Here. Take it."

"Why did you steal it?" Dewey said.

"I had to." She choked back sobs. "Now I'm going to lose my job. What am I going to do?" She buried her head in her hands.

"I don't care about a diary," Dewey said. "That's not my department. Murder is."

"You don't understand. Now it'll get out."

"What are you talking about?"

"Astrid, breathe, okay? Breathe. I'll help you any way I can," Michaela said.

After taking a few deep breaths, Astrid calmed down enough to continue. "A week ago, I received a text from a number I didn't recognize. It told me I had to steal the diary, or part of my past would come to light, and I'd lose my job."

"What part?" Dewey asked.

A pained expression crossed Astrid's face. "When I was a teenager, I was picked up for indecent exposure. A bunch of us watched some old seventies movies and saw people streaking. We thought it would be fun, but it didn't turn out that way."

"Were you arrested?"

"No. The police sent me home with a warning, but it doesn't make a difference. What would it look like for a children's librarian to have that in her background?"

"What were you supposed to do with the diary?"

"Put it in a plastic bag and tape it under a bench in the courtyard, then send a text."

"Can I see your phone?" Dewey scanned through the texts, jotting down the information he needed before handing it back. "Wait here." He pulled out his own cell and walked out into the hallway, closing the door behind him.

Astrid looked at Michaela. "I don't know what to do. I love my job. I love the kids."

"The diary's back in the library. As long as this doesn't have anything to do with the murder, no one needs to know."

Dewey returned. "We're checking on the phone now. Ms. Grimm, please stay here." He motioned for Michaela to join him in the hallway. They moved to one end and talked in quiet voices.

"Whoever texted her had to know something about her history," Michaela said.

"Could have known her family or been around when she was growing up."

"Doesn't seem like this has anything to do with the murder, but…"

"We can't be sure." Dewey paced the hall, head bent down in thought. He stopped, seeming to come to a decision. "Follow me."

They returned to the conference room where Astrid still sat, staring down at the table. She looked up when they entered.

Dewey sat next to her and said in a quiet voice, "Here's what I'd like you to do. After you leave, put the diary where you're supposed to and send that text. Then go home. We'll take it from there."

"What about…?"

"No one's hearing anything from me." He opened the door and motioned for her to accompany a uniformed officer to get her fingerprints taken. After giving instructions to another officer, he said, "Time for Mr. Cleary."

"I'll head back to the other conference room. Let me know if you need me for anything."

Michaela waited in the room while Melville Cleary went with the detective for his interview. She paced the floor and thought about the case. The choice of weapon indicated a spontaneous crime. The shoving of the body into the machine seemed to be making a point of some kind. Was Beverly to blame? Could she have had an argument with Janice that got out of hand and resulted in death? Or had Janice caught Astrid stealing the diary? And why had the library director asked Michaela to meet her? Had she discovered Astrid was being blackmailed and wanted to know what the police would do about it? The possibilities swirled through her mind. She stared out the window, struggling to put all of the pieces together in a way that made sense.

She gazed down at the courtyard below and spotted Astrid leaving the building, then sitting on a bench, taping the diary under it when she thought no one was looking. Not long after she left, the visible police presence was gone. Michaela was sure an officer or two was observing the scene, waiting for the culprit to arrive. She drew away from the window and waited, too. Before long, she heard a commotion outside. She glanced down at the courtyard to see Jacob Magruder with the diary in his hands, a uniformed officer holding one of the man's arms.

She hurried outside, arriving moments after Dewey.

"Tell this man to unhand me," Jacob said.

"May I?" Dewey motioned toward the diary. Jacob reluctantly gave it to him. "Care to explain why you made Ms. Grimm steal this for you?"

"I don't know what you're talking about. I found it."

"How did you know it would be under the bench?" The detective took out his phone and called the number Astrid had texted. A faint ringing came from the PR man's pocket.

"Going to answer that?"

"It can wait."

Dewey hung up, and the ringing stopped. "Care to explain?"

"It's my family's diary. I have every right to it."

Michaela widened her eyes. Another person related to John Melville. Interesting.

"You couldn't have simply asked for it?" Dewey said.

"Janice wouldn't give it to me. She said it belonged to the city. She was a very stubborn woman."

"So you decided to steal it. Or have someone do it for you."

Jacob threw up his hands. "She volunteered."

"After you threatened her."

"A little persuasion, that's all."

Michaela bristled. "You can't toy with people's lives like that. Whatever proof you have, hand it over."

"Look. I didn't have anything on her. I figured it was worth a shot. She seemed too good to be true. I thought she might have something in her past she didn't want anyone to know about, so I bluffed that I knew what it was." Jacob held out his hand. "Diary, please."

The entitled jerk acted as if he had done nothing wrong. Michaela flipped through the book. "I wonder what family secrets are in here you don't want to get out."

"It's a family diary. I have a right to it."

"What about Melville? It's his family, too," Dewey said.

Jacob snorted. "He says he's family, but I haven't found any evidence of it. Believe me, he isn't who he says he is. Can I go now?"

"For now. But we're keeping the diary."

Jacob glowered at them, then left.

"I doubt he had anything to do with the murder," Dewey said. "As annoying as he is, Magruder has no motive. He was getting the diary."

"What do you think about what he said about Melville? About him not being who he said he is."

"Worth looking into. I'll put a rush on his prints."

But, when they went inside, they discovered Melville Cleary had left without giving them.

"Suspicious," Michaela said. "Must have slipped out during the commotion in the courtyard."

"He's hiding something," Dewey agreed.

"Did he have anything interesting to say during his interview?"

"Didn't raise any red flags. Seemed pleasant enough." He cocked his head. "Kept his hands on his thighs the entire time. Didn't take a sip of the water I brought him either."

"He was avoiding touching anything."

"Now I really want his prints," Dewey said. "How about the other conference room? Did he touch anything in there?"

"The arms of the chair he sat in, but it's not going to help. He rubbed his hands over them, smudging everything. I thought it was nerves. Now I'm wondering." An idea popped into Michaela's head. "I think I know a way to get them."

Dewey listened carefully to her proposal.

* * *

The next day, the police released the library so the staff and volunteers could finish preparing it for the grand opening the following day. As soon as everyone arrived, they gathered downstairs near the town-history display to pay tribute to Janice Appleton. After they all had a glass of sparkling cider,

Beverly Beckley, the new interim library director, proposed a toast. "To Janice. Gone but not forgotten."

Everyone raised their glasses in response. Afterward, people gathered in small groups, chatting before starting work.

Michaela walked around, taking pictures, then approached Melville, who stood in front of the case containing the diary, staring down at it. "I bet you're glad to have the family diary back in its place."

"What? Right. Yes, it's good to see it here." He took a sip from his glass. "Nice of you to arrange the tribute."

"Me? Beverly took care of it, though I might have done some gentle prodding."

He raised an eyebrow. "She must have been in a good mood."

"She got what she wanted."

"For now," he said. "Any news?"

Forcing a sad expression on her face, Michaela shook her head. "This is one that may never be solved."

"Too bad."

"I was wondering if I can take a picture of you next to the diary? I've taken everyone else's." She mentally crossed her fingers, hoping he wouldn't say no to her request.

"Of course."

Melville put his glass down on top of another case, steps away from the one with the diary on it. Michaela put her identical glass next to his and arranged the photo so he'd be on the far side of the case. A crowd gathered to watch.

She quickly snapped several photos with her phone. "Thanks. I'll send you one."

Before he could pick up his glass, several others—all related to members of the police force—insisted on taking a photo with him. Michaela turned and grabbed Melville's glass off the table, holding it by the top edge, and made her way through the stacks, ending up at the east entrance, where Dewey waited for her. He emptied the glass, then put it in an evidence bag and left while she returned to work.

Later that day, Michaela was shelving books in the children's section when she received a text from Dewey to meet him outside. They sat on a bench in the courtyard.

He handed her a report. "Prints came back to a Jefferson Tate."

"That was the name on the note in Janice's pocket." She scanned the information. "He's wanted in Albuquerque for embezzlement. That's where she was from. She must have recognized him."

Dewey nodded. "That's probably what she wanted to talk to you about. Maybe she wasn't sure it really was him. He's changed quite a bit."

Michaela looked at the photo and nodded. "Dyed his hair gray, shaved his beard, and lost weight."

"He must have thought she recognized him and silenced her before she could tell anyone her suspicions."

"I suppose she didn't want to involve the police officially in case she was wrong. She probably figured I could make some discreet inquiries."

"There's more," Dewey said. "The print on the murder weapon is his."

"She must have turned her back on him, never thinking she was in any real danger. Or maybe she didn't know he was there. If he came in very early, hoping to surprise her when no one else would be around..." Michaela sighed and returned the folder to him. "When are you arresting him?"

"Right now." Dewey stood up and approached Melville as he exited the library. He didn't resist when the detective led him away.

At the grand opening of the library the next day, Michaela picked up a glass of wine and wandered through the stacks, admiring the result of all their work. She stopped and watched Jacob Magruder standing by the diary, talking to the local press about his famous ancestor.

Dewey stepped up beside her, a glass in his hand. "He's enjoying himself."

"Guess he changed his tune about disclosing family secrets."

"He's a PR guy. He can put a spin on anything." He looked at her. "Thanks for your help. Felt like old times."

"Anytime." Michaela took a sip of her wine. "I think, though, that the city should do a fingerprint background check on all its employees from now on, don't you?"

"Already in the works." Dewey held up his glass. "To a job well done."

CRIME DOESN'T PLAY

By Norman Klein

Part One: Mnemonics

I t had been more than a year since my last vacation, and I was beginning to feel it. More important, my family—wife Maria and thirteen-year-old daughter Gracie—needed a change of scenery. Maria was particularly worried that I was seeing too much of the sordid side of society that was endemic to being a police detective. She worries a lot about me, and it's one of the things I love about her. Three days later, we were on a plane to Los Angeles to visit a few relatives and to see the sights: subways to nowhere, faux outdoor villages like The Grove, to which everyone has to drive and park in order to experience neighborhood, and, of course, all the beaches. We decided to stay in Santa Monica, where at least the ocean looked real.

Less than a day passed when things took an unexpected but typical turn. At nine that morning, a Mr. Arnold Brecht regained consciousness at Cedars-Sinai Medical Center. He'd been beaten the prior evening during a burglary that followed a reception at his home. Now, he was babbling nonsensical word combinations.

Brecht, who had amassed a fortune in oil exploration, was a famous collector and connoisseur of art and antiquities. As he was advancing in age, he had recently announced that he would donate his considerable stash to several local museums to fill significant gaps in their various collections. He then went on to host the soiree at his home, which was attended by a who's who of guests. Invitees included important museum representatives from the Getty, the Hammer, Norton Simon, the Huntington, and MOCA—the Museum of Contemporary Art. All stood to benefit from Brecht's largesse. There was also a smattering of literati from local university art and English departments. Dress was formal, and the catering top-notch. Even the string quartet was composed of notable performers recognized by all and lauded for donating their time for such a charitable event.

Given the festive mood of the evening, it was especially shocking the following morning when the housekeeper found Brecht unconscious. Itemization of the stolen goods revealed a seeming hodgepodge: a few small but valuable etchings, a Hokusai sketchbook, some Roman coins and other ancient baubles, a few well-known and valuable first editions, including one each by Twain, Darwin, Dickens, and Cervantes, and one seemingly obscure volume from the end of the seventeenth century by d'Armancourt, a name not on the tip of anyone's tongue. To further confuse, a signed copy of Ginsberg's *HOWL and Other Poems* had also been purloined. A strange collection—but one that could easily be carried away.

We were staying at Shutters on the Beach, which on a detective's salary was quite a splurge, and I had caught only a quick glimpse of the ocean when a call came from the Beverly Hills Police Department. When I explained what they wanted, my wife's response was daggers (why always daggers?) and a muttering that sounded something like, "Don't you dare." I was surprised they knew I existed. But, what the heck, curiosity brought me to their building on Rexford Drive, where I discovered that my bureau chief at NYPD had learned of the assault. Knowing I was always rambling on about art, food, and trivia in such a cryptic way that no one could understand, he couldn't resist inflicting me on his old friend and colleague Barbara Steele, who just happened to be the Beverly Hills police chief. It was as an act of collegiality that the BHPD chief had called and invited me to "drop in" and give an opinion. I reviewed the inventory of missing objects and then asked to visit Brecht at Cedars-Sinai.

When I arrived, I was surprised to see how many rooms had been vacated on the floor to accommodate him and how tight security was. I was told that staff had been singled out and reminded and warned not to share any information about the patient's status. Apparently, this repetition of obvious policy was intended to avoid the embarrassment and legal action that followed leaked details related to the birth of Kim Kardashian and Kanye West's daughter at this facility some years earlier. Once cleared, I entered the room and saw Brecht.

His forehead was bandaged, and his gray hair was disheveled. He appeared at least fifteen years older than his reported sixty-five, with deep bags under his eyes. Brecht didn't seem to understand why everyone was there and appeared slightly disoriented but oddly affable. I listened as he repeated the same baffling collection of words: "ostriches and crooked poles," "thirty days hath September," "screwed," and what sounded like "darning box." Nonsensical babbling or a fascinoma riddle? I thought the latter. The visit clearly wasn't going to be any more productive at this juncture, so I headed back to headquarters. There, I asked to see the list of attendees at the big event. All the guests seemed on the up and up, and since the event had been well publicized, the perpetrator could be anyone from anywhere, but definitely someone with an odd sense of value and esoteric tastes.

Later that night, Maria, Gracie, and I watched the evening news. They had spent a wonderful day at Disneyland and were now hearing about some random shootings of a high school athlete in Los Angeles and of some workers in rural North Carolina and then a report of another "disappeared" child in Utah. The news, incessantly repetitious, was the same everywhere. The juxtaposition of Disney with all that mayhem wasn't lost on Gracie, who suddenly proclaimed that she now understood the opening line from *A Tale of Two Cities*, "It was the best of times, it was the worst of times..."

Yikes! Out of the mouth of babes.

The next morning, thanks to Gracie's comment and a lot of thinking about what Brecht had been saying at the hospital, I was back in Beverly Hills taking a second look at the guest list. Previously, I'd noticed and now confirmed that one Charles S. Carton, a literature professor at USC, was on the list and had attended. A quick Google search revealed the S. was for Sidney, and I felt certain of what I had realized.

The police chief looked doubtful, her rich brown eyes narrowed, when I told her Carton was the culprit and that I was certain thanks to Brecht's babbling. What he'd been saying, I told her, was actually a recitation of mnemonic devices, rhymes, and word associations.

"'Ostriches' was a reference to a mnemonic for the periods of the Paleozoic. 'Can Ostriches Slide Down Crooked Poles,' matches up with Cambrian, Ordovician, Silurian, Devonian, Carboniferous, Permian," I said. "And those periods were named by Adam Sedgwick, who trained and later reviled Darwin, who wrote *On the Origin of Species*. Moving on to 'thirty days,' it was part of the well-known rhyme for the number of days in the months, which was popularized in 1697 by Charles Perrault, using the pen name d'Armancourt, in his *Histoires ou contes du temps passé: Contes de ma mère l'Oye*, better known as the *Mother Goose Tales*. You're probably familiar with 'Le Petit Chaperon Rouge,' uh, 'Little Red Riding Hood,' 'Puss and Boots,' 'Cinderella'..." I was on a roll. "Ah, but I digress. What we heard as 'darning box' stumped me for a while but was really a reference to two characters from Dickens's *A Tale of Two Cities*. 'Darning' equals the character Darnay, also known as *Charles* Evrémonde, and 'box' is another word for carton, the last name of the book's main character, Sidney Carton."

Chief Steele was staring at me wide-eyed, so I hurried on.

"Brecht was referring to some of the missing volumes with his first two clues and to the thief with the last one. I thought his mutterings might provide a solution to the theft, and when my daughter mentioned *A Tale of Two Cities*, I recalled that one of the guests at the event was Charles S. Carton. Since Brecht's stolen Dickens novel was not *A Tale of Two Cities*, yet he clearly was pointing us to one of it characters, I figured his reference to Charles Carton must refer to a real person, as the guest list bore out."

"But, but those clues don't really have anything to do with each other. And Dickens was the main clue? Mnemonics? Are you nuts?" the chief bellowed and then added, "So, what about 'screwed'?"

"Gracious madam, I that do bring the news made not the match," I responded, and then, to properly misquote, I added, "So, go shoot the messenger."

The chief gave me that same exasperated look that I always get in New York, so I threw in, "And 'screwed' was Brecht's reference to his own situation and, of course, to Ginsberg."

It took some explaining—and emphasizing that the victim was Arnold Brecht—to get a judge to act quickly. Armed with a search warrant, BHPD entered Carton's home and found the stolen items. An arrest quickly followed. Apparently, the theft was motivated by vanity when Carton saw the Dickens tome on the shelf. Because of his name, Carton had always identified with Dickens. Later, I told Maria what had transpired. She gave me another familiar look and said, "You really need help."

The following day, I took the family to Venice Beach, where we saw fortune tellers, body builders, a turbaned guy on roller skates playing the guitar, a man swallowing an inflated balloon, a bare-chested, loin-clothed man juggling three balls while a three-foot boa constrictor adorned his neck; and all kinds of people wearing, and not wearing, all kinds of clothing.

After about an hour, our blasé thirteen-year-old said, "I think that's enough. Can we go home now?"

A week later, a package arrived at our home from Beverly Hills, containing a copy of *A Tale of Two Cities*—a first edition—and with it a short note that read, "Come see me next time you're in Los Angeles. Thanks, Brecht." I gave the book to my daughter since she'd provided the clue.

* * *

Part Two: The Giraffe's Long Neck

"Steam bath," was all my partner mumbled, and that summed up the general feeling in the squad room.

Tempers were short as the "real-feel" temperature approached 105 degrees in Manhattan. Oddly, it was so oppressive that even criminals decided to conserve energy and let the city melt down on its own. The chief called me in and informed me that he had received an odd request. The Beverly Hills police chief had asked if I could take some "vacation" time in his city and that Arnold Brecht would cover both my salary and benefits through a handsome gift to the NYPD. It was a polite request that had already been approved by my city. Highly irregular but intriguing—official but unofficial. I began to worry if I was going to be on personal retainer to the rich and famous. All I could glean from the chief was that it was personal and not just about a blow to the head and some stolen junk.

Later, I discussed it with Maria, who rolled her eyes and muttered "ha" and "more books, I s'pose." But unlike her reaction the last time the BHPD requested my assistance, this time I detected only affection laced with the sarcasm. More surprising, she said she approved of the trip and gave me her blessing. I was sure the look on her face suggested she planned to remodel the kitchen while I was gone. Since our daughter was leaving on Saturday for several weeks at summer camp, I thought it would be less expensive to have my wife come along for the ride, especially since I always benefit from her ability to maintain perspective and stay calm. She jumped so quickly at the opportunity for more California beach time that I knew she had played me by capitalizing on my remodelophobia.

I went to the small bedroom to kiss Gracie goodnight and saw the Dickens volume on her nightstand. It was propped up at an odd angle on a set of house keys with a glass of milk precipitously balanced on it. As I approached this *catastrophe en devenir*, she stretched and knocked the glass over. I lurched forward, and as she began laughing, I realized it was a gimmick glass.

"Now, where'd you get this little trick," I asked.

"Oh, Mom and I picked it up on Forty-Third Street. Neat, huh?" She was in hysterics.

Back in the living room, I said, "That child is going to give me a heart attack. By the way, did you guys buy anything interesting today?"

All I got was a simple "Nope."

A week later we were again at Shutters Hotel in Santa Monica, but this time in a grand suite sans child.

"Now, don't solve whatever it is too fast. I could get used to all this complementary spa stuff." Those were Maria's final words of encouragement for the evening, and from the look on her face, I knew she meant it.

Late the next morning, I was off to see Arnold Brecht to find out what all the mystery was about. When Brecht greeted me at his four-acre wooded estate, I barely recognized him. The only time I had seen him was at the hospital, when he was delirious and looking old and disheveled. Now, he appeared fit in a way that belied his advancing age. We segued to the library, where a variety of crustaceans graced our lunch. The room was truly impressive. Just the shelves on the nineteenth century alone signaled a complete history of science. There were works by Cuvier, Lyell, Spencer, Huxley, Darwin, Lamarck—it seemed endless. I thanked him for the Dickens volume and told him about my daughter's comments. He laughed and pointed to an empty spot on the shelf and said that it reminded him to call me if the need arose.

After all the pleasantries, Arnold—he insisted I call him that—related his sad tale. His daughter, Lisette, was doing research at the Huntington Library, where she met and later became engaged to a highly regarded neurobiologist at Caltech. He apparently went for a run in the San Gabriel Mountains two weeks ago and fell to his death at a precipitous turn of the trail. Two hikers spotted the body in a ravine when their dog wouldn't stop barking. The autopsy revealed nothing unusual. It was determined that the fall resulted in a fatal neck fracture along with a blow to the head and some other broken bones. The accompanying scratches and abrasions were attributed to the foliage encountered in the fall. There was nothing unusual here, so I asked Arnold why he'd gone to all the trouble of arranging for my "vacation."

"I guess I don't like loose ends. This is about my daughter's happiness, so I take it personally. His name was Richard Altman, and he was a fine young man. An experienced runner and mountain biker. There's something about this that just doesn't feel right. Lisette said that he had never been on that trail before and only found out about it from a colleague, someone named Jason Leopold, with whom he'd had words in the past. I don't know, like I said, I don't like loose ends. I'd like you to also take this personally, and, from what I hear, you will."

"I can certainly do that, ask some questions, see if I can get a feel for this," I said.

I went through the list of Richard's possessions from the day he died. His driver's license said he wore corrective lenses, but none were found on his person or in his car. A gold chain with a Saint Christopher medal—said to protect travelers—had also been recovered at the scene, and a photo of it next to the body detailed its disposition. While it could have been torn off in the fall, I felt that it warranted a question. I called Lisette, who said she was so distraught that she hadn't noticed it in the photo. She also said it was strange, as Richard was Jewish. This was, indeed, an odd find, given his religion.

That there was no comment on this omission in the Park Service report may have been due, in part, to the complexity of who was in charge of the investigation. National Park Service, FBI, local police, or the county sheriff? Interestingly, none of the departments with possible jurisdiction was the Beverly Hills PD, but given Arnold lived in Beverly Hills, I understood Chief Steele involving herself in this case. Anyway, back to who *was* in charge. If it looks like an obvious accident, the Park Service doesn't call in their Investigative Services Branch. Apparently, rangers had seen nothing suspicious, so the ISB had not been called in. The county medical examiner's office concurred, finding the death to have been accidental. Since I also don't like loose ends, I went to the accident site with some volunteers early the next morning to get familiar with the area and look for the glasses. No luck, but then the area was pretty rugged.

That afternoon, I stopped in at Richard's Caltech lab. I was hoping to get a sense of him, even though I wasn't sure how that might help. I also wanted to meet that colleague who suggested the trail. I was especially interested in the "words" they'd had and why Richard would suddenly use a trail suggested by someone with whom he'd had a misunderstanding. Everyone I encountered praised Richard's character and humor and commented on the quality of his work, which they described as "brilliant" or other superlatives. At Arnold's request, the lab had been left untouched since the accident—it helped that he was well-known in the college-endowment arena. After looking through

Richard's personal effects, I went to Jason Leopold's lab.

The office was fairly typical for a university professor but with little personal decoration. Hanging on the wall were his BS and PhD diplomas. My eyebrows went up. During my own university years, I'd never seen diplomas in a professor's office, and this struck me as a plea for respect. There was one photo of Leopold in cap and gown at a Caltech graduation, his thin face lacking emotion. There was also a chart depicting the evolution of Homo sapiens dating back two million years to Homo habilis. The only other wall hanging was a picture of Leopold in running gear and sporting a necklace with a Saint Christopher medal that appeared identical to that found at the crime scene. I suddenly had to work at appearing blasé.

Leopold greeted me in a way that seemed too solicitous, and there was something in his praise for his colleague that smacked of insincerity. I wanted to be certain that I wasn't being influenced by Lisette's remarks, so it was time to employ my irritating fishing technique.

"Did you and Richard work together on any projects?" A nice, innocuous opening.

"No. Richard was into some new stuff on epigenetics. Not really my cup of tea. I guess I'm more into straight-ahead evolution," he said, keeping it short and simple.

"You mean this epigenetics stuff contradicts evolution? What kind of research was he doing?" Just baiting the hook for any loose fish.

"Well, no. It doesn't exactly contradict evolution. He was doing some work with methyl groups attaching to DNA. The idea of passing on acquired characteristics is simply something that makes me uncomfortable," he said.

There was something about his being uncomfortable that made me uncomfortable. Maybe there were some fish to fish after all, so I threw him a fallacious red herring. "Sort of like Lamarck's theory that giraffes developed and passed on longer necks because they kept reaching for leaves in higher branches?"

"Absolutely not. There are no meiotic or mitotic heritable changes not related to regular genetic inheritance." He was still relying on his scientific hoity-toityness but was employing a time-worn sentiment.

"But giraffes do have long necks," I said, and just to rub it in, I added, "Is that what you argued about? This epigenetics versus what you call straight-ahead evolution?"

"No, we didn't really argue. We sometimes discussed our differences. And by the way, Lamarck was a fool. And who told you we were arguing anyway?" Again, that uncomfortable comportment.

"Just curious. Did Dr. Altman get a lot of funding for this research?"

"He was getting too much if you ask me. He was everybody's darling and for that nonsense. My own work was losing funding. My grants are drying up. My own reputation. My own work. My own repu…" He trailed off.

Leopold was clearly invested in this, and his complexion and nostrils revealed agitation and anger. The worm had found its mark.

"Well, Lamarck was no fool, and he's often misrepresented. You're only focusing on his second law regarding evolution. Lamarck was a lot more than that. Even Steven Jay Gould was a fan." Reeling him in.

"Hey, you seem to know a lot more than giraffe anatomy. What's going on here?" He looked a little shocked.

"Nothing, really. Simply my own liberal education getting in the way. One of my own foibles, I guess," was my quiet response.

"Well, a little historical knowledge doesn't trump solid science," and he was back on his high horse.

"And this epigenetics stuff is very different from multidonor mitochondrial DNA therapy, which is also heritable, isn't it? He wasn't doing that, was he? So, he wasn't dealing with that whole ethical slippery-slope business of genetic engineering for eugenic or cosmetic purposes, was he?" The coup de grâce?

"Huh? Well, maybe they're different. But to me, it's all fooling around with nature. I guess the mitochondrial stuff is more, I don't know. I don't like any of it. It's all unnatural and should be stopped, and people studying it should be stopped. I mean this is… How do you…? Why are you…?" And then he fell silent.

I changed the subject and pointed at the picture of him in running gear. "Interesting medal. Looks quite old and unique."

"Family heirloom," he replied.

An oddly curt response for a cherished item.

"A curious thing," I said. "When they found the body, Richard's eyeglasses weren't on him. I've arranged for a search party, including Boy Scouts, to go back with me to the accident site to give it a more thorough combing. Maybe we'll find some other evidence of how this could happen to such an experienced runner. We'll be going up the trail day after tomorrow. Well, thanks for all the info." And the trap was set.

On my way out of the building, I stopped at Richard's lab and left my prescription sunglasses on his desk.

That evening, I was back at the "accident" scene and left a replica of the necklace, with a slight scratch on it as an identifying mark, where it could be easily recovered.

Two days later, we searched the now correctly labeled "crime scene," and one of the boys recovered my sunglasses. The necklace and Saint Christopher medal were gone. By this time, the police chiefs from Beverly Hills and Pasadena—where Caltech is located—had contacted ISB. All were on board for the showdown. I went back to Jason Leopold's lab accompanied by Arnold, who wanted in on this one, a Pasadena detective, an ISB agent, and a sheriff's deputy. Imagine the hubris—Leopold was wearing the medal and looking smug.

"Did you find what you were looking for?" Leopold asked.

"Yup. Lucky too. That was my favorite pair of sunglasses. Funny how you can know so much about genetics but didn't think to wipe your thumbprint off one of my lenses. We checked the videos for the day of the death from several stores that are on the way to the trail and identified your car going and returning at all the right times. We also had an ISB agent—that's the investigation division of the National Park Service—ready to pass you on the trail yesterday, and it's interesting that you knew the exact location on that trail to deposit the glasses and retrieve the necklace. The spot wasn't marked. Doesn't look good, Jason."

There was a long pause, and I saw resignation settle on his face. Then, "Yeah, I did it." Anger laced his voice. "My whole life has been devoted to slow evolution, and this jerk was threatening it all. He was popular. He was getting funding. He was getting recognition. He was getting grad students. He was getting everything. After all my years of work, he was getting all the attention!" He took some deep breaths, getting himself back under control. "When you pulled that mitochondrial DNA stunt you threw me off, and I guess I panicked and thought you just might be clever enough to find something incriminating at the scene, especially after your comments about the necklace. It was torn off during the altercation, and I didn't have the forethought to search for it at that time."

"And my glasses?"

"*Your* glasses." He sneered. "I left the glasses to throw you off since they belonged to Altman and didn't incriminate me."

"Yeah, well. As my father would say regarding your failed eyeglass/necklace deception, '*No me da gato por liebre.*' Don't give me cat for rabbit. And you have a PhD in what?"

"You know, you think you're pretty smart. You think you know a lot about history and science, but even that knowledge is skewed, and you don't know beans about epigenetics."

"Skewed? Skewed?" I had to calm myself. "Given the circumstances, that's a pretty lame insult. Maybe I'm just smart enough to not be threatened by new ideas or good science. I also knew enough how to piss you off and get you, you son of a bitch. And you fell for the oldest plant-some-evidence trick in the book. You are a pusillanimous prick and a pockmark on the face of science, and I do mean that in its true etymological sense."

His face reddened. And since he'd impugned my scientific knowledge, I decided to "academic" him.

"Hoisted on your own petard." I misquoted Hamlet. "I hope you get the irony of your Saint Christopher medal in all this."

I couldn't believe how quickly he'd folded. Says a lot for the power of the ego.

That afternoon, Maria and I had lunch with Arnold. He turned to my wife and said, "You know, I like your husband's style, but half the time, I don't know what the hell he's talking about."

"Don't worry about it, Arnold. When I first started dating him, I would check his references but quickly learned that it wasn't worth it. I'm afraid our daughter is becoming equally annoying."

"Well, I can't tell you how much Lisette and I appreciate what your family has done for us getting closure. So, I'd like to do a little something for you."

"No more books," my wife joked.

"Okay, okay. You folks can come use my library whenever you want. But what I'd really like to do is make some of my other homes available to you whenever you want to vacation, if my family isn't using them. I have places on Martha's Vineyard and in London and Paris. I even have a little pied-à-terre in Roussillon, where I like to go and read, and my wife goes to paint, though we don't get there much anymore. I figured you'll be reluctant to ask me personally, so I instructed my secretary to take your calls regarding this and grant whatever."

"Roussillon?" I said, excited. "That's in the Vaucluse. I remember reading *Village en Vaucluse* in college. When I later glanced at the introduction to the second edition, I noticed that Wylie reveals the real name of Peyrene and that Samuel Beckett lived there for a time. It's what got me to read *Waiting for Godot*. I barely got through that damn book. I'm lucky that Proust didn't live there. Tried to read him anyway, yeesh."

"Oh God. There he goes again," they said in unison.

"What. Why didn't you just tell me to stop?"

They then had a good laugh at my expense.

Later that night, in bed, I said, "Funny about that fake glass of milk."

"You deserved it."

There was a wicked smile on her face. She and Gracie had fooled me nearly two weeks ago, but she knew exactly what I was talking about. Yet another reason I love her.

Then she said, "Holy revelation. That Peyrene-Roussillon thing, that's why you always check things like book editions, you sneaky little crime solver."

Caught by the wife.

Several weeks later, we received a package with a familiar return address. The note accompanying the first editions of Lamarck's *Histoire naturelle des animaux sans vertèbres* and Beckett's *Godot* simply read, "I couldn't help it."

Maria raised an eyebrow. "Well, let's get even and spend the weekend on the Vineyard."

What a strong sense of justice. Maybe the wife should always get the last word.

UNBEATABLE

By Melinda Loomis

D aisy Campbell, professional pet psychic, stared intently at the massive chestnut colt warily eyeing her from the inside of his stall. The gold nameplate on the door of the stall identified him as Frontier Justice, not that he needed any introduction. He was the biggest thing in horse racing since Secretariat.

But before she could form a question for him, a voice blared in her head. *"I like carrots!"*

Daisy groaned. As impressive as he was, the big colt sounded like an idiot, not the champion whose upcoming race promised to be the triumphant conclusion to a remarkable career. He'd never lost a race, ever, and if he could take the Santa Anita Handicap, he would not only retire unbeaten, but would also become the all-time top money-winning American racehorse.

"Okay," she thought to him, "You like carrots."

"And I like to run! I run fast!"

She sighed. "Yes," she said out loud, "yes you do."

"WHAT?" Millie shrieked. "What did he say?"

Daisy glanced unhappily over at the colt's owners—the Holmby Hills socialite who was strung higher than any of the racehorses housed at Santa Anita and her dull but ridiculously wealthy husband, Ed.

Whatever his mental challenges, Frontier Justice could, in fact, run *very* fast. It was what he was bred, built, and trained to do. Daisy wondered if he knew his upcoming race would be his last, before he was retired to stud, when it was hoped he would spend years to come spawning little Frontier Justices who also ran fast as lightning.

There had been no reason to think his winning streak wouldn't remain intact. He was in peak condition, and victory seemed preordained until a couple days earlier when his jockey, Rob Cushing, had fallen off him during a workout and tragically ended up crushed beneath the big colt's hooves.

The average thoroughbred weighs about eleven hundred pounds—a little over half a ton—and Justice was big for his breed. It was a lot of weight on the jockey's small body, and it was over instantly. Daisy had heard that some idiot dubbed it "death by hoofbeats" on Santa Anita's Facebook page, and there was the usual internet outrage over the tastelessness of the comment until the track's social media team deleted it and blocked the offender.

Millie, seeing her dream threatened, had decided an animal psychic was just what was needed to make sure Justice wasn't traumatized and would stay focused on the race that would cement his legendary status. Daisy had noticed Millie seemed more concerned about her horse and his place in racing history than his jockey's tragic fate.

"Well, what did he say?"

"Millie, please, hang on a sec," Daisy pleaded.

Along with Millie and Ed, the colt's trainer, T.J. Fitzgerald, and groom, Lou Hawkins, were hovering, along with an unhappy representative of the racing board. Daisy couldn't tell if he was more concerned about Rob's death, the bad publicity it had generated, or the presence of a pet psychic. Whatever the case, a crowd was not welcome in Daisy's line of work. Each person present was that much more of distraction for the animal. Plus, T.J. and Lou had made it crystal clear they greatly disapproved of Millie hiring a pet psychic, causing some friction with Millie and, by extension, Daisy.

"Where's Rob? I like Rob! I don't like Millie! I want to kick her yappy little dog into the next barn!"

Daisy smiled. Justice was referring to Zip, the vocal purse-sized dog Millie was always clutching to her bosom. But as annoying as he was, the yappy little dog had sold Millie on Daisy's abilities.

She had been recommended to Millie by a friend who'd been impressed by Daisy's read of her late cat. Zeus, the beloved orange tabby, had died unexpectedly, and Casey, his distraught owner, had needed reassurances that he'd had a good life and was happy in the afterlife. After looking over some photos of Zeus, at first Daisy could only give the expected platitudes—the cat had enjoyed his life, had died a peaceful death, and was at peace in kitty heaven. But what proved Daisy's ability as far as Casey and Millie were concerned was when she commented, "Zeus misses riding in the convertible."

"I don't have a convertible, and even if I did, I didn't take the cat out for car rides," said Casey, adding, "Except when we had to go to the vet, and he hated that."

Daisy was insistent. "I see him sitting in the front seat of a convertible, and he's having a blast. It's one of his favorite places to be. Sorry, *was* one of—"

She was cut off when Casey began sobbing. "My neighbor's car," she gasped. "He parks it out on the street sometimes with the top down, and I had to get Zeus out of it a few times." And with that, Daisy had established her credentials.

That didn't stop Millie from "making sure" by having her read Zip first. Daisy had learned that not only did Zip loathe Millie, but he wasn't particularly pleasant himself. In fact, he was so rude during their reading that instead of relaying his complaints, Daisy told Millie that the dog adored her and everything about his life. "He feels like he won the owner lottery. Don't change a thing," she cheerfully advised while Zip yapped up an angry storm. Millie was thrilled. Daisy had passed the test and was on her way to Santa Anita.

Daisy returned her focus to Justice. "I'm sorry," she thought to him, "but Rob isn't coming back."

The colt didn't respond but swung his head to the left and pinned his ears back, which Daisy knew was a bad sign in horses, an angry threat. She looked over to see what had prompted his displeasure and saw a diminutive man sporting a wide smile approaching them.

"Oh, Woody," Millie said. "This is Daisy. She's our pet psychic."

Daisy knew that Wendell Woodman had been Justice's original jockey early in the colt's career before Rob Cushing took over. While remaining unbeaten, Justice suffered a couple of uncharacteristic close calls, barely clearing the finish line in front of his opponents as opposed to his usual multi-length blowouts. Woody lost the mount to Rob, at which point Justice rediscovered his crushing speed and resumed his dominant winning ways. An untimely injury had cost the colt his one shot at the Kentucky Derby and, thus, the Triple Crown. But after he recovered, he had continued to run like a machine, and Rob and Justice became a legendary pairing among racing fans, on par with Ron Turcotte and Secretariat.

Woody greeted Daisy with a look she knew well. It said, "Psychic...yeah, right." An actual eye-roll wasn't necessary. She could feel it.

"Millie wants to make sure Justice isn't distracted by Rob's accident and is focused on the race," she explained to Woody.

When she turned her attention back to the colt, she saw that he had disappeared into his stall. This wasn't going well at all. Between the number of people present, the horse's apparent lack of intelligence and understanding, plus the repeated interruptions, Daisy didn't know if she would be able to accomplish much, if anything, with him.

"Poor Rob," the unimpressed Woody said, and Daisy couldn't help thinking he didn't sound the least bit upset about poor Rob. She wondered if Woody could be the jerk who'd posted the idiotic "death by hoofbeats" comment. He seemed like the type.

In his stall, Justice snorted. "Woody?" Daisy quickly thought to the horse. There was a brief something, but before she could get a grasp on it, it was squashed, followed by a dejected *"No...Rob. I want Rob."*

"What do you have against Woody?" she thought emphatically. Again, the same dejected tone. *"I want Rob."*

"What's going on?" Millie demanded.

"He wants Rob," she told Millie. "I'm not sure he understands why Rob's not here."

Millie looked troubled by this information. "It's not going to affect the way he runs tomorrow, is it?" she asked. Daisy marveled at her callousness.

"Does he have anything to say about me?" Woody smirked.

Daisy smirked back at him. "Nothing. He just keeps asking for Rob. Sounds like Rob's the man." She relished both Woody's displeased sneer and Millie's concerned frown.

* * *

To Daisy's surprise, Millie and Ed invited her for dinner. But her puzzlement faded away as Millie spent the entire meal picking Daisy's brain about Justice's frame of mind.

"He wants Rob," Daisy reiterated.

"Well, he can't have him. And God knows I'd give that horse anything he wants or needs, but he's going to have to run for Woody," Millie said. "What does it matter, anyway? He's can't be beat. He would win with *me* in the saddle."

But maybe not with Woody. "Why was Woody given the mount when Justice didn't run well for him in the past?"

Ed jumped into the conversation. "There were only a few days until the race when Rob...got hurt. Woody's at least familiar with Justice. We thought it was better than someone who didn't know him at all."

Daisy thought a brand-new rider might have been a better idea, given Justice's antipathy toward Woody. But if Millie took her up on the suggestion and he lost the race, they would blame her and possibly smear her reputation. She decided to stick to her own area of expertise.

"Is it too late for me to go back and try again to get him to understand the importance of running fast for Woody tomorrow?... This time without a crowd?" Daisy asked.

Millie brightened at the idea. "I don't see why not. I'll call T.J. and Lou."

* * *

When Daisy arrived at the barn, Lou excused himself by telling her he was going to go grab a bite. Millie had gotten the message through to let Daisy have time alone with the horse.

Justice poked his head out of his stall door.

"Carrots!"

Crap, Daisy thought, I should have brought carrots. The colt was an elite athlete and probably on a strict diet, but a furtive snack might have made him more talkative. She wondered if there might be something in the vicinity, but Lou had left, and it might look odd if she was seen rummaging around. "Sorry, buddy," she thought to the colt, "I forgot."

Justice gave her a forlorn look.

"Let's talk about Rob and Woody," she thought.

"Are you coming to my race? I run fast! I always win! I never lose!"

Daisy had read horses before. Most of them were aging and beginning to experience physical issues, and their owners wanted to know what could be done to ease them comfortably into old age. She had found most of these horses to be intelligent and soft-spoken. One of the owners had described them as "live-and-learn" animals that got wiser with age, and Daisy's experiences with them had borne this out.

Justice was by far the youngest horse she'd ever read. A powerful, excitable four-year-old whose life revolved around running in circles as fast as possible. An equine jock of whom depth and intellect wasn't required. His job was to run fast, and that was pretty much it. Daisy wasn't sure how much she could reasonably expect from him.

"You have a huge race tomorrow, and you've never been beaten. Does it really matter if it's Ron or Woody riding you?" Daisy asked.

Justice snorted, then turned around into his darkened stall. All she could see now were his heavily muscled hindquarters, and she had the distinct feeling of being rudely dismissed. The conversation was over before it had begun. What she wasn't clear on was if he was displeased because she'd brought up Woody's name or because she had neglected to bring him carrots.

* * *

The next day was race day. A Westside girl for life, Daisy took the 405 to the 134 to the 210 for the second day in a row. She got off at Baldwin and headed south to the track, where she was greeted by an extremely anxious Millie. The woman was such a wreck, Daisy wondered if she would make it through the day. It would be a huge relief when the race was over, and Millie could stop worrying about Frontier Justice securing his lofty place in the racing world.

The Santa Anita Handicap would take place on a typically warm, beautiful spring afternoon in Arcadia. Crystal-clear blue skies, with the San Gabriel Mountains serving as a stunning backdrop to the historic racetrack, set the scene for what everyone expected to be a dominating wrap-up to Justice's brilliant career. Daisy marveled at the postcard-quality setting, at how close the mountains were, and thought she might venture east of the 405 more often.

Millie had asked Daisy to join them in the paddock in case Justice gave off any signs of distress. But when he strolled in, led by T.J., she got a completely different vibe from him than before. Gone was the dopey man-child who wanted carrots, bragged about his speed, and mooned over his lost jockey. He was sharp and focused. The rippling muscles under his chestnut coat made him an imposing figure even among the elite field, and his demeanor was cool as a cucumber.

Daisy turned to Millie, who was almost crushing Zip in a fit of nerves. "I'm not getting anything in particular," she explained, "but his mind is good. *Really* good. He's calm and focused and ready to go." Millie's eyes filled with tears of gratitude at the good news.

Woody strode confidently into the paddock, waving to the jostling crowd, smugly relishing his return to Frontier Justice's glorified orbit. Daisy thought it was a bit unseemly, considering how he'd obtained the ride. Then, she was overwhelmed by a malignant loathing. It came from Justice. Grinning like an idiot, Woody patted him roughly on the rump, and the colt pinned his ears.

A few seconds later, when T.J. boosted Woody up into the saddle, Daisy half expected the horse to buck him off, but Justice swiveled his ears forward and relaxed. He was confident, fearless, and Daisy couldn't help but be amazed that this regal creature was the same goofball with a carrot jones that she'd been unable to engage in a simple conversation. Whatever he might be in the barn, Daisy mused, he was all business when it was time to hit the track.

T.J. gave his horse a gentle pat on the neck, and Woody and the colt ambled away out of the paddock to meet up with their lead pony and a date with destiny.

Daisy followed Millie, Ed, and T.J. to their box. The stands were packed, as was the infield, and the crowd was antsy with anticipation, thrilled at the potential to witness a historic moment in horse-racing history. Frontier Justice was California-bred, and he was going to go out on top in front of an adoring home crowd.

Justice loaded calmly into the starting gate. When the final horse was in, the crowd's roar swelled so loudly that Zip began yapping along with them.

Then a bell rang out, the starting gates clanged open, and the field of horses bolted forward. "They're off," the announcer bellowed, barely heard over the crowd.

Daisy had heard T.J. tell Woody to follow the same strategy used in every one of Justice's previous races: Keep him off the lead so he wouldn't burn out too soon, leaving him with enough energy for his trademark overpowering stretch run. When the horses hit the top of the stretch, the big chestnut colt would be turned loose to leave the rest of the field scrambling in his wake, fighting for second. But until then, Woody had to keep Justice in the middle of the pack, not allowing him to fall so far back that he would be boxed in, unable to thread his way through the other horses when it came time to make his move.

Through binoculars, Daisy could see Justice fighting the tight reins that held him back. He wanted to run.

As the field went into the final turn, Woody loosened the reins, and Justice began to surge past the other horses. One, then another, and another. It was what the crowd had been waiting for, and the roar became a din. Daisy couldn't help getting caught up in the thrill. She screamed along with Millie, Ed, and the crowd, "*GO, JUSTICE, GO! GOOOOO!*"

At the top of the homestretch, Justice took the lead. But he didn't break away from the pack. He remained barely ahead, the other horses on his heels. Daisy felt the crowd's energy shift, the sudden collective feeling of dismay that this race wasn't the sure thing they'd thought. Pulling away, far way, was what Justice was supposed to do next. But it wasn't happening.

Woody's response to this unexpected development was to whack the colt on the hindquarters with his whip to get him moving. Startled, Justice jumped, then, thrown off his stride, stumbled. For a horrific split second, Daisy thought he was going down, but he regained his stride and powered down the stretch toward the finish line.

But he did it without his jockey. The unexpected stumble dislodged Woody from the saddle as Justice galloped away without him. The horses and riders following closely behind didn't have a chance to react, and Woody vanished beneath the thundering hooves of the tightly packed field. The crowd howled in horror, Millie shrieked, Zip yipped, and Daisy's heart pounded along with the sound of the relentless hoofbeats.

She watched Justice rocket past the finish line lengths in front of the closest horse, but disqualified due to the loss of his rider. Instead of pulling up, he thundered on, hooves beating the earth.

As the colt galloped relentlessly, Daisy sensed an animal happier than any she'd ever encountered, in spite of the loss of his second rider within a week, much less his place in racing history. Loose reins rippling in the wind, Justice ran exultantly, gaining speed as the shocked crowd began to cheer him on again, until a trio of outriders surrounded him and brought him to a halt before he came around to where the fallen Woody was being attended. Seemingly oblivious to the disastrous outcome, Justice pranced happily as the outriders hustled him back to the barn.

Once the horse had been taken off the track, Daisy turned her thoughts to the question of how one horse could accidentally kill two riders within the space of less than a week. She wasn't sure she wanted to know, but she also knew her curiosity would get the better of her.

* * *

It was hours before the crowds and media finally thinned out. Millie, devastated and hysterical, was bundled off to the comfort of her palatial Holmby Hills estate. Daisy wondered if she was more upset about the double lost glory of owning an undefeated champion and an all-time money winner, Woody's unfortunate fate, or the whispers that T.J. told Daisy were already starting up that Justice was cursed. Racing people were a superstitious group, and the idea of a curse might take the shine off of Justice's upcoming stud career. The glorious future Millie had envisioned for her horse had at least partly died on the track with Woody. Even Lou seemed spooked and accepted T.J.'s offer of a couch to sleep on rather than staying in the barn, leaving an uneasy security guard to watch over the horse.

That night, with the barn finally deserted—even the security guard had found an excuse to wander off—Daisy approached Justice's stall. Completely unfazed by the day's tragedy, he was calmly munching a mouthful of hay. After a few seconds, he poked his head out over the stall door.

"I bet you have some questions for me."

Daisy was stunned. Not just at what the horse had thought, but his tone—it had completely changed from the previous times she met with him here. She almost wished he would start babbling about carrots and running fast and how much he loved Rob Cushing. This new voice was odd, not quite sinister, more like completely in control, and very much the opposite of what she'd previously encountered with him.

But he was right. She had questions.

"It wasn't an accident, if that's what you're wondering. And neither was Rob."

At that unexpected news, Daisy backed away from the stall, horrified. He was a killer, she thought. A cold-blooded killer. And here she had thought him so simpleminded, so harmless. How could she have been so incredibly wrong? She had never misread an animal that badly, never before feared an animal she worked with. It was terrifying, and she had no idea how to deal with it.

"No, no, it's not what you're thinking." A calming tone now.

Part of Daisy wanted to bolt, to run away from this horse, this barn, the whole crazy situation. But there was also a part of her that couldn't help be curious, that had to finish the job, see it through. She glanced at the clasp on Justice's stall. It seemed secure, but she kept her distance just in case.

"Relax. You're safe. But I need you to do something."

"What?" she blurted out loud.

"I told you I loved Rob. You've met my owners. Millie is ridiculous, and her husband is the most ineffective man I've ever known. T.J. is okay, and Lou's a good man, but Rob was the best. It was almost like he could read my mind—not like you do, but almost. Woody was the worst. He was a mean, rough rider, so I ran slow on purpose so they'd replace him. And they did. But he didn't take it well."

Daisy wasn't sure how to process all this, although she did notice he had referred to Woody in the past tense. All she could think was, "So what was up with the dumb-animal act?"

"I was afraid you'd figure out my plan and stop me."

"Your plan?"

"I saw Woody lurking around the tack room a few nights ago. The next day, when I was saddled for the workout, I could feel something was wrong. But nobody noticed, and I couldn't tell them. I tried to go slow in the workout because I was afraid the saddle wasn't going to hold. But Rob thought I was being lazy and pushed me, and then the saddle slipped, and he fell under me. I tried not to hurt him, but I ended up trampling him..."

Daisy felt a surge of the horse's grief over Rob's fate.

"And you thought Woody tampered with the saddle?"

"I know he did. Something broke, and Rob fell under me."

"But that's murder! Why would he do that?"

"To get the mount back. He carried a grudge—T.J. and Lou talked about it a lot. And it worked. Look who got the call."

Daisy nodded and thought, "The guy who used to ride you. Better than someone who's not familiar with you at all, with just a few days until the race."

"Then they showed up with you. By then, I'd made my plan, but I was afraid you'd find out, so I tried to block you by yelling dumb things at you."

"It worked," Daisy admitted.

"I couldn't take the chance you'd warn Woody."

201

"If you'd said something the day we met, I could have asked someone to take a closer look at that saddle. Maybe they would've realized it had been tampered with."

"I thought they would check it because of what happened, but they didn't seem interested."

Daisy nodded absently, and then the light bulb went off. The presence of the unhappy rep from the racing board hovering around during her reading suddenly made sense. "They were afraid of bad publicity for the sport," she said. "It's not nearly as popular as it used to be. Heck, they mowed over Hollywood Park a few years ago and built a stadium on it. Santa Anita's the last track left in LA. I guess a murder would be even worse publicity than an accident, and the sport doesn't need any more bad publicity."

Justice tossed his head. *"So it was between Woody and me. But I want you make them look at the saddle. Get them to make the connection."*

But there had been something else at stake. "What about your unbeaten streak?" Daisy asked. "And the money title? You threw that all away."

Justice looked like he might break out in laughter. *"So what? I don't care about trophies or money or records. I'm a horse. I like running and bucking and eating. And I loved Rob. I miss him."*

"You could have just thrown the race..." Then it hit her. "It was your last race. You wouldn't get another shot at him."

The colt's big brown eyes gleamed.

Daisy wasn't sure exactly what to make of the things he'd told her. Her animal reads usually involved much simpler conversations. Things like *More treats! More walkies!* and *I miss riding in the convertible!*

Justice snorted for her attention, his imperious mood restored.

"As far as I'm concerned, I won. I beat Woody."

"Frontier Justice," Daisy said out loud. "Still undefeated, in a way."

"I told you last night. I always win. I never lose."

Daisy marveled at the irony. Woody had caused Rob to be trampled by his own horse. Then that horse sent Woody under the hooves of the rest of the field, where he was crushed by the thundering herd.

The colt seemed disinclined to offer up any additional thoughts but eyed her expectantly. *Very* expectantly. Daisy wondered how he knew. Maybe he'd caught the scent, or maybe he had a gift of his own. He certainly communicated as well as any animal she'd ever read when he wanted to. Either way, it put a huge smile on her face.

She reached into her backpack, pulled out a carrot, and offered it to him. He bit into it and munched happily, never breaking eye contact.

"Justice is served," she told him, wondering if he'd get the double meaning. The big colt winked at her.

BYLINE FOR MURDER

By Nancy Cole Silverman

I knew Barbie Bivens, and I would be competitive the first time we met. It was 1996, and I was a junior reporter at the *LA Times*. I was pulling into the paper's parking lot one morning when I spotted a car backing out of a space. Before I could slip in, Barbie, in her white BMW convertible, raced past me and stole the spot. I remember staring at her personalized license plate—GO USC—as she stepped out of the car.

"Snooze, you lose!" She flashed a venomous smile in my direction.

Bitch!

Barbie and I had started working on the paper at about the same time. I'm a UCLA grad. Those of us from Westwood refer to our crosstown rivals as spoiled children. In return, they call us coddled toddlers. But like our cars, Barbie's gold-pack BMW versus my dilapidated old Toyota, we couldn't be more different. She's a long-legged, redheaded actress wannabe. I'm a short, dark-haired, and slightly overweight news junkie. My beat was general assignment for the Main News section, while Barbie's beat, probably because her daddy was a successful talent agent, was in the Entertainment section—a.k.a. fluff news.

Flash forward two years—to '98—two turbulent years in which a number of senior reporters had been laid off due to decreased readership and shrinking ad revenues. Every day, I worried I would come in and find an empty box on my desk along with a pink slip.

So, when Harry Simms, my balding editor, called Barbie and me into his office, I was anxious. And then totally blown away. He wanted Barbie and me, Madison McKay, to work together.

Mimi Howard, an Oscar-winning superstar, had been arrested the day before for the murder of her television series costar, Steve Sloan. It was the paper's page-one story above the fold. A neighbor had called the police when he noticed that Sloan's front door was wide open and his dog was loose in the yard, barking. The police arrived, found Sloan's body in a puddle of blood on the living room floor, conducted a search, and found a gun registered to Mimi in the bushes. When they interviewed the caller, who lived right down the street, he said he had been walking his own dog when he saw Mimi leaving Sloan's house early that morning. He hadn't mentioned it when he called 911 because Mimi "seemed so nice on TV," and he hadn't wanted to get her into trouble. Between the gun and the dog walker's eyewitness report, that was enough for the police to arrest her.

The police arrived at Mimi's home within an hour of discovering Sloan's body, and she was immediately arrested and taken into custody. Ordinarily, a suspect would have been processed and transferred to the country jail, where they would await court proceedings. However, Mimi's attorney was quick to respond, and because it was still early in the day, he managed to expedite proceedings and, within hours, had arranged for Mimi to come before a judge where formal charges were filed. Mimi's attorney managed to get her out of jail on a $750,000 bail bond, which might have been unusual for anyone else. But this is Hollywood. The rich and famous play differently here, and big bucks roll faster than the heads of major studios. After claiming that Mimi posed no threat to the public and surrendering her passport, she was released without ever seeing the inside of a jail cell, but the case loomed large.

Simms had assigned follow-up stories to Michael James, the senior reporter who wrote the page-one story, except he had called in sick that day with the flu, so Simms needed someone else to follow up.

"Mimi's agent has scheduled a press conference on the plaza outside her offices in Century City in an hour. Madison, I need you there. Barbie, you get in touch with the Sullivan brothers, who produce Mimi's show. Find out what's going on, and feed it back to Madison."

"What?" Barbie stood up, her face red as her hair. "Why is *she* lead?"

Simms barked, "Because this is a news story, Barbie, not entertainment." I smothered a smile. "You work together or not at all. Maddy, I want an update on my desk for tomorrow's paper before five o'clock. You got that?"

"Got it." I could feel Barbie's eyes bore into my back as I walked out of Simms's office. Given a chance, Barbie would rip me to shreds, and she'd be damn slow in sharing anything she found. I wasn't optimistic.

* * *

I got to the press conference in time to see Mimi seated on the dais behind a tree of news mics. Her husband, Greg Howard, and teenage daughter, Erin, sat next to her. Flanking them was a beefy guy who looked like a bodyguard, and her attorney, whose picture had been in the paper that morning. Mimi's agent, Nona Meyer, introduced herself and motioned for Mimi to join her at the podium. Mimi stepped up with Greg and Erin at her side. It is always interesting how a child can resemble both parents. Erin had her mother's strong cheekbones and her father's curly brown hair. Greg rested his hand on his wife's shoulder, his head bowed, while Erin looked nervously out of the crowd. Mimi dabbed a tear from beneath her dark glasses, then cleared her throat.

Cameras clicked.

"I want to thank you all for coming today. This isn't easy. There are no words to say how—"

"Did you kill Steve Sloan?" a reporter shouted. Then, another joined in. "The cops said they found your gun. Did you shoot him?"

Mimi shook her head. "Of course not. I had no reason to shoot Steve. But I am aware that the police found my gun. I don't know how it got there. I lost it weeks ago."

"Why didn't you report it?"

"I…I don't know…I—"

"Is it true you and Sloan argued because you backed out of your contract?"

Nona stepped forward and pushed Mimi aside. "I'm sorry, we're not taking questions. We're here because Mimi insisted we—"

"Honor Steve." Mimi grabbed one of the mics in front of the podium. "But that's not the only reason. I asked you here because I'm being framed. I didn't murder Steve Sloan. And I'll do whatever I can to ensure justice is done."

* * *

I scribbled Mimi's exact words in shorthand in my notebook—a likely headline quote for tomorrow's paper—then grabbed my camera for a quick photo. The newspaper had sent an official photographer to cover the story, but I always like to carry a camera with me, just in case. Typically, I would download the digital files from my camera to my computer when I returned to the office. With any luck at all, I might have captured the money shot for tomorrow's front page.

Directly ahead of me, a group of radio and TV reporters focused on Mimi, while behind me, a group of fans held signs. *We love you, Mimi.*

The story was bigger than I thought. I wasn't just reporting the facts. I was investigating them. This was my big chance. If Mimi was being framed, I needed proof of who might have framed her. Another actor, maybe? Someone she had screwed out of an award or another part? Hollywood is full of vipers. I picked up my cell and tried to call Barbie. But my call went to voicemail. I left a message.

"Mimi claims she's being framed. Call me when you get this."

Rather than head back to the paper. I decided to stop for a quick bite at a convenience store while I reviewed my notes. While at the checkout counter, I noticed a couple of sleazy weekly tabloids with photos of Steve and Mimi on the cover. The stories had nothing to do with the murder, but I thought they might be helpful. I paid for the rags and headed back to the car, where I skimmed the stories, complete with pictures that had been taken while filming *Double Agent*, a hugely successful television franchise with a husband-and-wife team played by Sloan and Mimi as secret agents, who, week after week, risked it all to secure world order and peace. To her fans, Steve was Mimi's on-screen husband and, according to the gossip sheets, despite Steve's playboy lifestyle—of which there were plenty of rumors—a welcomed third wheel in their marriage. Mimi, Greg, and Erin were Steve's off-screen family, best friends, and traveling companions, and they all spent much of their free time together. I was about to toss what I thought was nothing but tabloid trash into the back seat of my car, which was cluttered with empty soda bottles and candy wrappers, when I noticed a picture of Steve's house.

I immediately recognized it. Practically every interview Sloan had done since he catapulted to A-Lister status had been held there. The house had floor-to-ceiling windows and was built around a pool with magnificent views of the city. Perched on the edge of a Hollywood Hills cliff, it was a perfect fit for Sloan's alleged swinging-single life.

I glanced at my watch. It was barely noon. I had plenty of time to drive up to walk the perimeter of the scene of the crime, get a feel for what had happened, and still be back to the paper in time to get a response from the police or the DA's office to Mimi's claim about being framed, then file my story.

* * *

The canyon roads are twisty and narrow, and on a clear day, from some angles, it's possible to see the ocean. The homes, some on stilts, jut out over the cliffs, defying gravity with awesome views. It didn't take me long to find Sloan's house, and as I parked my car down the street, I noticed what looked like a paunchy, aging ex-rock star out walking a frisky yellow Lab. When he bent down to bag the dog's poop, I could see a greasy gray ponytail hanging halfway down his back. *Could he be the same dog walker who had called the police?*

I stopped, identified myself as a reporter, told him I'd like to take a few notes, and asked if he had seen anything unusual the morning of the murder.

"I already spoke to the cops, but since you asked, yeah. There was a white Mercedes convertible parked in the drive next to Sloan's Porsche. It was early, around five a.m. I usually take Baxter out for a walk 'for the sun's up. He was doing his business when I noticed it. Then I saw some woman rush inside. Didn't think much about it at the time. Figured it was one of Sloan's ladies. He's got quite the reputation, you know."

"Did you get a look at the woman?"

"Not really. She had a baseball hat on. Couldn't see much."

I glanced back at the drive. The black Porsche was parked on the far side of the carport, leaving space for a second car to pull between the house and Sloan's car. It would have been easy for whoever the woman was to rush inside.

"Couple hours later, Baxter needed to go out again, and this time, I see Mimi in her blue convertible Bentley pulling out of the drive."

"And Mimi, you're sure it was her?"

"Aside from the car, there was no question. Once you've seen Mimi, you don't forget her. That hair, that curly mane of hers? It's her trademark. Couldn't miss her. Not with the top down on that car."

I knew he was right. Some stars, despite their attempt to walk around wearing oversized sunglasses and baseball hats, never can hide their identity.

"And then, after you saw Mimi drive away, you and Baxter, you returned home?"

"Yep. We did."

"And you didn't see anyone else around the house, not until you saw Mimi leave?"

"Not a soul. But I knew somethin' was wrong. It just didn't feel right. So I called the police, and the next thing I knew, they were on my doorstep asking questions. That's when I told them about Mimi racing out." A squirrel scampered across the street, and Baxter started pulling on the leash. "I'm afraid you'll have to excuse me. Sometimes, this guy's more than I can handle."

"Wait. Can I have your name?"

"Already gave it to the cops. Don't want my name in the paper. Never know these days what people might do."

* * *

I left Sloan's house and was back at the newspaper by one thirty, enough time to ask the police about the white Mercedes and Mimi's and claim that she was framed, write my story, and have it on Simms's desk by five o'clock. I still needed to touch base with Barbie. She had yet to return my call, and I had no idea if she'd been able to talk with Mimi's producers or if they knew Mimi thought she was being framed or who might be framing her.

But, as I pulled into the parking lot, I saw Barbie headed to her car.

"Hey, where you going? We need to talk."

"I'm running late. I'm due in Malibu for a celeb cocktail party at five, and I need to rush home and change. I emailed you my notes and left some stuff on your desk."

"What about the Sullivan brothers? Did you talk to them?"

Barbie shook her head. "They're not talking. But I am friends with some of the crew, and if the stuff they told me is true, there's bad stuff going down. Some guy was selling drugs on the set, and when Mimi found out, she was furious. She went to the Sullivans to complain and got the guy kicked off the lot. And now, everybody's waiting to see who she goes after next. She's not exactly loved."

"Anyone say anything to you about Mimi's relationship with Sloan?"

"Not anything that I'm going to want you to put my name to. Most of it is cheap gossip anyway." Barbie flipped her hair from her shoulder. "Besides, Simms assigned you the lead. You figure it out. I'm not burning my sources. Anyone knows I've talked to you, and they'll never trust me again."

Barbie left me in the parking lot, and I went and checked my email for her notes, which amounted to nothing more than a biographical history of Mimi's movies and awards, followed by a brief paragraph stating Mimi had been married to Greg Howard for eighteen years. They had one child, Erin, age sixteen. On my desk was a stack of old tabloids with a note attached. *Not much here, just a lot of stuff we wouldn't print.*

Frustrated, I sat down and recapped what I'd learned from Mimi's press conference that morning, her tearful tribute to Sloan, her surprising outburst that she believed she was being framed and had lost her gun, and—equally as dramatic—had not reported it. Then I started making calls.

Simms stopped by my desk before I finished my story and told me that Mimi was scheduled to be arraigned first thing in the morning and that James, the *Times* senior investigative reporter, would likely be out sick again.

"Make sure you're at the courthouse plenty early. Story like this, the place will be crowded."

* * *

Officially, Mimi had already been formally charged with first-degree murder in Sloan's death, and today's arraignment, the second in as many days, was for the purpose of allowing Mimi to enter a plea. I settled back into my seat, fully expecting after Mimi's press conference yesterday for her to enter a plea of not guilty.

However, things didn't go as planned.

The bailiff entered the courtroom. "Court is now in session. The Honorable Judge Anna Rosenberg presiding."

I took out my notebook and pen as Judge Rosenberg took the bench.

The judge instructed those of us in front to sit. People in the back of the room—including several reporters I recognized—stood huddled together while she read the charges. Murder in the first degree.

Judge Rosenberg then asked Mimi to stand. "In the matter of the State versus Howard, Ms. Howard, how do you plead?"

"Your Honor, I wish to enter a plea of guilty. I murdered Steve Sloan."

What? There were gasps throughout the courtroom. I looked at Mimi's husband, Greg, sitting directly behind her, with their daughter next to him.

"Mom. No!" Erin reached for Mimi.

"Order in the court!" Judge Rosenberg pounded her gavel.

Greg put his arm around his daughter and whispered in her ear.

The judge waited for the room to settle. "Ms. Howard, you do know that by pleading guilty, you lose the right to a trial."

"I do."

"And you understand what giving up that right means?"

"Yes."

"Has anyone forced you into making this plea?"

"No, your honor."

Mimi looked over her shoulder at her husband and daughter, then nodded toward the door. Her intent was unmistakable. *Get her out of here.*

Mimi's attorney whispered in her ear, then shot Greg a warning glance. *Leave.*

I rested my notebook against my chest and watched Greg hustle Erin from the courtroom. I didn't stick around to hear if Judge Rosenberg set a date for a sentencing hearing. I would get that information later. For now, as far as I was concerned, the story I wanted had just walked out the door, and I wasn't about to let it get away.

* * *

Erin stood outside the courtroom, looking like she wanted to run back inside and scream at the judge. But her father put his hands on her shoulders. She needed to keep it together. Then, rolling her eyes, she stomped off.

Her father yelled, "Where are you going?"

"What do you care!"

"Erin. Please."

"I'm going to take a piss, okay?"

I followed Erin to the bathroom and waited at the sink until she came out of the stall and washed her hands.

"You okay?" I handed her a paper towel.

"Who are you?"

"I'm a reporter. And I know a fix when I see one. I don't believe your mother killed Steve Sloan."

"Why do you care? Steve deserved to die."

Huh? "I thought Steve was like a member of the family."

"If you want to believe all that tabloid crap, yeah. Too much of a member."

I wasn't sure if she was in shock or if I was looking into the face of a victim of child abuse. Or maybe she was high. She was undoubtedly angry. I reached into my backpack for a tissue. "Did he…did he hurt you?"

"No. It's not like that. Steve broke up my family, and I hated him for it."

Erin's eyes began to tear up. I handed her the tissue. "You okay?"

"I'll be fine." Erin wiped her eyes. I waited to ask my next question.

"Do you know what happened? Did your father shoot Steve?"

"Are you joking? My father wouldn't shoot Steve."

"You're sure?"

"Reporters! You're all alike." Erin shook her head. "My dad wasn't even in town. He went to scout locations for a new movie for my mom. I was going to go with him until—"

Erin stopped abruptly.

"Until what, Erin?"

"Until nothing. I shouldn't be talking to you."

"I get that. But with your mom pleading guilty, everyone is going to think she killed him. If she didn't…"

After standing silently for at least thirty seconds, Erin said, "Dad told me he was leaving my mom for Steve."

I leaned back against the counter. This wasn't the news I expected.

"Go on."

"I left my dad at the airport. I was furious. I took a cab home and spent the night in the guesthouse."

"And your mom, she didn't know you were there?"

"She had no idea. I wanted to be alone."

There was a heavy pounding on the door, followed by a man's voice. "Erin, hurry it up in there. We need to leave. Now."

"That's my dad. I've got to go."

"Wait." I grabbed her arm. "Your mom's gun. She said she lost it. Do you know where?"

"Last I saw it, it was in her purse when she went for a fitting at the studio. She's always got a lot of bags with her and never pays much attention. Anyone there could have taken it. I've gone through her bag a hundred times when I needed money. But the police found it in the bushes at Steve's. And it's got my prints on it."

"That's why your mom pleaded guilty. Because she thinks you murdered Steve?"

Erin wrenched her arm free. "Wouldn't you?"

* * *

Wishing I had recorded that conversation, I chased after Erin and her father and asked if he wanted to make a comment. He turned, his face bright red.

"Stay away from my daughter! I catch you around her again, and you'll never work for another paper in this town—ever."

I hurried to my car and jotted down as much as I could recall of what Erin had said, then I returned to the paper. I needed to talk to Barbie and found her alone in the break room, making herself a cup of coffee. Upon seeing me, she turned her back.

"Why didn't you tell me about Steve and Greg? You must have known."

"Come on, Madison. You can't be that stupid. All those pictures in the tabloids? Sloan with Mimi. Greg and Mimi. Sloan with Greg? They're all just for show." Barbie took a stir stick from the counter and sat at one of the small tables. "The studio's been covering it up for years. I'd be screwed if I said anything. You know how things work in Hollywood. Some publicists are paid to promote things. Others to keep things quiet, and any reporter who reports differently is out."

I sat at the table opposite Barbie. "Okay, I get it. Greg's gay. But who gives a damn? This is Hollywood. It's not like he'd be the first gay man to come out of the closet."

"It's not just that."

"Then what is it? Yesterday, Mimi announced she was being framed, and this morning, she pleaded guilty to murdering Steve Sloan. What's going on?"

"She pled guilty? Wow. I guess it doesn't pay to sleep in." Barbie paused, then said, "Okay, so here's the story. Two years ago, the Sullivan brothers started to get concerned that expenses for *Double Agent* were getting out of hand. The sets. The travel. Their costs had skyrocketed, and they ended up bringing in an investor. Suddenly, money was no longer a problem. The brothers were driving exotic cars. Taking expensive vacations. Buying new homes. I was on the set one day when one of the crew pointed the investor out to me. They called him Candy Don. And I can tell you this: he wasn't one bit interested in the show. He was dealing nickel and dime bags to anyone who wanted them. So, I wasn't surprised when I heard that Mimi and Steve had gone to the Sullivan brothers and accused their investor of selling drugs and the brothers of laundering money."

"So, what happened?"

"Mimi got the guy barred from the set, and for a while, things calmed down. But then she found out that this sleazebag had slipped Erin some weed, and Mimi flipped out. That's when rumors started to circulate among the crew that the producers were threatening to expose Greg's affair with Sloan if Mimi didn't shut up."

"And did she?"

"Shut up? Yeah. But when the season wrapped, Mimi refused to sign on for another one. She probably figured the Sullivans wouldn't come after her once the show was over, even though she'd screwed up their money machine. Then she called it quits with Greg and told him she's done covering for him."

"You're getting all this from the crew?"

"Yeah, they blamed Mimi for the show being canceled. They're pissed."

"Then any one of the crew or the cast might have threatened Mimi."

"I don't think so. They're gossipmongers, all of them. But murder? I don't think any of them would go that far. The Sullivans are another story. They knew Mimi was meeting with Steve the day he was shot."

"How do you know that?"

"Her agent, Nona, called me a few days ago and said the Sullivan brothers wanted Mimi and Steve to do an interview, an exclusive for our Entertainment section. A tribute to their long and successful series, and she asked me to do it. It sounded odd, knowing what I did about how the

215

cast and crew felt about the show's sudden end. But this is Hollywood, and everyone wants to put a spin on things, so I said yes. I mean, I wasn't about to turn it down. It was a big opportunity."

"I get that."

"I was on my way to Sloan's house for the interview when I saw all the police activity, and I couldn't get through. There were cops and crime-scene tape everywhere. The road was blocked, and I had to turn around. There was nothing else I could do. I tried to call Steve, but he didn't answer. I had a feeling in the pit of my stomach that something awful had happened, and then I heard later that Sloan was dead."

I rose from the table. "So, the Sullivan brothers knew Mimi would be at Sloan's house that morning."

"Exactly. And so did Nona and probably Erin and her father."

"Yes, but why would Nona frame Mimi? Mimi was her meal ticket. Greg was in love with Sloan, and Mimi was no longer standing in their way. So I don't see either of them shooting him."

I pulled my notebook from my backpack and flipped through my notes. "Erin said she left her father at the airport after he told her he was leaving her mother for Steve. She said she wanted to be alone, so she went home and spent the night in the guesthouse. She swears her mother didn't know she was there." I tapped my pen against the notebook. "Do you happen to know what type of car she drives?"

"A white Mercedes."

"A convertible?"

"Yeah, it looks a lot like mine."

I skimmed back through my notes. "I spoke to a witness outside Steve's house. He described seeing a white car in Steve's driveway around five a.m. and a woman rushing inside."

"That can't be. He's got to be lying. He couldn't have seen anything at that hour. It's pitch black. Just who was this witness anyway?"

I shoved my notebook into my backpack again. "He wouldn't give me his name, but I think I need to find out."

"Where are you going?"

"To Sloan's house."

"I'm coming with you."

"Fine, but I'm driving."

* * *

"Jeez. No wonder your car looks like a piece of crap." Barbie gripped the handrail as we slipped in and out of traffic from downtown to the Hollywood Hills. "What do you think this is, bumper cars?"

I handed Barbie my cell. "Call Simms. Tell him we're going to Sloan's house to question a witness—"

"You think we might need the police?"

"I don't know." I glanced at Barbie. Random thoughts raced through my mind. Barbie's car looked like Erin's. Barbie was supposed to be at Sloan's house the morning of the murder. Maybe despite telling me differently, she had been. Maybe *she* shot Sloan. I know it was stupid, but I couldn't stop myself from thinking it, so I finally asked, "Did you do it? Did you shoot Sloan!"

"Are you crazy?" Barbie reached for the wheel. We struggled, and I pulled to the curb, two doors down from Sloan's house.

"You can't possibly think I'd murder Steve Sloan. Why would I do that?"

"I don't know. I haven't figured that out yet."

"Don't waste your time." Barbie looked out the windshield and suddenly scrunched down in the seat.

"What's wrong?"

"Up ahead. The black SUV. In the driveway? It's the Sullivan brothers. And that's Candy Don with the briefcase."

"That's Candy Don? The guy who looks like an ex-rocker?"

Barbie nodded. "That's him."

I reached into the back seat for my camera. "This is perfect. He's the witness. The dog walker."

"Maddy, what are you doing?"

"What do you think I'm doing? I'm going to take a picture of the Sullivan

217

brothers with their so-called investor, Candy Don, standing in a driveway two doors down from Sloan's house."

"Are you crazy? They'll see you?"

"They don't know who I am. They'll think I'm some fan, taking pictures of Steve's house. Stay here. Anything goes wrong, call nine one one."

I took my camera from my backpack and walked toward Sloan's house. But I hadn't counted on Baxter. After I got out of the car, Baxter ran from the driveway where the Sullivans and Candy Don were talking—*that must be Candy Don's house*—and started yapping at my heels.

I jerked my leg away and clicked off several shots of Sloan's house, then snuck in a shot of the Sullivan brothers and Candy Don. Moments later, Candy Don, with his briefcase in his hand, came chasing after Baxter.

"Hey! Stop kicking my dog."

I snapped a photo of him. "Tell your dog to stop biting me."

"I know you. You're that reporter. What are you doing here?"

"Taking pictures. What do you care?"

I guess Candy Don didn't like my answer. He stepped forward aggressively, closing the space between us. "Well, it just so happens I do care. I don't want you 'round here. This is private property."

"Not here, it's not. I can stand in the street and take pictures of every house I want."

"You can think that all you want, lady, but I'll show you different."

He lunged for my camera, but I jumped out of his reach. Candy Don went reeling to the asphalt, and his briefcase skidded into the street.

We both looked at the briefcase, then back at each other, and in the instant our eyes met, we knew what the other wanted. Candy Don crawled on all fours toward the case. But I was faster, and in a couple of seconds, I put my foot on top of it.

Meanwhile, the Sullivan brothers leapt into their oversized SUV and started to reverse out of the driveway. But not before Barbie jumped into the driver's seat of my beat-up Toyota and pulled up directly behind them, blocking them in, taking the full force of the monster SUV against the Toyota's passenger side just as two patrol cars pulled up with their lights flashing and sirens blaring. *Wow. In this neighborhood, the cops came fast.*

I picked up the briefcase, unsnapped the lock, and looked inside. Greenbacks. Lots of them.

"Care to explain what this is all about?" I asked Don.

"You really think I'm going to tell you?"

I smiled disingenuously. "I don't imagine you would. But if I were you, I wouldn't let those two friends of yours talk to the cops first. You know how it goes. First to talk usually gets the deal."

"Outta my way." Candy Don pushed me aside and hobbled back toward his house with Baxter at his heels.

Barbie, the Sullivans, and the cops all stepped out of their respective vehicles at the same time. With one hand covering her face—like the Sullivans couldn't figure out with those long legs and all that red hair that she was friggin' Barbie Bivens—she ran to me. "Are you okay?"

"I'm fine. What about you?"

"All good."

"I'm happy to hear that. But did you have to wreck my car?"

"You think another dent on that junker is going to make a difference?"

"Says the woman who drives the fancy BMW." I looked back at the cops, who were heading our way. "You call them?"

"Simms did. After you got out of the car, I called and told him where we were and that things looked like they might get exciting. Simms said he didn't like that and called Hollywood Division, asking them to do a drive-by, just in case."

* * *

It was after deadline by the time Barbie and I had returned to the paper and hammered out a front-page story for the next morning's edition. Simms held the presses for it. *Drug Dealer Charged in Death of Hollywood Star.* It was the first of several stories we ran in the following days, including one with the headline *Judge Vacates Mimi Howard's Guilty Plea, Charges Dropped.*

The best part was that Barbie and I had the exclusive about Mimi's discovery of the Sullivans' money laundering and murder-for-hire plot to eliminate Sloan and hush up Mimi. Not that they had reason to kill Sloan, but since people knew they had a beef with Mimi, having her murdered could've left them exposed. But having Sloan killed and Mimi blamed enabled them to get their revenge against her, at least that's what the prosecutors eventually argued in court.

Barbie and I never printed a word about Greg and Sloan's affair. We figured we'd leave that for the tabloids. Ultimately, the Sullivans and Candy Don were sentenced to spend the rest of their lives behind bars. Baxter went to live a life of luxury with Don's ex-wife, and Sloan's dog moved with Greg into his new house. It was nice to know neither Greg nor the dogs would be alone.

As for Barbie, some things never change. She still steals my parking spot.

About the Authors

Gail Alexander, a graduate of UC Berkeley, saw the world as a flight attendant with Pam Am and later wrote for the screen. She had four books published in 2024: *Flower: The Story of Flower, the Skunk, in Walt Disney's BAMBI Movie*; *There's a Crack in the Constitution*; *Rainbow to Heaven*; and *House of Secrets and Lies*. Gail and her husband, Stan, live in Southern California, where they raised their two boys: Windsor Castle, a white Pom, and Barkley Oxford, "BO," a Bichon. Gail acknowledges Sisters in Crime as the first to refer to her as an author, and she is sincerely grateful.

Paula Bernstein is a physician, a scientist, and the author of the medically themed Hannah Kline Mysteries. Her short stories have been included in the anthologies *LAst Resort*, *Avenging Angelenos*, and *A New York State of Crime*, and published on Short-Story.me and Fiction on the Web. She has been an active member of Sisters in Crime and served as president of the Los Angeles Chapter and chair of the California Crime Writers Conference. Her nonfiction publications include *Carrying a Little Extra, A Guide to Pregnancy for the Plus-Sized Woman* (Penguin), and *Woman to Woman, A Gynecologist's Guide to Your Body* (Bantam). Her website is HannahKlineMysteries.com.

Anne-Marie Campbell is a former French professor who lives in Southern California. She currently writes mysteries that plunge readers into the heart of Paris, where a spirited American French professor solves murders in locations that include skull-packed catacombs, the sultry Moulin Rouge dance hall, and bougie catwalks with killer couture. Her novels are flavored with French wine, cheese, pastries, and *merde alors...* French swear words, too. Anne-Marie is a member of Mystery Writers of America and Sisters in Crime. In August 2023, her short story "Palms Up" was published in the Anthony Award-winning anthology *Killin' Time in San Diego*.

Jenny Carless began her writing career in environmental nonfiction. Now she concentrates on suspense, typically with a focus on wildlife and/or the environment. Jenny's happy place is the African bush, which is the inspiration for most of her fiction. In addition to being a writer and safari addict, Jenny is a curious explorer and amateur wildlife photographer. She is a member of Sisters in Crime and Mystery Writers of America. Her website is jennycarless.com.

Ken Funsten, CFA, is twice-married with two only-children—each unique. His careers have included librarian, teacher, punk-rock journalist, stock analyst, corporate executive, and hedge fund manager. His most important life-changing event was at age ten, smacking his new "birthday" bike into a tree, lying in a coma for a week, then lying bedridden off and on for a decade, during which time, Ken hardly aged physically but lay reading Homer, Heller, Freud, Chandler, Updike, Altsheler, Dumas, Tolkien, Burroughs, Robbins, Miller, Melville, Poe, Cain, and Camus, to name a few. His website is yourfunsten.com.

Daryl Wood Gerber, an Agatha Award-winning author, is best known for her nationally bestselling mysteries, including the Literary Dining Mysteries, Fairy Garden Mysteries, and Cookbook Nook Mysteries. In addition, Daryl writes suspense novels, including *The Son's Secret*. Her short stories have appeared in a number of anthologies: *Mystery Most Theatrical*, *Infinity*, *Fish Tales*, and more. Her website is darylwoodgerber.com.

Sybil Johnson's love affair with reading began in kindergarten with "The Three Little Pigs." Fast forward to college, where she continued reading while studying computer science. After twenty years in the computer industry, Sybil turned to a life of crime writing. Her short fiction has appeared in *Mysterical-E* and *Spinetingler Magazine,* among others. She also writes the Aurora Anderson mysteries, craft-based cozies set in the world of decorative painting. Originally from the Pacific Northwest, Sybil now wields pen and paintbrush from her home in Southern California. Visit her at authorsybiljohnson.com.

Norman Klein is an emeritus professor of anthropology at Cal State, LA. He has conducted research in Venezuela, Western Europe, China, Indonesia, and in rural and urban communities in the United States. After publishing the usual academic books, book chapters, and articles (including a piece for *Psychology Today* titled "Is There a Right Way to Die?"), he felt it was time to start writing fiction on purpose.

Aimee Kluck writes about bold female crime busters: homicide inspectors, nosy neighbors, and wise elders who avenge crimes. Her work appears in *Murder Most International, Shotgun Honey, Punk Noir,* and *Inkd Publishing: Noncorporeal.* She has completed a murder mystery novel, *The Last Cut,* which takes place in San Francisco during the cocaine-crazed 1980s. She is a member of Mystery Writers of America, Sisters in Crime, Women's Fiction Writers Association, and the Short Mystery Fiction Society. Catch her dancing in the streets or at aimeekluck.com.

Melinda Loomis was born and raised in Southern California. Her short stories have appeared in anthologies from the Los Angeles, San Diego, and Guppy chapters of Sisters in Crime. Visit her online at melindaloomis.com.

Kate Mooney is an award-winning advertising copywriter. Over the course of her career, she's had the privilege of working on brands like BMW, Cottonelle, HP, and Fiat. Originally from Chicago, Kate currently lives in San Francisco with her husband, son, and dog.

Nancy Cole Silverman retired to write fiction after twenty-five years in news talk radio. Her crime-focused novels have attracted readers throughout America, and her short stories have appeared in numerous anthologies.

Nancy writes the Carol Childs and Misty Dawn Mysteries (Henry Press), and the Kat Lawson Mysteries (Level Best Books). For more detailed information, visit nancycolesilverman.com.

Meredith Taylor retired from clinical psychology to a life of crime—on the page, at least. She published "Avenging Superheroes" in the 2021 Sisters in Crime Los Angeles anthology *Avenging Angelenos*. With Gay Toltl Kinman and Susan Rowland, she edited the 2023 SinC LA anthology *Entertainment to Die For*. Mysteries with Ali Marchant—therapist, professor, and reluctant sleuth—will arrive shortly. Meredith is a past board member of SinC LA. She lives in Los Angeles, where her poor (old) house has calmed down. Mostly. She is very pleased to join *Angel City Beat*.

Jacquie Wilvers is a member of the Sisters in Crime Los Angeles, Orange County, and Guppy chapters, the California Writers Club, and the Authors Guild. Jacquie lives in Southern California with her husband and two Rottweilers. She likes to create characters who misbehave and enjoys reading other writers who do the same. In real life, Jacquie has never wielded a ball-peen hammer, which is a good thing, as no good can surely come from that! She enjoys traveling, reading mysteries, and spending time with friends and family. She is currently completing her first book-length manuscript and can be found at JacquieWilvers.com.

AUTHOR WEBSITE:
   www.sistersincrimela.com